Reckless

by

Priscilla West

Table of Contents

Chapter One

TROUBLE

I'd been expecting a quiet Saturday night out at the bar, but it was fast turning into chaos.

I waited with bated breath, the sound of my own heartbeat pounding in my ears, the anticipation in the air so dense I could cut it with a knife. I couldn't see the stage from where I was sitting because the audience was near shoulder-to-shoulder packed, but from the eerie—almost reverent—silence that passed over the crowd, I knew the band had taken the stage and were about to play.

Then I heard something.

A thump.

Followed by another.

And another.

The bassline echoed off the walls, resonating with the crowd's thrumming energy, its infectious rhythm building in a slow crescendo, raising the excitement in the bar higher and higher.

The explosive sound of drums broke through the bassline and people began shouting and pumping their fists in the air to the beat like an angry mob. I looked to Jen for her reaction and saw her eyes wide and mouth in the shape of an 'O'.

I wanted to see the band badly. I'd been to enough rock concerts to know that half the performance was the music and the other half was in the way the band worked the stage. They must've been a local act because I didn't know what they looked like and hadn't seen them perform before.

After getting up from my barstool and stupidly jumping a few times on my four-inch heels—which only got me closer to twisting my ankle than seeing the stage—I realized we'd have to get closer.

"Come on!" I shouted to Jen.

Yanking my purse off the counter, I grabbed her hand and headed toward the crowd. Distantly, I registered a voice behind me saying "I have a really bad feeling about this, Riley!" but I ignored it.

It had started as a typical night out in downtown Manhattan with my co-worker Jen. On our way to our usual drinking spot, we took a detour and stumbled across a sign advertising for the Wallabee Pub—a grungy dive bar that must have been one of the last places in Manhattan where Jen and I had never gone on a Saturday night. The sign had a cartoon kangaroo dressed in a tuxedo and sporting a purple mullet. It was cute and we felt adventurous, so we decided to check it out.

I'd been in the middle of complaining to Jen about a new travel assignment I'd been given at work-when things in the bar quickly got weird.

A guy appeared on stage and announced that "The Cocks" were going to play a secret, impromptu show in ten minutes. As soon as the words came out of his mouth, pandemonium erupted. People started screaming with excitement and flooding the dance floor in front of the stage. Phones, lit up by thumbs, looked like fireflies in the dim lighting, a few girls fainted, at least one vomited, and Jen and I sat at the bar, completely dumbfounded. Curiosity led me to look up the band on my phone, but I scowled when all the search hits that came up were pictures of dongs.

I pulled Jen into the crowd, and something whizzed by our heads, making us do a double-take. Was that a shot glass? We shouldered on, but before we even got past the first row of people, a flurry of beer mugs, bras, and shirts bombarded us. People were undressing and alcohol was flying. My pulse began to race. The situation was quickly turning into one of the wildest concerts I'd ever been to.

And I'd been to Coachella.

"I'm getting half a Victoria's Secret store thrown at me!" Jen shrieked, pushing her glasses higher on her nose.

The night felt crazy even to me—I couldn't imagine what Jen must think of the crowd here at the Wallabee. Other than the occasional night out for drinks to release work tension, Jennifer Benton fit the straight-edge image of a professional accountant to a tee—pixie haircut, thick glasses, and pant suit included. Since I was more lively and rebellious, we complemented each other well; I pulled her out of her shell, and she pulled me out of trouble. Well, at least some trouble, anyway.

"Suck it up!" I said. I knew this wasn't really her scene, but tonight, we were going to let loose. It was hard to see in the low lighting, but I pulled her along as we dipped, ducked, dived, and dodged our way through the hail of clothing falling around us.

Just when I thought the worst was over, a thin white material enveloped my eyes. "Ugh! I got some guy's underwear thrown in my face!" I cried, throwing the garment off into the crowd and spitting cotton threads from my mouth while Jen laughed at me. Not only were the girls getting wild, but apparently so were the men—the few that there were. I shuddered, imagining the half-naked guy who owned it flopping up and down to the beat, his penis doing the same.

"I think we should turn back to the bar, Riley. This is dangerous!"

"No, we can't give up!" I said, pulling my friend along. "I've seen worse. We'll be fine!"

We squirmed past feverish bodies, avoiding randomly thrown paraphernalia while the pace of the music increased. Our urgency grew with the beat and within moments, I'd lost both my heels and had torn the hem of my little black dress. My breathing was ragged, and I was sweating like I'd just been in a sauna, but I didn't care. Curiosity was my kryptonite, and I was determined to make it to the front of that stage—minor setbacks be damned.

Right as I elbowed my way past a pair of headbangers, the music stopped.

A moment passed in complete silence. Then, a distinctly masculine voice broke through.

And this is how it feels when I lose myself in you
And this is why I'm caged and bound, frozen by your secrets
And this is where we hide, when we're lost inside
And this what I do to fight my way back to you

The tone was intimately low but carried a dangerous edge of intensity, effortlessly shifting between smooth legato and fierce gutturals as the beat picked up again. High-pitched female screams from the crowd followed each verse.

I'd been to a lot of concerts, but I'd never heard a voice like that before.

Heart racing with more than anxiety, I was suddenly reminded of an old myth I read in high school: man-eating half-bird-half-woman creatures who would use their beautiful voices to lure men to their doom. Back then, it seemed like a silly story— what voice could have that effect on people? But now, listening to another soaring chorus, I was beginning to rethink that opinion.

Was I listening to a male Siren?

Jen and I continued fighting our way to the front. I no longer had to pull her along, rather, she was pushing me forward, the Siren's voice taking effect on both of us. I released my grip on her hand for just a moment and a rush of sweaty bodies separated us. I spotted her among a flurry of guys and girls jumping up and down, banging their heads to the beat.

"Jen!!" I cried, as I shouldered my way to her. People thrashing to the music's rhythm moved in front of me and blocked my view. I lost sight of her.

"Riley!"

I barreled toward the direction of her voice. As I caught a brief glimpse of her plastic frames through a narrow gap, I stretched my hand out to her.

Her hand extended—almost far enough, but not quite. I touched the tips of her fingers then she was pulled away by the sea of people. "Go on without me!" she cried as bodies collapsed on the opening.

"Nooo!" I tried to push my way back to Jen, but it was like trying to swim through raging rapids. My pulse raced, and my stomach knotted. She'd been right. This was a stupid, dangerous idea. I should've listened to her. I wanted to give up on getting to the stage and focus instead on getting Jen and myself out of the crowd and back to safety. As I shouldered past a girl on top of a guy's shoulders—a teetering, terrifying human totem pole in the middle of the crazy crowd—the Siren began singing again.

Give yourself to me
I still need you
I'm falling, falling hard
Give yourself to me
I will save you
I'm falling, falling
Give into me

Give into me

His voice was hauntingly beautiful, each verse devilishly raw and sublimely angelic. The chorus filled me with such intense yearning I began to doubt my own sanity.

His voice beckoned me, and I felt compelled to respond. Thoughts of my friend were quickly overpowered by fantastic lewd images of the possible owner of such a mind-blowing voice. I turned around and began heading for the stage.

I'm sorry, Jen. He's calling me.

I silently made a vow. I'd get to the front. For the both of us.

Leapfrogging over someone who was kneeling down and crying, her hands clasped together in prayer, I bumped into the back of a topless girl. Before I could apologize, she turned to face me. Her silver hair showed her age, and there was a crazy look in her eye along with foam teasing the edges of her mouth. "You're not getting near my husband!" she screeched, pushing me backward.

There was no way Granny Cujo could be the singer's wife. I considered using my pepper spray necklace on her but quickly decided against it—using it in such a cramped space meant I'd get hit along with everyone else.

Before I could contemplate the situation further, she balled her fist and wound back. Adrenaline rushed through my system. I instinctively ducked her punch and stumbled forward, disappearing into the horde of people in front of me.

"Get back here!" I heard her shriek from behind me like a banshee. My heart beat pulsed in my ear a thousand times a minute, my lungs burned, and my bare feet ached. Only moments ago, I'd been complaining to Jen about my stupid job assignment, and now I was running for my life. Between the naked people and the rabid granny, the situation was insane.

But I couldn't stop moving toward the stage.

The crazy woman's voice grew faint, overpowered by the thumping music and the sound of my own breaths. Squeezing past a flailing guy who was desperately trying to hold his kicking and screaming girlfriend from rushing the stage, I broke out to the front section of the audience. There were still rows of heads in front of me, but I could at least see the stage.

It had nearly killed me in the process, but I'd made it.

After a few quick, panting breaths, I raised my eyes to the stage and nearly fell backward at the sight of the man singing.

Holy. Fuck.

Towering in front of the mic stand, he exuded a near-tangible aura of intense sexual energy. I was forced to squint, as if the spotlights shining down came from *him*, not the ceiling. Lean but packed muscles in his arms rippled as he jammed his guitar. Flowing black hair framed equally dark eyes beneath arrogantly slashed brows. He had a sharply angled nose, full lips, and a thin layer of stubble covering a jawline that could have been chiseled out of granite. I'd never seen a man so savagely gorgeous. It was difficult to describe him as anything but a god—a rock god in a dark v-neck and black leather pants.

My breath caught in my chest as my heart danced in my ribcage. I figured he'd be hot—judging by his voice, he had to be—but confronted with the full visual effect of him performing, I realized he wasn't just hot. No, he was beyond hot. He was *scorching*.

A feverish heat ripped through me as he passionately belted a verse and whipped his shoulder-length hair back. He jammed a chord from his hips, closed his eyes, and belted out another powerful verse, sending the crowd reeling. Each move gave the impression of raw animal magnetism. He didn't just ooze sex. He *was* sex, made flesh. Every motion of his figure, every movement of his lips, the way his inky hair tossed against his marvelous features, and those eyes—those intensely dark eyes—it was as if he was directly fucking every woman in the crowd with his gaze.

He started scanning the audience. He gazed over my section, but he paused and turned back to look right at me.

My heart stopped.

Our eyes locked as he began singing the down-tempo bridge.

Something passed in the air between us, and I could've sworn I saw a spark in his eyes. A charge of electricity ran through me. Then, just like that, he finished the bridge and shifted his eyes to a different section of the crowd, freeing me from his gaze.

Had it been my imagination?

I looked around and saw glazed eyes staring at him. Maybe I wasn't the only one who'd thought he had made eye contact.

Stepping away from the mic, he bent toward the front row and pulled an eager brunette onto the stage. She took a seat in a chair at the center. Other girls tried to jump onto the stage with her, but burly security personnel in the front row managed to hold them back—though it looked like they were struggling.

The Siren set his guitar down, took the mic off the stand, and sang to the brunette, crooning seductive notes as she squealed and gripped the edges of her chair tightly. I felt a pang of jealousy, wishing I'd been the one he'd chosen to bring on stage. Midway into the second chorus, the brunette moaned in ecstasy, slid off the chair and collapsed to her knees with her head back, lids closed, and thighs clamped together— clear signs of an orgasm. A shiver moved through me. My last boyfriend couldn't make a woman come if he had half a sex toy store and a map at his disposal. This guy could do it with just his voice.

The brunette slumped on stage, apparently no longer able to stand. Members of the stage crew had to come out and carry her away, but she had the biggest smile on her face.

Shaking my head, I was starting to regain my senses. It was clear that any "connection" I'd imagined earlier was all just part of the show.

The Siren picked his guitar back up and returned to the mic stand. He started another song.

I stood there watching, listening. Entranced. I was vaguely aware of other members of the band, but in the middle of such a stunning performance,, my attention only focused on him.

He sang about pain and pleasure, desperation and elation. The lyrics seemed deeply personal. I vaguely wondered whether he wrote them himself and if so, where his inspiration came from.

When the set ended, I felt emotionally drained. How many songs did they sing? Two? Twenty? I didn't know. I only became aware of the passage of time when the music stopped.

The male Siren unslung his guitar, tossed it backward to his bandmate, and hopped off the stage to the dance floor.

Without so much as looking back toward the stage, his eyes searched the crowd and then locked back onto mine just like earlier in the set. Tension coiled in my stomach as he began taking steps in my direction.

Toward me.

I wanted to move but couldn't; it was impossible to pry myself from his gaze. The sea of bodies, rather than mobbing him, parted to create a path between us, the burly arms of security guards keeping them at bay.

The girl I passed earlier who was struggling against her boyfriend's grasp squeezed past security, approaching the god from his right. Another girl approached from his left. They each latched onto one sleeve and yanked on the fabric. Within seconds, their panicking boyfriends were at their sides, tearing them away. But the girls held on tight and the god's shirt split down the middle, one half going to each girl.

He didn't react, and his steps didn't falter. He continued moving toward me, his dark eyes maintaining their hold on mine.

My breath hitched in my throat. He was shirtless now, and I could see a melange of tattoos splayed across his sculpted chest and along his muscular arms. Nipple rings jostling with each step, he closed the distance between us.

I tilted my head up to look at him as he stopped a foot in front of me. My mouth dried and my throat constricted. He was so close I could smell him. Nerves in my head were misfiring and bolts of desire were shooting through my core. The scent of his sweat was like an aphrodisiac, warping my senses until all I could think about was the sweat of our bodies tangled together.

My heart was beating a million times a minute, and I was afraid it was going to explode from my chest. I opened my mouth to speak, but no words came out. My brain was a jumbled mess, coherent thought mixing with visions of me licking his bared skin from head to toe.

He tilted his head.

Oh my god. Is he going to kiss me? In front of all these people?!

My eyes closed, and my lips parted. The surface of his soft lips brushed across mine as his mouth moved to my ear. The warmth of his breath tickled the tiny hairs on my ear.

"Backstage. Twenty minutes."

I opened my eyes to see him walking past me toward the door that led backstage, leaving me in shock.

Almost simultaneously, the face of every woman around me contorted into a jealous scowl. A few had what looked like pure hatred in their eyes. Two of them were the girls that had pieces of the god's shirt. I then realized that they each had a broken beer bottle in hand and were rushing toward me.

The crowd was still densely packed, leaving nowhere to escape. My eyes darted toward the exits, but after a split second, the reality of the situation sunk in.

I was going to die.

Chapter Two

BAMBOOZLED

Through a buzzing haze, I heard a faint voice crying out to me. What was it saying? It sounded like "snack on a chip", but that made no sense. *Why would it say that?*

SMACK!

A blow landed across my cheek, sending me reeling. I reached out and grabbed ahold of the counter to stabilize myself before I fell on my ass.

"Snap out of it!" I heard Jen's voice.

"Ouch, that hurt!" Grasping my burning cheek, I blinked a few times and realized I was sitting on the same barstool I'd been sitting on earlier. Jen was beside me, a look of concern etched on her face. Wasn't I just near the stage? Had it all been my imagination? "Was it all just a—"

"No, it wasn't a dream, you numbskull," Jen grumbled, holding an ice pack to the right side of her face. "You see this?" She pointed to the cracked lens on her glasses. The skin beneath was already beginning to swell. "That's real. I'm pretty sure it's gonna be black and blue in the morning, thanks to you."

"Wuh?" I mumbled, looking around and seeing that the bar had returned to its normal state prior to the band taking the stage. Except for a few stray thongs on the floor, it was as if the chaos during the show never happened.

"You left me to fend for myself! I got elbowed in the face by some naked douchebag. Then I ended up saving your ass from some crazy chick trying to cut you with a broken bottle. I had to carry you back to the bar and I tell ya, you may look small, but you're freaking heavy! I should've left you there."

Still recovering from the fog in my head, I squinted my eyes and rubbed my temples. "Ugh . . . What happened to the crazy girl?"

"Her boyfriend grabbed her and pulled her away. Maybe he chloroformed her or shot her with a tranq, I don't know. Good for him if he did. All I know is she's gone."

The haze over my mind cleared, and the situation sunk in. "Wow, you saved me. I owe you big."

"Damn straight you owe me! And you can start by telling me what that rock god whispered in your ear."

For a moment, I debated whether I should tell her the truth in case she turned into a jealous psycho like some of the other girls did, but I quickly dismissed the thought. Jen was as level-headed in the workplace as she was in her relationships with men, which was more than I could say for myself. "He told me to meet him backstage in twenty minutes." Saying the words he'd whispered into my ear sent a dark flutter through my stomach.

Her left eye widened. "No way. For what? To hook up? Why'd he single you out among all the raving female fans?"

"I—I don't know! I mean, it did happen, right? I didn't hallucinate it, did I?" It wouldn't surprise me if the whole episode had only happened in my mind. The rock god's performance had driven more than a few women batshit crazy.

"Unless I was hallucinating too, it definitely happened. Everyone near the stage saw it," Jen said. She took a deep breath. "So what are you going to do?"

I raised an eyebrow and shot her a wicked smirk. "What do you think?"

"No, Riley. Don't." She shook her head disapprovingly. "I know you have a habit of thinking with your vagina instead of your head, but you almost got yourself killed just a few minutes ago!"

"But I didn't," I replied. I might've occasionally hooked up with hot guys that didn't have a lot of other redeeming qualities, but I wasn't going to apologize for liking sex.

"You think he's worth the danger to your life?"

"For one, you're overreacting. And two, that's a stupid question," I scoffed. "Did you see him? I mean, really look at him? Because the answer is obvious."

She sighed deeply. "Through one eye, yes, I saw him. He's attractive for sure, but not hot enough to throw away your common sense. Please promise me you won't go. I'm not going back there to save you if you get into trouble."

"You're acting like my mom," I groaned.

"I'm acting like your friend," she responded, her voice somewhere between gentle and concerned. "This wouldn't be the first time I've had to help you out from trouble because you got mixed up with some tattooed bad boy that turned out to be from prison."

"That was one time!"

"One time too many."

I sighed. She'd been referring to Danny, a guy I'd met online and ended up dating for a few weeks. Ever the worrywart, Jen had looked up his background and discovered he'd done a year in prison for theft. I understood that a guy having a few blotches in his past kind of came with the 'bad boy' territory, but there was a difference between dark and dangerous and just plain dangerous. And that's where I drew the line.

"Look, I'm pretty sure this guy's not from prison considering he's a rock star. Worst he's probably done is some drugs, which is par for the course for a rocker."

"You're really intent on becoming a groupie, aren't you?"

"What? No. That's not what this is—"

"Then what is it? Don't tell me you're expecting to sit down with him over a cup of tea and talk about your mutual interest in music when you're back there."

I stuck my tongue out at her. "There's probably going to be sex, sure. But so what? I'm not going to sleep with him just because he's some semi-famous rocker. It's not like I get a thrill out of fucking famous people. I don't even know his name!" I exhaled deeply, regaining composure. "He's simply an attractive member of the male species who has expressed his interest in me, and I'm attracted to him as well."

She eyed me skeptically.

"Okay," I admitted, looking away. "So it happens that he's also a rock god. But there's a difference between being a groupie and being a self-respecting girl deciding to hook up with a guy she's attracted to."

Jen sighed and put a sympathetic hand on mine. "Rye, you know I'm not trying to clam jam. I'm just concerned about you. I know you like putting on a strong face, but I've seen you get torn up over one-night stands in the past, and I don't want to see you get hurt this time—physically or emotionally."

"Ugh." I knew I wasn't going to win the argument. I appreciated her concern, but if I'd wanted my mom at the Wallabee telling me what to do, I'd have invited her. "Fine, fine. I promise. I'm not going. Happy now?"

She raised a brow. "You sure?"

"Yes, I'm one hundred percent sure. You're right, Jen. I have a tendency to get myself into trouble when it comes to hot guys, and I promise not to do it this time." I held up one hand as if swearing an oath.

She studied my expression for a moment, probably waiting to see if I'd crack. Fortunately she wasn't looking behind my back, otherwise she'd have seen my other hand with fingers crossed. "Good. I'm going to use the restroom and to make sure that my eyeball is still in its socket. Don't go anywhere, okay?"

I gave her my sweetest smile and nodded. "Okay."

Tapping my toes against the floor, I waited impatiently for her to take her leave. I considered eating a lifesaver while I waited but decided against it because they made me sleepy.

When she finally disappeared around the corner, I left two twenty dollar bills on the counter, told the bartender to keep Jen's ice pack fresh, and began walking toward the large metal door that led backstage.

Jen was probably right about the danger, but what she didn't know was that I was already in trouble. With the heated ache between my thighs building to a near-threatening level, I figured my body was in danger either way. And given a choice, I'd rather go out with an orgasmic bang.

***

I tried the handle on the door leading backstage, but it wouldn't budge. It was locked. After knocking a few times without a response, I grew impatient. I figured there would be a security guard watching the door, especially considering the fans' behavior during the show, but apparently there wasn't. Or at least he wasn't at his post.

An idea popped into my head.

Fuck it, I thought. *What's the worst that can happen?*

I plucked a hairpin I kept in my purse, inserted it into the lock, and shimmied it until I heard a distinctive click. I breathed a sigh of relief. *Thanks, internet research.* My lockpicking skills had come in handy before—not just for breaking and entering, but also whenever I lost my keys during a wild night out.

After opening the door and stepping through, I found myself in a quiet corridor with lighting equipment strewn haphazardly along the ground. The place looked so abandoned I practically expected a tumbleweed to roll across the hallway. Had the band left already? Was I too late?

The sound of boots echoed down the hallway, and I gathered it was coming from the far end. Realizing that it was the guard returning to his post from a piss-break, I ran in the opposite direction, grateful that losing my heels earlier made my footsteps near silent. I could've waited for the guard to return and explained why I'd picked the lock on the door he'd been protecting, but in an environment where crazy fans wielded broken bottles to stab other people, I worried he'd taze first and ask questions later.

I turned the corner at the end of the hall and nearly ran smack into someone.

"Hey, watch where you're going!" a female voice said.

Two blonde girls with large chests, pencil-thin waists, and long legs stood idly beside a green door. Both wore matching red dresses with necklines that plunged in a "V" down to their waists, revealing ample side-boob. Then again, maybe I was the one who was dressed inappropriately. My little black dress had been ripped along the hem and one strap was broken, leaving me feeling bedraggled and a little embarrassed. After a moment, I realized that the girls were twins, and they were both shooting me nasty looks.

It was the left one who had spoken; I noticed she had a tattoo on her chest that said "Tiffany". The other one had a similar tattoo, but it said "Amanda". They probably got mixed up often enough—and wore revealing dresses enough—that they decided to get permanent nametags inked onto their chests.

"Oops, sorry. I can be a klutz sometimes," I said.

"That's obvious," Tiffany said.

I was more interested in finding the Siren than I was in her response, so I craned my neck to look past them down the new hallway I'd entered. There was a door at the end with a red "EXIT" sign above it. Other than the conspicuous green door on the left next to the twins, there was only a set of restrooms along the right wall. I scratched my head, wondering if I'd taken the wrong path. "Hey, do you guys know where I can find the lead singer?"

The girls exchanged looks between one another. "He's busy right now. And he'll probably be busy for the rest of the night," Tiffany said with an air of smugness. "We can tell him you stopped by though."

I narrowed my brows. "You know him?"

"Uh. Yes," Tiffany said, condescension dripping from her voice. "We're like this." She crossed her middle finger over her forefinger.

"Like this," Amanda echoed, mimicking the same gesture.

I eyed them doubtfully. I noticed on the green door behind them that there was a silver star mounted above the center.

"Is he in there?" I asked. "Are you guys waiting for him?"

"That's right," Tiffany said. She and her sister each crossed their arms in front of their large chests, clearly becoming impatient with my questions. "Like I said, we'll tell him you stopped by. So hurry and run along now." She made shooing motions with her hand. "I suggest you fix your dress while you're at it."

Groupies.

I probably should've realized it sooner, but I went to shows for the music and the crowd, not the hotties in the band. I'd never been backstage before, but it was all starting to make sense now. While I had to pick a lock and avoid detection to get back here, they probably flirted their way past security for a chance at having a threesome with a rock star. Whereas I was chosen, they probably weren't.

"Fix yours first," I replied. "Get some self-respect while you're at it." I stuck my tongue at her.

Tiffany gasped. A grimace on her face, she raised her hand and pulled her shoulder back. For the second time tonight, I was going to be smacked across the cheek, but this one was going to be much harder. Tiffany swung her arm at me. "You bitc—"

The door opened and a large hand shot out and grasped Tiffany's arm. A tall, imposing figure stepped out from the entrance.

He was wearing a fresh pair of black leather pants, but he hadn't yet replaced the shirt that had been unceremoniously shredded from his body earlier. With his sculpted muscles, rippling abs, and the tattoos along his arms and chest exposed, the ache I'd experienced before returned and amped up to a painful degree. His olive-toned skin was damp, and his silky hair draping along his shoulders looked wet and tousled in a deliciously sexy way, making me wonder if he'd just gotten out of a shower.

"I'm disappointed," he said to Tiffany. The cool, controlled tone sent a heated shiver through my core. "You're not playing nice."

She looked up at him, speechless. "I—I'm s-sorry." Her other hand shaking, she pointed a finger toward me. "She started it."

Those dark eyes shifted to me and pierced me with a searing gaze. "You," he said, his voice rough yet velvety.

It was one thing imagining him, but it was a whole different thing being in his presence. He couldn't have been more than a few years older than me but he carried himself with an air of authority befitting someone much older. Someone world-experienced. Scarred, but not jaded. I was drawn to him like a moth to a flame.

I'd met my fair share of hot guys, but I'd never met one hot enough to unsettle my composure. This Adonis in leather pants was proving to be the exception.

His sharply angled brows raised slightly. "How did you get back here? I was about to tell the guard to let you in."

I tried my best to keep my voice steady. "I, uh, picked the lock."

His gaze intensified. I suddenly felt exposed and naked before him. Vulnerable. As if he had direct access to my innermost private thoughts. Could he see his effect on me?

I thought I'd be crushed beneath the weight of that stare, but a hint of a smile touched the corners of his lips. "Interesting. You like getting into trouble, don't you?"

I wasn't sure whether he was referring to my lockpicking skills or my life in general. "Only the good kind," I said, trying my damnedest to steel myself against his allure. "I didn't start the trouble back here though."

His smile faded, and he turned his attention back to Tiffany—who was probably on the verge of wetting herself in more ways than one. He dipped his nose close to her ear and sniffed her neck like a predator assessing the fear in its prey.

She closed her eyes and released a faint noise that sounded like something between a moan and a yelp.

"You lied to me," he growled.

Her eyes widened. A look of terror flashed across her face. "I—I . . ."

"That's strike one," he warned, his tone wielding a dangerous edge. He released his hold on Tiffany and her arm hung limply by her side. He looked at me again and narrowed his brows. "You're not hurt, are you?"

The deep concern in his voice caught me off guard. "Um . . . nope."

Other than almost getting punched and stabbed during your show and now almost getting bitch-slapped. . . no, of course not.

His eyebrows remained furrowed. "You sure? Your clothes are ripped. And you're not wearing shoes."

His left brow had a diagonal slash across the middle. The scar only added to his mysterious allure, and I briefly wondered how he got it. Maybe he was a fighter that moonlighted as a rocker. Judging by the conditioning of his body, I could imagine him throwing punches in a boxing ring or grappling in a cage or even riding bare-chested on a steed with a sword in his hand. He certainly had the hair for the latter—his dark locks could probably make the heroes on the covers of my mom's old romance books jealous. I could also see him in my bed wrestling me beneath the sheets—both of us, hot, sweaty, and naked.

"Yeah . . . it's kind of a long story. I could tell you in private, though." I gave him a suggestive smile and winked, hoping he'd take the cue to dismiss the other girls.

He grinned back. But there was a twinkle in his dark brown eyes that made me wonder what was going through his mind. "I'd like to hear it. Come inside." He gestured to the green room behind him. "I'll be there after I handle this."

Tiffany and Amanda watched me, their jaws nearly on the floor. I flashed a smile at the twins, returning the smugness they'd given me. Then I went inside.

It was called a "green room", but a quick scan revealed there wasn't a single green item in the space except for a fake potted tree that was as tall as me. The walls were a lush crimson, while the hardwood floor was covered with a soft Persian carpet. There was a full-length mirror at the back next to a bathroom, a comfortable-looking tan leather couch to the side, and various food and drinks on a rolling cart next to the armrest. I'd been expecting instruments, clothes, makeup, and drug paraphernalia scattered about the space, but this resembled a classy hotel room.

Given how the bar had looked, this room was completely out of place. I guess they really pampered their performers.

I started feeling excited—almost giddy—at the thought of the Siren. I'd be tapping that soon. It'd been a while since I last got laid. And I was eager to break the dry spell.

Examining myself in the mirror, I heard footsteps then the door closing.

I pivoted on the balls of my feet, enthusiastic. "So glad you got rid of those—" I saw the Siren enter with each of the twins at his side. His hands were at the small of their backs, guiding them inside. My neck jerked. "Uh, what's going on?"

He smiled at me. "Line up. I want a good look at each of you."

"Huh?" Confusion swept over me. Did I miss something?

"You heard him," Tiffany chimed as she lined up on my left, while Amanda stood to my right, leaving me sandwiched between them.

The rock god stood in front of us, assessing. I could feel his gaze gliding over my profile. He casually shifted his attention between me and Tiffany, then me and Amanda. A nauseous feeling swirled in my belly. Was he seriously comparing us? No way . . . He *chose* me from the crowd to meet him backstage while these girls were just groupies . . .

A nervous sweat began to break out on my skin. A million thoughts and concerns raced through my mind. Equally anxious and offended, I found myself becoming self-conscious. How could I possibly stack up to the Barbie twins? They'd probably had enough work done to buy some plastic surgeon a summer house in the Hamptons. All I had was a torn-up dress and some scented body wash.

"Relax," the rock god purred darkly to me. "You're squirming." His voice flowed over me, filling me with a restless energy that only stoked my irritation.

When I saw the knowing smile on his face, an awful thought hit me. *I wasn't the only one he chose.* The twins had probably been told to come "backstage in twenty minutes" just like I had, so he could have the privilege of comparing us and choosing the best.

I'd been played.

My face burned. A wave of disgust and embarrassment washed over me for being made an unwitting participant in this perverse beauty contest. I was way too old to fall for this shit, but I'd wanted so badly to believe I was special. I'd called myself a"self-respecting girl deciding to hook up," but from where I was standing right now, the "self-respecting" part seemed like a lie.

Gah! I always fall for jerks. I needed to return to Jen and apologize for lying to her and bolting. If I walked away now, I could at least salvage what was left of my dignity.

I threw my hands up. "Alright, fuck this. I'm leav—"

"You." He pointed at Tiffany. "And you," he said, pointing at Amanda. "Leave." He gestured to the door. He turned his gaze to me and pointed a daunting finger in my direction. "You. Stay."

I halted mid-step, speechless.

"Wait, we'll do anything you want!" Tiffany and Amanda both pleaded in unison. "Both of us. Use us. We'll let you stick it anywhere! Please!"

"You're not what I want." Jax was speaking to the twins but his eyes never left mine.

"But, I only had one strike!" Tiffany pleaded.

"And you're out. Leave." His authoritative tone left no further room for argument.

As Tiffany and Amanda left the green room and turned the corner, I could hear Amanda yelling at her twin for ruining their chances at getting laid by the hottest man in the history of rock 'n' roll. The door closed.

With their departure, that just left me. And him. Alone.

Chapter Three

HOT-HEADED

We stared at each other for a moment.

"You're an ass and your music sucks," I shot at him before turning to leave.

"Wait a second." He caught me by the arm, his hold gentle but firm. "I know you're upset. But listen, I was just messing with you," he said with a smile.

The skin to skin contact sent electricity up my arm and scorched a few of my brain cells. Shaking my head, I pulled away from his grip. "Messing with me?" I asked. I folded my arms across my chest and stepped back to put some distance between us. "So, do you do this after every show? Ask multiple girls to come backstage, line them up, and check out their tits and asses to see which one you'd want to take into the green room and bang? I guess you either fuck them or you just fuck *with* them instead."

He smiled nonchalantly. "I only asked you to come backstage. I didn't ask those other girls. They showed up on their own." Turning to pick up a towel hanging over a nearby chair, he began drying his hair with it. "But yes, I was fucking with you. I thought it'd be fun to see your reaction. And it was."

Ugh, the nerve of this guy. Even though I was pissed off, I didn't really suspect he was lying; in fact, it made a lot of sense. The tightness in my forehead relaxed slightly. I wasn't as angry as I was before, but still, it was a pretty dick thing to do for a joke. "Are you serious? Why would you do that?"

He finished drying his hair and gracefully draped the towel across the back of his neck. He looked irritatingly self-assured and lethally sexy. "You caught my attention when I saw you fighting your way to the front during the show. You're bold," he said, grinning, "and I like that. I wanted to push your buttons."

It was a compliment and an admission of assholery all rolled into one.

I smiled wryly, secretly pleased by the compliment. "Well, congrats, you succeeded. You do know that still makes you a jerk, right? Doesn't matter how hot you are."

His mouth twitched, and his eyes strayed briefly toward the ceiling in thought. "If that's how you feel about it, how about I make us even."

I was still mildly pissed. Even though I now knew he'd been playing a joke on me, I hadn't changed my mind about leaving and calling it a night—the damage had been done. "And how do you plan on doing that?"

He took a step forward, entering my personal space. I touched my pendant instinctively. "Just so you know, this necklace is full of pepper spray. So don't try anything funny." I intended it to be less of a threat and more of a warning against doing something else douchey.

He raised a brow. "Oh?" He reached for my star-shaped pendant and fingered it curiously, touching my fingers gently as he did so.

His hands were soft, but the pads of his fingers were rough with calluses, probably from playing guitar. Embarrassed by the thrill of pleasure I felt from his touch, I let go of the pendant. "Yeah."

Smiling, he moved his attention from my necklace to my face. He gently brushed a strand of my strawberry-blonde hair away from my cheek with his finger. I shifted on my feet but didn't pull away; I didn't want him to see his effect on me. "You know," he said, "with the necklace, the hair, and the attitude . . . you're quite the package, Pepper."

A thrill shot through my core and I raised my brows. A glint from the overhead lights reflecting off something hit my eye. I looked down at his spiky belt. It was unclasped and hanging loosely around his waist; he probably put it on in a hurry after getting out of the shower. My hands clenched against the urge to run my fingers over the shiny silver studs. If I was going to be "Pepper," then "Stud" fit him well.

"So what I'm suggesting," Stud continued, "is an eye for an eye. Since I ogled you, I'll let you ogle me."

I narrowed my brows. "That's not an eye for an eye—I'm not having you line up next to other guys with bigger muscles and longer cocks."

His mouth curved in displeasure. "Look around. There's no one else here, so we can't do that. You're just gonna have to settle for something else."

"Well I'm not settling for what you're offering. If you're gonna offer something, it had better be higher stakes."

"Higher stakes? Let me think about it . . ." He looked toward the ceiling, once again lost in thought.

I took the opportunity to stare at the sculpted pecs in front of me. They were at eye level, and I couldn't avoid looking at them—even if I'd wanted to, which I didn't. Although I was ogling him, it was hardly the same situation as the one he'd put me in. So I felt no shame.

He had sexy nipples, and the silver rings that hung from them only added to the effect. My gaze slowly trailed down his bare torso to the chiseled contours of his abs.

Gawd. Dayum.

They were so well-defined that I could've sworn they were airbrushed. I imagined that if the rock star thing didn't work out, he could always make a living as a human cheese grater in a pizza kitchen.

I got to his navel—an innie—and from there began a trail of fine dark hairs that led down the center of his pelvis, disappearing into the top of his low-rise pants. Hard lines on the edges of his hips angled downward in the shape of a "V". It seemed like everything was pointing toward his crotch—which was impressive, from what I could tell. The tightness of his leather pants left little to the imagination. Even if he did line up next to other guys, I wasn't sure there *were* any guys with bigger muscles and longer cocks.

An unwelcome desire grew in my core the longer I looked at his body. I gulped. *Maybe I should forgive him.* Stud's ego was huge, but his cock might almost be just as big . . .

As I thought about his cock, his hands drifted to his fly. He easily unclasped the top button, and yanked down the zipper.

I caught a glimpse of bare skin and my mouth dropped. *He wasn't wearing any underwear.* "W— What are you doing?!"

He smiled. "Making us even. You wanted higher stakes. Here it is." He ripped back the leather flaps, exposing himself. I cupped my hand over my mouth, shocked. The treasure trail I'd followed earlier continued down his pelvis, fading into a patch of neatly-groomed pubic hair set above a massive cock that hung halfway down his thigh.

OMG.

Cheeks burning, I picked my jaw up off the floor and collected myself. "This is the opposite of making us even. You humiliated and embarrassed me with those trashy groupies. But this isn't embarrassing you. It's more like you flashing me!"

Stud raised his scarred brow. "Embarrassed or not, I'm naked. You weren't. We should be more than even. In fact, I think you owe *me* now."

I couldn't help a laugh from escaping. "Owe you? Owe you what? A slap in the face?"

"We can start with a kiss."

A puff of air escaped my lips. His persistence blew my mind. But a part of me found it admirable. Charming, even. And if he hadn't acted like a douche and then made it worse with his misguided attempt to make up for it, I would've been all over him in a heartbeat. He shot me an arrogant grin, and I realized his stubbornness rivaled my own. Debating him would be fruitless. Still, I couldn't leave with him having the last word—not after all of this.

Taking a deep breath, I decided to get even on my own terms.

"Okay, a kiss," I said.

Stud's eyes widened. He looked at me doubtfully for a moment. I gave him my sweetest smile, and he seemed to buy it. "Good," he said. "Glad we could get this resolved."

I could tell he was still skeptical about my quick change of heart, so I trailed the tip of my finger down his chest seductively. The excitement I felt from touching him made me wonder if I wasn't seducing myself at the same time. "Me too," I purred.

He grinned slyly and cupped my cheek. "You're dangerous," he said with a low, intimate voice. Traces of a vibrating rasp hinted at his velvety vocal timbre. I wouldn't have believed it if I hadn't witnessed it earlier in the night, but I knew that with his voice alone he could make a woman come.

I licked my lips to wet them. He tilted his head, his lips hovering perilously close to mine. My pulse beat erratically. "So are you," I breathed, just before our eager mouths collided.

Electric pleasure coursed through me. The kiss deepened, our tongues darting out to softly clash against one another.

His hand fisted my hair and he pulled me deeper into the kiss. I gripped his ass and squeezed firmly. With my other hand, I reached down to touch his flushed skin. He groaned into my mouth, and my moan echoed his in response. Using feather-light touches, I stroked him until he stiffened, his full erection hot and needy against my palm. A sizzling ache heated the area between my thighs. My toes curled against the Persian carpet as I struggled to resist the urge to grind myself against him. I wanted him. Badly.

Summoning every ounce of willpower I had, I pulled away, breaking the kiss.

"What are you doing?" he asked, his voice dripping with frustration and desire.

"What does it look like?" I took a step back and smiled at him. "I'm giving you blue balls. *Now* we're even."

With that, I stepped toward the door and left the rock god alone with his boner.

Chapter Four

HUNGOVER

BZZ! BZZ! BZZ!

An incessant beeping woke me up the next morning. I kept my eyes closed, trying to silence the noise through mind power alone.

It didn't take me long to realize that I didn't have superpowers. I pulled the pillow tighter against my head, but since I was completely hungover, concentrating only made the pounding in my skull worse. The annoying ring tone meant one thing and one thing only: a message from work.

Argh, it's probably Palmer finally giving me the details of my assignment.

After giving the rocker blue balls in his green room, I'd filled in Jen on both my encounter with Stud and this mystery work assignment. Apparently, Hans-Peterson needed me to travel for an urgent, last-minute assignment but they couldn't give me any details by the time I left the office on Friday.

So now I get to spend my Sunday morning dealing with work. Fantastic.

Groaning, I rolled over and grabbed my phone off my nightstand. The email was clearly from Palmer because the subject line was written in all caps. I opened it and quickly skimmed it.

When I finished, my heart was beating fast.

This wasn't just any assignment. I wasn't going on special assignment to Chicago or Seattle. I was going on the road as a tour accountant . . . with a band.

Memories from the night before came flooding back, in brief, bright flashes. My thoughts immediately jumped to the taut muscles of the sultry rock god. *Jesus Christ, Riley, get ahold of yourself.* Hans-Peterson only worked with high-profile clients that could afford our rates, not small-time bands that played in hole-in-the-wall bars on a Saturday night. Besides, the email referred to the band as "HC" and Stud's band was called "The Cocks." All the wishful thinking in the world wasn't going to make that bolt of lightning strike twice.

I went back to reviewing Palmer's memo. It looked like one of my biggest tasks was going to be managing and curbing expenses. Checking out the dozens of attachments, I saw that each one was a zipped file full of numbers, spreadsheets, contracts, and tax forms.

Even though I'd been inundated with information, I couldn't find anything that explained what the hell HC actually stood for. I did a quick Google search, but the only results that came up were those for hemorrhoid creams. *Whatever, I'll find out tomorrow.*

As I scrolled through one of the spreadsheets, a call came in. I smiled when I saw the name: Kristen, my ex-roommate, was just about the only person I could tolerate when my head was spinning.

"H-Hello?" I answered, trying my best to sound normal—which was tough, considering my mouth was as dry as a cotton ball. I took a big gulp of water from the glass I'd left out the night before and it was like finding an oasis in the desert.

"Hello, yourself, sleepyhead," Kristen said, sunny as ever and sounding like she'd been up for a few hours already. "Do you want to call me back when you're a little less of a zombie?"

I cleared my throat. "No, no, it's fine. I'm good." We'd both been busy the past few weeks, so in spite of my throbbing headache, I was eager to catch up with her. "What's up? How's Vincent?"

"Pretty busy as usual, but he's starting to slow down, delegate more responsibilities to his VPs. He's really trying hard to make things work for us, and I'm really grateful for that."

Her hubby was a busy man. It had actually been a sticking point earlier in their relationship. "And how's the baby?"

"It's getting pretty real, Rye," she said. "I can already feel her kicking . . . which is actually why I was calling. I wanted to go over some ideas I had about the baby shower."

It was still over a month away and she had a professional planner taking care of all the details, but as one of her best friends, I had a major role as a sounding board.

She went through a laundry list of minutiae that required my personal opinion. Even with my hangover, I did my best to offer up what few ideas I could muster. I was so happy for her and Vincent; I just knew they were going to be amazing parents.

After settling on some choices, she asked, "So what else is new with you? Wait, do you have a guy there?" Her voice crackled with curiosity. "I'll let you go if you do. Tell me first, though, just say yes or no."

"Nope, no guy. Just me and the pillows." I yawned, throwing off the covers and looking at the other side of the bed, which was empty except for a small, pink cylindrical object.

Just me and the pillows and . . . my vibrator!

I faintly remembered leaving the bar with Jen and then coming home and being so ridiculously turned on after my encounter with Stud that I couldn't fall asleep. I shook my head, disappointed in myself—I must've eventually dozed off, drunk on alcohol and high on battery-operated orgasms. My plan to give him blue balls had ended up being a double-edged sword, but I was still the victor. After all, he knew nothing about what I'd done between the sheets.

"Oh? No crazy night then?" Kristen asked, sounding slightly disappointed. "Don't tell me you're starting to settle for quiet nights in."

Pulling myself out of bed and rubbing my temples, I dragged my feet toward the kitchen. I intended to make my patented hangover cure: broccoli, oatmeal, orange juice, a banana, and yogurt—all thrown together in a blender.

"I can have quiet nights in when I'm dead." As I made it to the kitchen and started preparing my smoothie, I began telling her about my outing with Jen last night, making sure to highlight the show and how I dealt with the crazed fans. The more I told her about the night, the more my excitement grew. "Kris, I'm telling you, it was bananas! Some girl came right there on stage, just from this guy's singing."

She laughed. "*Sure.* Did he also get someone pregnant through eye contact? Maybe you?"

I scoffed. "No, that's just silly." I patted my belly to check anyway. He did send a fair number of dark flutters through my stomach last night . . .

I swallowed a large gulp of my smoothie and filled her in on the rest of the details—from the moment he first locked eyes on me to the look on his face as I left him empty-handed.

She laughed riotously. "If your past boyfriends are any indication, he sounds like he's just your type. When can I expect to hear about part two?"

"There's not going to *be* any part two," I grumbled. "Look, the guy was hot. *Muy* hot. *Tres* hot. But I am not going there. I can tell he'd be way more trouble than even I could handle."

"Well that's saying something."

Kristen had helped me through the fallout of some pretty bad choices in men. Cheaters, liars, and the occasional creep-job: the Riley Exes Hall of Fame would be a lousy place.

"So what else is new? How's work going?" Kristen continued after I had been silent for a while.

"Crazier than usual. I just found out this morning that I'm going to be some band's tour accountant for a few weeks. I just got this certification so I'm a little surprised they stuck me on an actual tour so fast."

"Whoa! That's great news, congrats! I didn't know you got certified in that. I'm not even sure I know what 'tour accountant' means. So you just manage their expenses and the money they make from their shows?"

"Yeah, basically. The band manager already put together a preliminary budget. In theory I'm just supposed to keep a close eye on the cash flow, make sure the band isn't overspending, and all that jazz."

"You must be excited! Travel plus partying equals fun. Well, with maybe a little bit of work in between. Sounds like your ideal job."

I nodded. "That's why I got certified! But we'll see. I'm hopeful, but I'm imagining there's going to be a lot less partying and a lot more of me jumping in front of guitars and amps to save them from being smashed on-stage. I'm probably gonna have to end up being a total hardass to make sure we stick to the budget."

"If anyone can do it, it's you." I could practically hear her wink over the phone. "I've worked out with you, I know you worked hard for that hard ass."

She always knew just what to say to put a smile on my face. "You know it, Kris. But seriously, I feel like I'm in a little over my head. You're in wealth management, got any tips for me?"

"Just one, and only because it's you: mixing business with pleasure is never a good idea," she said, chuckling.

I heard Vincent's voice protesting in the background—they'd mixed business and pleasure pretty frequently when they first met—and I laughed. "Don't worry about me, Kris. Some of us have self-control."

We both erupted in giggles.

By the time we said our goodbyes and I hung up the phone, I was feeling much more relieved. The smoothie had erased my hangover and talking to Kristen always brightened up my day.

Now that my headache was cured, I headed back into my room to pack. After rummaging under my bed, I retrieved a suitcase emblazoned with Louis Vuitton logos and set it down in the middle of my room. The bag had been my best thrift store find in years: fifty dollars for a suitcase that originally cost thousands.

I wasn't thrilled about Hans-Peterson sending me into a last minute assignment with almost no preparation, but I could definitely teach this band a thing or two about managing a budget.

Chapter Five

THE SUIT

"You the new suit?"

The guy questioning me looked like he walked right off the cover of a classic rock album: a tangle of brown curly hair with long sideburns, tinted sunglasses, a faded Led Zeppelin t-shirt, ripped jeans. The only modern thing on him was an expensive pair of STAX headphones slung around his neck. He looked to be in his late twenties, maybe early thirties. In his hands, he fiddled around with an odd electronic device that looked like a baby monitor mixed with a Geiger counter.

"Yep, that's me, Riley Hewitt, the new suit." As much as I would've preferred to have been dressed in casual attire in this summer heat, I was outside this Brooklyn warehouse on behalf of Hans-Peterson, so I was dressed in my typical work uniform: a pink blouse, blue pencil skirt with matching blazer, and black flats, with my hair pulled up in a tight bun. I'd be the first to admit that the outfit was better suited for an accounting convention than a rock concert tour.

"Riley the suit, I'm Chewie the drummer." He held out his hand and grinned like we were long-lost friends. A lingering odor of marijuana filled the air, and I suspected it came from him.

"Nice to meet you," I said, shaking what felt like a leathery baseball mitt.

Two roadies scurried past me on the sidewalk and tossed a few crates into the cargo bin of what must've been the Taj Mahal of buses. Three levels high, wide enough to take up a full lane, and covered in shimmering gold paint, it looked like a bus that had been injected with steroids and given to a Bond villain to dip in gold. *How does that thing even fit under bridges?*

When the initial awe wore off, numbers began swirling around in my head as I started considering how much it had to cost. Driver, fuel, maintenance, cleaning, and who knew what else. The tour projections in my files indicated profits, but I wondered how that was possible with such an expensive bus. The sight of the glittering behemoth left me with a nagging feeling that this assignment wasn't going to be easy.

The next thing I knew, Chewie started moving the weird device up and down as if he was scanning me.

"Uh, what are you doing?" I said, instinctively holding up my hands behind my head. "This is all starting to feel a little like the TSA."

"You can leave your hands down," Chewie said nonchalantly. "I'm just checking you out for ghosts. This is the same detector Lady Dada uses when she goes on tour."

I looked at him skeptically. "That has to be a joke, right?"

"For fifty grand, it'd better not be a joke," he said, checking the read-out. "Nope, you're cool. No ghosts here."

"So why would Lady Dada use a . . . wait, did you just say fifty grand?!" I couldn't believe that bogus device had cost so much.

"Well yeah," Chewie said as if I was the dense one. "You get what you pay for. No way I'd go with one of those cheap detectors that couldn't detect a ghost from a thetan. Only suckers would get those."

An anxious feeling settled in my stomach. "And did you use your own money, or did you expense it to the tour account?" Although I felt like an old teacher scolding a naughty child, I was here to do my job— not play Ghostbusters.

"Oh great, here it comes." He rolled his head back and groaned. "This was a legit band purchase. A rampant ghost on the loose will do a lot more damage than fifty grand and we don't have ghost insurance."

I wanted to slap my forehead but managed to restrain myself. If I'd met this space case in a bar, I would've laughed and given him a high-five, but this situation could quickly turn into a nightmare if I didn't put my foot down early. The band could walk over me with thousand-dollar ectoplasm-resistant boots and go bankrupt, and before I knew it I'd be out on the streets, holding up a sign reading "WILL DO TAXES FOR FOOD."

Still, it wasn't as easy as just putting my foot down, because I didn't want to be seen as the enemy. Honey always caught more flies than a flyswatter. I took a deep breath. "Chewie, I understand your concern about ghosts, but you're not seeing the big picture. I wouldn't want to be sucked into a TV and spit out with birthing fluid all over me, either, but we can't afford to pay for every contingency we see in a movie. What if a UFO crashes into the bus? There's no insurance for that. We just have to balance the risk with the expense. And I'm here to make sure we do that, so that at the end of the day, you guys get the money you deserve."

He furrowed his brows and scratched his chin. "Yeah, I guess you're right. Didn't think of it that way. The less we buy for the tour, the more weed I can get. Got it."

That wasn't really what I'd meant, but it seemed close enough for now. "Great," I said. "Oh, by the way, do you have any receipts or bills you could give me? I want to make sure all the important papers are kept in a single, safe place."

Chewie laughed, and it ended with a bit of a cough. "Only papers I'm in charge of are the rolling papers."

"Um, okay. Who should I speak with to get started then?"

He stroked his chin. "That'd be Jax. He's the man in charge around here. Wish I could be more help, but I'm only here to rock n' roll," he said, wiggling his fingers on an air guitar. "Jax'll be here soon enough though. Knowing him, he's probably busy fighting off a horde of women."

I was hoping the person in charge would be more responsible than Chewie, but it sounded like Jax was probably even less responsible. *Great.*

A ding came from Chewie's pocket. He pulled out a shiny, gold-plated iPhone and read the message. "Okay guys," he shouted so that everyone could hear. "We're shipping out soon, so let's shake a leg." Chewie turned to me. "I'll take your suitcase on board. You can wait for Jax on the bus if you want."

I held my hand up like a visor and looked at the blue sky. It had rained last night, leaving puddles here and there, but the gray clouds were nearly all gone, allowing the sun to shine through. "It's a nice day out, so I guess I'll wait for him here."

"*Suit* yourself," he said. I chuckled as he took my luggage and hopped onto the bus.

I took a deep breath, inhaling the crisp summer air. This was going to be some assignment. Judging by the exorbitant bus, the fifty-thousand dollar ghost detector, and the gold-plated iPhone, I could already tell that reining in the expenses was going to be a pain in the ass with a capital "P". But if I'd learned anything from the past three years at Hans-Peterson, it was that no matter how difficult the assignment, I'd always figure out a way to handle it.

I watched the roadies trying frantically to finish loading up all the gear into a trailer attached to a separate, smaller bus that had a psychedelic paint job and an assortment of rust splotches.

I walked over to one of the roadies stacking up empty boxes beside the warehouse, curious to see what he was doing. He was middle-aged with stringy hair and a wiry build.

"Looking for something?" he said, catching sight of me.

"Oh, nope," I replied. "Just killing time waiting for someone named Jax."

"Ah, I see. Trust me, you'll know when he's around."

I stared at the stack of empty boxes that looked like a modern day Stonehenge, wondering if it would've been easier to collapse them instead. The beautiful tower was just begging for someone to run into it, destroying all the hard work it took to build it.

When the roadie finished what he was doing, he locked the trailer, and he and all the other roadies piled onto the school bus.

What was just a flock of busy people was now a barren landscape. I was the only person left on the street. For a Brooklyn neighborhood on a Monday afternoon, the long city block was eerily empty and silent. Nothing but overfilled garbage cans along the curb and a few small saplings lining the sidewalk.

As I enjoyed the view of the skyscrapers in the distance, a crowd of people rounded the corner down the block. A group of at least a dozen men ran together with one person in the lead. *Was the marathon today?*

As the runners sped down the sidewalk toward me, I noticed that none of them were wearing numbers clipped to their shirts—and there wasn't a pair of running shorts in sight. No, it wasn't a marathon. It was a mob, and they were headed in my direction.

The throng of men appeared to be chasing someone in a white tank and black jeans. I couldn't make out his face from this distance, but I could tell from his figure that he was fit. A few of the men behind him were waving around wooden baseball bats. It looked so much like Frankenstein's monster getting chased out of town by angry villagers that I half-expected to see some of them carrying pitchforks and torches.

The guy being chased ran past a line of garbage cans and pulled each one down behind himself, spilling trash everywhere. The first chaser jumped over a rolling can, clearing it with ease. A fat guy followed, leaping to clear the debris, but caught his foot on a trash bag and fell flat on his face. A third man hurdled both the fat guy and the garbage, and the remaining men did as well. Tossing over the garbage cans had been a smooth move, but it couldn't stop them all.

As the mob's target approached, his jet black hair flowing wildly around his head, I noticed colorful sleeves of tattoos covering both of his bare arms. My eyes focused on his face—long, flowing black hair and a peppering of stubble—and then it clicked.

It was him!

Stud—the rock god, the male Siren—was the grand marshal of the carnival of chaos running full speed down the pavement. I didn't think I'd ever see him again, but there he was, racing in my direction with at least a dozen people chasing after him.

As they approached, the crowd's unintelligible shouting crystallized into words: "*Fuck you, motherfucker!*" "*Gonna beat your ass!*" The men chasing him were clearly not his adoring fans. I was no stranger to swearing, but even their vulgar cries made the hairs on the back of my neck prick up. These guys were seriously *pissed*.

Stud lingered in place for a moment, looking back at his pursuers. They were about to run right past me on their way to the bus when one of the men heaved his bat like a throwing knife. Stud jerked to the right to dodge it, changing his course. While he kept looking back to the mob of angry men, he was now running in a straight line toward me.

"Oh no. No, no!" I shouted, waving my hands frantically in front of me.

He turned his head to look forward. "Shit!" he yelled as I turned sideways and scrunched myself, bracing for impact.

He swerved out of the way at the last second, crashing into the tower of boxes and sending sheets of cardboard flying in all directions as he tumbled along the pavement. Groaning and rubbing his head, he staggered to his feet and faced me. Dark eyes squinted. "Pepper? What the hell are you doing here?" Hearing him say the nickname he'd given me sent an unwelcome flutter through my belly.

I was just as surprised as him. "What the hell are *you* doing h—"

"Now we've got you, you fucking scumbag!"

A brown haired guy running at full speed leapt into the air, launching himself like a torpedo at Stud. Stud fell onto his back and kicked his legs upward, sending the guy somersaulting into the air and landing with his head poked through a cardboard box. Stud flipped onto his feet then immediately ducked. A punch passed above his head, and the assailant lost his balance. Stud balled his fist and landed an uppercut against his jaw, sending him flying off his feet and then slumping back to the sidewalk in a lump of skin and clothing.

Another man arrived and landed a blow across Stud's jaw with a loud crack. The excruciating sound sent a tense dagger down my spine.

Stud quickly spit out some blood, then pivoted right in time to dodge a baseball bat to the skull. Stud retaliated with a swift punch to the batter's gut, sending him staggering backward into another guy, and then another, all of them collapsing to the ground like dominoes.

The fat one who had tripped over a trash bag earlier threw a jab, but Stud blocked it with his forearm. Stud absorbed another guy's kick to the torso with a primal grunt, then clocked the fat guy in the face. The fat guy wobbled for a split-second and fell backwards, hitting the ground with a heavy thud.

"You think you could get away with this, asshole?" screamed a guy holding an aluminum bat, nostrils flaring and eyes crazed. Although Stud was holding his own pretty well, there were too many of them for him to handle by himself. I began to fear for his life.

"Stop it!" I screamed as the blood rushed from my head. "Stop fighting!" My cries went ignored as two guys rushed at Stud. I frantically looked around to see if anyone could help out, but everyone was already on the bus far away.

I heard a bone-crunching slam, turned back, and saw more crimson drops splattered across the sidewalk. I couldn't tell whose blood it was. This was like the flip side of Saturday night—instead of women throwing panties and having orgasms, these men were throwing punches and hurling obscenities.

While Stud's back was turned, a goon with dreadlocks snuck up and wrapped thick arms around Stud's neck, squeezing him like a boa constrictor smothering its dinner. I couldn't tell if he was trying to choke Stud or break his neck. Stud grasped for his attacker's arm, trying to pry it off, but it wasn't budging. When I saw Stud's face turning a bluish-red, my entire body filled with dread.

He was going to die.

Adrenaline overruling fear, I tore off my silver locket and ran toward Stud. "CLOSE YOUR EYES!!" I shouted to him.

He closed them, and I squeezed my locket, blasting fifty milliliters of industrial-grade capsaicin into the eyeballs of the guy choking him.

Dreadlocks screamed in pain, releasing his grip to claw at his own face. "My eyes! My eyes!"

"You little bitch!" someone growled behind me.

I spun around and saw a scowling blonde guy winding up to punch me. I screamed and took a step back, tripping over my flats, dropping my necklace, and landing in a puddle of dirty gutter water. My bun came undone and hair clouded my vision.

A strong grip wrapped around my wrist from behind. "Get away from me!" I screamed, rolling around and kicking my legs and splashing water everywhere.

"Stop it!" he yelled.

"No!" One of my kicks landed in what felt like his crotch. He groaned in pain but didn't release his hold on me. *I should've worn heels!*

"Stop fighting me, dammit!" The next thing I knew, I was in the air, hoisted over a huge shoulder.

Brushing wet hair from my face, I realized we were moving away from the brawl. Panic shot through my veins.

He was kidnapping me.

"No! No! No!" I wailed at his back with my fists, trying my best to aim my blows at his kidneys, but his body was hard as fucking stone, and his firm grip around my waist only tightened. It was like being carried away by a gorilla.

"You idiot! It's me!" Stud's voice pierced through the adrenaline. My thrashing faltered. I blinked a few times and realized Stud was carrying me away from danger. The blond guy who had almost punched me was chasing after us. I feared he'd catch up, but when I looked back, I saw we were gaining on him. Stud was faster—even with me on his shoulder.

We reached the bus, bounded up the steps, and the doors slammed behind us.

The angry mob charged the bus, slamming their fists against the windows. One of the attackers reared his bat back and took a hard swing at the window in front of me. I screamed and shielded my face with my forearm. The bat shattered, sending splinters flying, but the glass didn't so much as wobble.

Thank god for this expensive-ass bus and its bullet-proof windows!

"Go, Bernie!" Stud shouted to the bus driver.

The driver stepped on the gas with a loud roar and we drove off, leaving the enraged mob in a cloud of sooty exhaust.

Chapter Six

ON THE BUS

"Put me down!" I demanded, adrenaline still coursing through my body. I was still over Stud's shoulder, his arms tight around my waist. His body was warm and he smelled good in that same way he did when I first met him, which only made my confusion and irritation worse.

He carried me further into the bus without saying anything, and I noticed a poster on the wall with bold letters that said "The Hitchcocks" with the silhouette of a raven perched above the "o".

So that's what "HC" stood for. Damn it, the announcer at the bar had used 'The Cocks' as shorthand; I should've made the connection sooner!

Closing the privacy divider behind us, he gently plopped me down on a leather couch.

"What the hell was that?" I asked as he straightened. "Who were those people?" I looked down at the damage. My blazer had a tear in one sleeve, my favorite skirt was puddle-splattered, and my hair was a wet mess, the tight bun I had earlier long gone. First day on the job—no, first *hour* on the job—and I was a wreck.

Stud calmly went to the wood-paneled bar a few feet away against the opposite wall and looked through a collection of liquor that would've made most bars proud. Picking up a bottle of Stoli, he poured himself a drink with a slight shake in his hand, spilling a few drops on the counter. His chest rose rapidly with each breath, silk hair damp against his shoulders. I watched him as he drank while looking outside at the passing cars; I was astonished that he was ignoring me, or at least taking his sweet time before answering.

"Hello?" I said, raising my voice to get his attention.

He put the tumbler to his lips again and tossed it back.

He's drinking vodka instead of answering me? I clenched my hands over my skirt in frustration. "Dude, hello??"

He finished a gulp, set the glass down, and turned back to face me. A few damp strands had fallen across his face, and he looked at me from behind inky locks. "The girl I slept with the other night . . . apparently she had a boyfriend," he said casually.

My eyes widened. "Are you saying I almost got beaten to a pulp all because you're a homewrecker?" I asked. I thought about how I saved him from Dreadlocks and threw my hands up in exasperation. "I can't believe this! I should've left you to get choked out by the Predator."

"Hey, if I'd known she had a boyfriend," he said gruffly, "I wouldn't have done it. She lied to me."

"Oh *sure*," I said, though it wasn't hard to imagine a girl lying to get into his pants. Compared to the lengths women went through on Saturday night to be with him—myself included—lying was a small thing.

"I'm serious. Look, I didn't mean to get you involved," he said, downing the last of his drink. Then he looked at me carefully. "Wait there for a second."

Reaching into a nearby cabinet, he pulled out a first aid kit and came over to the couch, where he knelt in front of me. "You're hurt. Let me take care of it."

His concern surprised me enough that I felt my irritation fading. I only had a few bumps and scratches, but I was still shaken after what had happened. I tried putting on a strong face. "I'm fine."

His eyes flicked to my arm. "No, you're not." He tried raising my right arm to see, but I pulled away when I saw a cut on his bottom lip. He was in much worse shape than I was.

"I'm fine," I repeated stubbornly. "It's just a scratch. Besides, you should take care of yourself first. I saw you take some hard hits."

"Shut up, Pepper," he grunted. "And let me see it." He tried lifting my arm again and, seeing how determined he was to care for my wounds before his own, I grudgingly let him. He touched the skin on my elbow gently and I flinched. "Hold still," he said with a calm but firm tone.

"Fine," I relinquished.

As he unpacked the first aid kit in front of me, I accidentally glanced at his eyebrow scar and then couldn't stop staring at it. I idly wondered if it came from a fight like the one we'd just had. On another face, it could've been a flaw. On Stud's, it gave him a dangerous, dark edge that made my heart beat faster.

Something touched my elbow. "Ow! Fuck! Motherfu—" He gripped my forearm firmly, holding me steady. I bit my lip, allowing him to finish cleansing the wound with hydrogen peroxide.

He blew softly on my skin, soothing the area before applying a bandage. "You had a pretty bad cut, but I cleaned out the dirt. Fortunately, you're not gonna need stitches."

"Thanks," I said, cheeks heated. I was more surprised by his tenderness than I was about the state of my wound. He didn't seem like the caring type.

"You helped me back there. It's the least I can do." Still kneeling, he pulled out some more supplies and began to tend to his own wounds.

"Do you need any help?" I offered.

Shaking the hair from his eyes, he smiled and shot me a curious look. "Do you know why this mess happened in the first place? It's because I trusted you that night."

My brows knitted together. "What?"

"I wouldn't have slept with that girl if you hadn't pulled that fast one on me, Pepper."

He's blaming me for all of this? My warm fondness for him evaporated quicker than the rubbing alcohol he was applying to his cuts. "Oh my god. Look," I said sternly, "first my name's not Pepper. It's Riley. Second, I'm not your boner's keeper."

His smile widened. "Riley, huh? I like that."

I waited for him to address the second part of my response. When he finished wrapping himself without answering, I realized his accusation had only been intended to push my buttons. *That jerk.* "Judging from what everyone around here says about you, you must be Jax. The *man in charge*," I said, using my fingers to make air quotes.

His smile faded. "You didn't already know?"

"No. I didn't know your name—or even the name of your band—until today."

He narrowed his eyes, looking genuinely perplexed. "You're telling me you showed up here without knowing who I was?"

"It's not my fault! Your label hired us last minute. All the files used the term 'HC' to refer to your band. I only now just figured out it stands for 'The Hitchcocks'."

"Wait," he said, his eyes widening. "*You're* the new tour accountant?"

Now I was the confused one. "What did you think I was?"

A moment passed and a devilish smile appeared on his lips. "Interesting."

Oh no. I knew that look. I'd seen it before, backstage at the Wallabee. It was the same one I remember picturing as I pleasured myself at the tail end of that night. "Whatever you're thinking, stop thinking about it."

The way his eyes grazed my figure made me begin to ache in other places. "I'm just thinking about what a pleasure it'll be working with you . . . " he said, the word *pleasure* rolling off his tongue like a silk ribbon, sensuous and inviting, ". . . if our first meeting was any indication."

Anxiety returned as the implications sunk in. I recalled Kristen's advice about not mixing business with pleasure and realized that I already had, even before my first day on the assignment. *God. Fuuuck my life*.

"Shh!" I hissed, holding my finger to my lips. I dared to lean closer to that beautiful face of his and whispered harshly, "I had no idea who you were at the time. Don't tell anyone that happened. I could be fired if my company finds out."

His devilish smile spread into a provocative grin. "Of course not. We'll keep it just between us."

The way he used the word "us" didn't sit well with me at all. I took a deep, calming breath.

"We might've had an . . . unusual introduction, Jax. But from here on out, our relationship's going to be strictly professional. That means no kissing. No flashing your cock at me. None of that. *Capisce*?" I said, jabbing my finger into the air for emphasis.

I needed to be forceful with him from the start. I needed to establish distance between us and

professional boundaries we wouldn't cross.
Otherwise, I could easily see myself being in more
trouble than I could handle.

He gently took my unsteady hand and clasped it
between his warm palms. "Everything you're saying
is exactly what I want to hear," he said evenly.

I blinked a few times. Did he just agree with me?
I'd mentally prepared a few more responses in case
he didn't get the message, but he seemed strangely
agreeable. "Seriously?"

"Yeah," he said, lifting my chin gently so I looked
directly into his eyes. "I like a challenge."

Minutes later, I was seated on the edge of the couch,
pinching the bridge of my nose, exasperated.

I'd tried talking sense into Jax after he'd made his
intentions clear, but it was like talking to a wall. He'd
got up, put the medical kit away, and said he was
going to have someone give me a tour of the bus
while he cleaned up. Then he disappeared upstairs.

Unbelievable. As if almost getting killed a few
minutes ago wasn't bad enough. Now the rock god
who I'd given blue balls to was my company's
client—essentially my boss in some ways—and he
was determined to finish what he'd started that night
backstage. The situation was even *worse* than I'd
imagined.

I could try talking to him again, I thought. But
given the track record between us so far, I'd probably
sooner convince Chewie that ghosts were fake than
convince Jax to find a different "challenge" elsewhere.
Feeling awful about the whole situation, I decided
cleaning myself up might help calm my nerves.

Searching the first floor, I found my luggage in a
small storage area, pulled out a spare skirt and tank
top, and went to the bathroom to put them on.

Because I was still covered in muddy water, I did a quick rinse of my hair and makeup. And then I reached into my purse for a badly needed lifesaver and ate it. When I finally came out, I was surprised to find a girl waiting for me.

"Hello!" she said with a light, lilting voice. Her figure was slim, and she was wearing black yoga pants with a matching tank top. Her tightly braided, bleach-blonde hair made her look like she had walked out of a punk video, but her huge, fawn-brown eyes softened the effect. "I heard you're our new accountant. And that you saved Jax!"

I'd been expecting Chewie to give me a tour since I'd met him earlier but this was a surprise in more ways than one. I didn't realize there was a girl in the band. Then again, there had been a lot of things I hadn't realized because I had been so focused on Jax that night at the bar. If it hadn't been for Jax's mesmerizing body, I would've recognized Chewie the moment I met him.

"Hi, I'm Riley Hewitt." I smiled and extended my hand. "He was exaggerating about the life-saving part. It was just a bit of pepper spray."

She chuckled and shook her head. "Just a typical day in the life of Jax Trenton. Women and men alike love him. But the men that have girlfriends hate him. You get used to it after a while. Sky Reynolds, by the way."

Sky made it sound like this was a regular thing for him. I grimaced. "Seems like his good looks are a curse."

"Blessing and a curse, I guess." She shrugged. "Wait a second," she said, squinting. "Do I know you from somewhere?"

An awful thought occurred to me. *Did she remember me as the girl Jax picked out from the crowd at the bar?* I laughed uneasily. "Probably not. I think I just have one of those faces."

"Hmm . . . I feel like we went to school together or something. Did you go to the Anderson School?"

I shook my head. "No, never." I'd heard of the school before—it was up on the Upper West Side, which was culturally and socially about a million miles from where I grew up on Staten Island.

Sky shrugged. "Ah, okay, my bad. I'm not so good with remembering people and I've seen so many faces from doing shows that it's almost always like: wait, haven't we met before?" She laughed, and I joined her. "So how much of the bus have you gotten a chance to see?"

I gestured to indicate the living area we were in. There was basically the kitchen, bar, bathroom, couch, and a small storage area for luggage. "This, mostly. Stud—I mean, Jax—didn't get a chance to show me anything upstairs."

One of her high-arched eyebrows rose when I called Jax "Stud," but she didn't say anything about it. "We'll start from the top, then," she said, taking my hand and leading me to the staircase. "So if you're a tour accountant, I'm guessing you enjoy music. Do you play anything?"

My cheeks warmed slightly. I was on a bus full of musical talent, but the truth was, I had almost none. "I mostly play Angry Birds," I said with a laugh. "I like listening to music, but every time I've tried playing an instrument, it sounded like a dying cat."

Sky chuckled as we took the stairs. Once we arrived at the top, she opened the door onto a large sundeck. Half-walls made the space open to the air, and I could hear the cars on the highway below us. A table and two chairs stood next to a bar—bigger and better than the one on the first floor—toward the front, and a larger, round table was at the back.

"This is incredible," I said, looking around in awe.

"You haven't seen the best part of the sundeck. This bus has the only one like it." With that, she stepped to the far side of the deck, and pulled the top off the table. When I saw what it really was—a hot tub easily big enough for four people—my jaw dropped in surprise.

"Are you kidding? A hot tub on a bus?" My mental calculator shifted into overdrive. It wasn't just the installation of the tub that I found extravagant. It was the chemicals, the electricity, the plumbing . . . It would be expensive to maintain even while operating perfectly. And if it broke . . .

She grinned. "Amazing, right? Use it whenever you want. It gets better." She pressed a button on the deck's back wall. A noisy hum began, and a shadow fell over the two of us from above.

I looked up to see a cover rolling over the bus, making a ceiling. I gasped. It was a *convertible*. I couldn't imagine what it had cost. I knew the details would be in the email from Palmer, but it was becoming increasingly clear that the band was spending their money as fast as they could possibly be making it.

"Now I know I'm dreaming," I said, trying hard to keep the disapproval out of my voice. I didn't want to get a reputation as the party pooper on my first day—I knew from experience that being too harsh, too soon with a client could lead them to hiding expenses from me. "Want to show me the other floors?"

"Suit yourself, but this is the best one."

She led me down the stairs, to the bus' second level—a cramped hallway with four narrow doors.

"All the bedrooms are here, along with another bathroom."

"Only three bedrooms?" I asked.

"Kev and Chewie share," she said, pointing to one of the doors. "Chewie's my big brother, and a pretty great drummer . . . even if I'll never say that to his face." She smiled. "Kev is Chewie's bunkmate, the band's lead guitarist, and a dead ringer for Ryan Gosling. But if you're smart, you'll never tell him that. He's a little sensitive about the whole baby face thing."

I made a mental note of it—but that wasn't the only reason I'd asked. "And . . . where will I be sleeping, exactly?"

"Well, the good news is, you've got a couple of options. Bad news is, they're all couches. You can borrow a pillow or two from me if you don't have any. I've got tons."

I was grateful. A pillow hadn't been on my packing list. "This, over here, is my room," Sky continued, her words fast and light. "I'll even open the door. Just ignore the mess, okay?"

She pulled open a door to reveal a bedroom not much larger than a closet. A double bed took up almost the entire floor, leaving a space in front of the mattress edge just wide enough to stand in. Rock concert posters, old and new, covered the walls. On the bed was a bass guitar, along with papers around it. As I looked a little closer, I noticed hand-drawn music notes, some scribbled out, on the papers.

"Wow. Do you write the songs for the band?" I asked, pointing to the papers.

"Me?" She laughed. "I just play bass. This is something I've been working on for fun." It struck me how different her life was from mine; I couldn't have imagined getting home from my job and working with more numbers just for the hell of it.

She closed the door to her room, and pointed to the third door. "That, over there, is Jax's room, AKA the Fortress of Solitude. He likes to go in there and hole up."

I stared at the door to his bedroom, finding myself curious. What was it like in there? A hot mess like what I've seen of him? Or clean like the green room from that night? Why was I even wondering about this?

Sky, seeing my gaze locked on Jax's bedroom door, raised an eyebrow. "I wouldn't go in, if I were you."

"Oh, I wasn't," I said hurriedly, hoping she didn't think I had a thing for Jax.

She shook her head, giving me a wry half-smile. "I know."

Her smile gave me pause. "Are you and Jax together? I mean, not that it matters, I'm just curious."

"Heh. No. Jax isn't exactly the 'together' type, with anyone," she said, wrinkling her nose. "The length of his relationships can usually be measured with a stopwatch."

From what I knew about Jax already, I wasn't surprised. "I guess it must be easy to move from girl to girl when you're a rock star," I said lightheartedly.

"It's not that," Sky said in a quiet voice. "Believe me. He was like this before he ever wrote his first song. I've known him since he was fifteen, and he's just not wired for real relationships—rock star or not. There's no soft, mushy core in Jax, and there never has been."

"Ah, I see." It was more candor than I was expecting, and yet another sign clearly pointing to Jax as bad news. The more I learned about The Hitchcocks' frontman, the more I resolved myself to keep him at arm's length.

I'd seen him for the first time just a few days ago, and in that time, he'd nearly caused a riot at his own show, flashed his cock at me, and been chased by a jealous mob. And in the midst of all that, I'd had my life threatened multiple times. He wasn't just a bad boy anymore; he was a very real danger.

When it came to a man as desired and dangerous as Jax, there was only one way I could keep both my job and my life safe. Look, but don't touch.

"Anyway!" She wrapped her arms around my neck and hugged me tightly. "I'm *so* glad there's another girl on this bus!"

I squeezed her back, realizing how much better I felt after having met Sky. She seemed like a kind, cool girl that I could hang out with, especially if I wanted an excuse to avoid Jax.

Chapter Seven

PUSHING BUTTONS

"What are you doing up there, Sky?" a voice came from the first floor—a masculine voice, but without Jax's velvety smoothness.

"They must have gone downstairs when we were up on the deck," Sky said to me. "Come on, let's go."

We walked down the steep bus steps to the living area. Chewie sat hunched over, looking at a metal machine in the middle of the room that I didn't recognize. Behind him stood a man with soulful, pale blue eyes and blonde hair. I realized in an instant that it must be Kev—the resemblance to Ryan Gosling really was uncanny. Next to Chewie's tripped-out persona and Jax's larger-than-life bad-boy presence, Kev's clean-cut look made him seem like the boy scout of the group.

In any other rock band, Chewie and Kev would have been the ones with admirers hanging off them. But compared to Jax, they looked like overgrown boys. A joint hung limply in Chewie's mouth as he twisted the machine's parts. His frizzy hair and big sunglasses were haloed with thick, skunky smoke. "Okay, I give up," he said, looking up at us hopelessly. "Either of you know how to work this?"

I looked at the machine, which seemed almost industrial. It was relatively small, and had an empty round part at the bottom. I shrugged. "I don't even know what it is. Sorry."

"Oooh!" Sky burst out, as gleeful as a kid. "Is that the new button maker?"

Chewie nodded. "It's supposed to be able to make a button a minute, but Kev and I tried for an hour up in our room and only managed to do . . . *this*." He gestured to the end table, where I saw two mangled buttons with The Hitchcocks' logo emblazoned on them. The paper with the band's logo was flapping away from the metal backing of the pin, which in turn was bent almost in half.

Sky looked at the twisted metal circles and laughed. "What did you do? Did you even bother reading the directions?"

Chewie lifted his sunglasses slightly, showing his brown eyes beneath. "Directions? We're men. No directions, no problem."

Kev sighed. "Also, we lost them."

Sky looked at him, dumbfounded. "You lost them?! Now we've got a useless button maker machine and we wanted to have the buttons ready for Chicago tomorrow night."

"Maybe it's a dud," Chewie said. "We might've just gotten a bad machine. We could throw it out."

I'd seen all kinds of wasteful spending on the bus—from the ridiculous hot tub to the insane quantities of top-shelf liquor—but this was becoming ridiculous. "Wait a minute," I said. "Are you seriously talking about throwing this out? Look, Chewie, how much can you sell a button for at the merch table?"

"Five bucks, I guess?"

"So if you could make a button every minute, that's *three hundred dollars per hour*. Can you really afford to give that up?"

Sky grinned at me. "You have to put this in terms Chewie will understand," she said, elbowing her brother playfully. "Chewie, the accountant says you could make an ounce of weed an hour."

"Damn," he said, shaking his head, "that's a lot. But that still doesn't mean I can figure out how to use it."

I pushed up the sleeves on my blouse. "Here, let me try. Let me see one of each of the supply parts." I looked for the back of the button first—that part was easy, it had a pin. I slid it into the machine, then put a blank piece of metal, artwork, and a cover over it. "That's gotta be the right order," I mumbled, half to myself. Nothing else would make it possible to see the artwork and have the pin in the right position. "Now we just have to figure out how to use it. If I just bring this lever here down . . . and then we . . ."

After a few seconds, I lifted the lever and brought out a perfectly serviceable Hitchcocks logo button. Smiling, I handed the masterpiece to Chewie.

"Far out," Chewie said then turned his head toward the stairwell. "Yo, Jax, we have a button maker!"

My smile faded and pulse quickened as Jax came downstairs, a towel wrapped around his waist. If he was wearing anything else, I couldn't see it. His muscled torso gleamed, and I had an unwelcome urge to reach out and touch him. "Good," he said with an approving nod toward me. "We've needed that."

His sudden appearance refreshed my mind of our last interaction, and my positive mood quickly soured.

As he went to the bar, Sky said, "Want to stay here and make buttons with us?"

He shook his head. "I'm going to my room to write. Instead of messing with buttons, you guys should be practicing the set—we've got a big show tomorrow and I don't want anyone blowing it." He locked eyes with me for a moment sending a flutter through my stomach before heading to the stairs with a couple bottles of Guinness.

As he walked up, I couldn't help myself from honing in on the firm contours of his towel-clad ass.

Wow. I'd been so focused on everything he had going on in the front—tatts, muscles, nipple rings, and all—that I hadn't taken a moment to appreciate the magnificent backside he had. My fingers flexed with a sudden urge to slap it.

When I stopped staring, I realized my mouth had been open and the band members were all looking straight at me.

"What?" I asked, hastily assembling a new button in the machine to hide my embarrassment.

Kev shook his head, smiling faintly. "It's just like watching a nature show—the mating displays of the alpha male, starring Jax Trenton."

"Mating display?" I said.

"He gave you that 'look'," Kev said. "Like he's marked you as his prey,"

"Well, he's barking up the wrong tree," I defended, not liking how accurate his assessment of the situation probably was.

Chewie lifted his sunglasses and looked at me with big brown eyes. "Yeah, man, but this is Jax. You don't even *know* yet."

"Ugh, I don't care if he's Casanova," I said, popping out a button and readying another one. "I'm not interested. He's really not my type."

"He's every woman's type," Sky said soberly.

The trio looked at me skeptically. Everyone looked like they wanted to say something, but they were keeping it in. The room was uncomfortably silent for a moment.

I cleared my throat. "So the buttons . . . what are you guys planning on doing about them?"

"Well we can't practice and make the buttons at the same time," Kev said, "I volunteer Sky."

She shot him a disapproving look. "Hey, I need to practice too! This is all your fault anyway, you and Chewie couldn't do it right the first time."

Completing another button, I sighed. I knew what I had to do. "You know what, why don't you guys go practice. I'll take over the button-making."

"You sure, Riley?" Sky asked.

"Yeah. This stuff has to do with money. So, in a way, I'm responsible for it."

Chewie and Kev, excited to have someone else working on the buttons, started interrupting each other to give me the supplies.

"Here, take the pins—"

"These are the covers—"

"And art—"

"And here comes Chewie with the metal!" Chewie said, using an exaggerated voice, which made me giggle. He brought the box of blank buttons down across his body in a sweeping arc like he was playing a power chord.

Kev burst into laughter and moved toward the steps. "Was that supposed to be a guitar? I've gotta go practice so I don't look like you."

"Sorry, man, I only play real instruments," Chewie said, getting up to follow Kev upstairs. "Like drums. That's a man's instrument."

Sky let out an exasperated sigh in their direction as they disappeared into the second level, then turned to me. "I've gotta go practice with these apes. Help yourself to anything in the fridge. And don't forget to get some sleep, even though the couches pretty much suck."

"Thanks." I was grateful for her. Even though Jax had made me feel more wary than welcome, I was starting to feel more at home on the bus, and Sky had a lot to do with it.

As the band scattered to their rooms upstairs, I settled in with the button supplies. The rhythms of instruments flowed around me; I could hear the faint thrumming of guitars along with Jax's velvety voice quietly echoing through the thin walls. In an attempt to keep my mind off him, I turned my body into an efficient, rhythmic machine. Assemble pieces, pull the lever, toss the finished pin in the big cardboard merch box. Assemble, lever, toss.

Jax "marking" me as his target and the outrageous spending aside, I was grateful to find that the rest of the band was pretty cool. This tour accountant gig was certainly better than sitting in a stuffy cubicle all day at Hans-Peterson. Although there was a hell of a lot of work to get done, I was oddly relieved by the prospect of having two weeks away from Manhattan.

Jax may have liked challenges, but so did I. With all the opportunities to keep myself—and my thoughts—busy, I couldn't help but feel a hint of smug satisfaction. He might've thought that he had the upper hand, leaving me to stew on our interaction this morning along with the image of that towel-clad ass of his. But between the two of us, I was definitely the craftier one.

Night fell, and the once-empty box was nearly full to the brim with buttons. After the first couple hundred, it had been easy to completely lose track of time—not quite as relaxing as yoga, maybe, but meditative in its own way. The only annoyance was the lever. It stuck just enough each time that I had to shove the machine with my shoulder, leaving me a little sorer with each button that went *ker-plink* into the box.

Small price to pay for avoiding Jax. Sky, Kev, and Chewie had come down for snacks periodically, but Jax never did. Fortunately.

Completing another button, my knotted upper back went into a full cramp. "Ouch!" I rubbed at the aching muscle and got up from the couch to stretch, only to hear my stomach growling loudly, reminding me that I hadn't eaten all day.

Looking around for food, the gleaming steel of the refrigerator caught my eye. When I opened it, I saw that The Hitchcocks' fridge was crammed with more pre-made sandwiches, salads, and reheatable meals than the band could possibly eat before it went bad. Imagining the amount of food that went to waste only made me crankier.

Sighing, I scanned the shelves, taking stock of my options, before spotting fresh fruit on the bottom level. I bent low to pick up what looked to be the last plum in the fridge. But when I reached for it, the fruit slipped from my hand, forcing me to bend further and lunge to grab it before it disappeared behind a case of beer. Cool air from the fridge wafted up the back of my skirt, welcome and refreshing.

"Looks juicy," a voice said behind me.

Straightening in surprise, I bonked my head on the shelf above me. "Ow! Dammit!" Massaging the back of my skull, I whirled around to find Jax leaning against the far wall looking exactly where my ass had been.

"Ripe, tender—must be delicious," he purred, arms crossed and stroking his chin. He nodded toward the fruit in my hand. "The plum, that is."

The dull throbbing on the back of my head was irritating, but him standing there looking smug and sexy made it so much worse. He was wearing black jeans that hugged his toned thighs and a matching black tank that exposed the sculpted contours of his broad shoulders. His preference for black suited his personality.

"You just made me hit my head, you jerk," I accused, ignoring his innuendo. His insinuation had clearly been bait, and I preferred to avoid playing into his hands.

"You're upset. And you hurt your head. Come here," he said in a casual tone. He pushed off the wall and spread his muscular arms, motioning for me to receive a sympathetic hug. "You need this."

The invitation was tempting, and I really could've used a hug, but I didn't want one from him. There'd inevitably be strings attached. And Jax was good at plucking strings.

"What I need," I said with a dismissive wave, "is my job, my paycheck, and for your band to stop spending so much money."

"I think you need more than you realize."

"Yeah, you're right." I pointed grumpily at my stomach. "Like food." I lifted the plum to my mouth and took a bite. "Mmmm . . . just what I *needed*."

He watched me chew with seemingly greater interest than the activity deserved. I heard his stomach growl then he swallowed hard. "I came here for a sandwich, but now you're making me want a plum."

I grinned when I realized I had the upperhand. "Too bad, this is the last one," I said with barely repressed delight. I couldn't resist the urge to get back at him for all the shit he'd put me through since this morning, so I raised the plum like a trophy. "And it's *all* mine." Bringing it back down to my mouth, I took an aggressive bite.

He'd been right—it was juicy, and my teeth sinking violently into the soft flesh made sweet nectar dribble down my chin. Too stubborn to wipe it off, I let it drip freely in defiance.

"Mmm," I moaned loudly. "*So* good."

His eyes narrowed as his arms fell to his sides. "You're teasing me."

"Me?" I mumbled, mouth full. "Why, I'm shocked you'd think I'd do such a thing." I batted my eyelashes at him obnoxiously. I was still chewing what I bit off from my previous bite, but I took another chomp anyway and rubbed my belly for good measure. I could tell from his expression that I was pissing him off. I wasn't ordinarily a petty person, but Jax was an exception; seeing him irritated by my antics brought me great enjoyment, since I knew he deserved it.

Without warning, he walked over to where I was, eyes focused intently on my mouth. His tattooed body and rippling shoulders set off alarm bells as he entered into my personal space. I could smell him— an earthy, rich, testosterone-loaded scent that was intoxicating.

An unwanted shiver of desire moved through me. I wanted to take a step back, but I held my ground. I couldn't back away. Not here. I couldn't show weakness around a man like Jax, or he'd try to take advantage of that weakness whenever he could.

I bit down on the plum again, savoring its juices and eyeing his presence warily. I searched his eyes in an attempt to figure out what he wanted, and when I saw the blaze in those inky irises, my grip on the plum tightened. If he wanted to take it, he'd have to use a crowbar to pry it from my fingers.

He reached out, cupping my face then brushing the side of my mouth with his thumb. He brought his thumb to his lips and sucked the nectar from the pad.

"I was right," he purred seductively as he savored the juice. "Delicious."

My heart skipped. *Oh no.* I was starting to feel it: that inescapable pull, the sheer force of his sexuality unleashed on me through those dark, haunting eyes. Somehow the situation had turned dangerously flirtatious—exactly what I didn't want to be doing if I wanted to have a job in accounting at the end of this tour.

"I—I really should get back to making buttons," I said, turning away. Taking one last bite, I tossed the pit in the trash, and went back to that dreaded machine. As I bent, trying to make sure I didn't give Jax any more upskirt views, my shoulder twinged again. "Fuck!" I cried, bolting upright as the muscle cramp intensified.

His eyes narrowed as he stared my shoulder. "What happened? Are you still hurt from this morning?" His voice was heavy with concern, the flirtiness from before gone.

"No, it's just this damn machine," I said, spinning my arm in slow circles. "It gets stuck, so I have to push it hard."

"Here, lay down." He gestured to the couch.

Feeling more achy by the second, I didn't have much of a choice. I slowly eased myself down on the couch with his help. When I settled into a semi-comfortable position on my back, I looked up at him seated on the armrest. "Thanks."

"Don't thank me yet," he said. His expression was unreadable as he swirled his finger. "Turn over."

My brows lifted. "And why would I do that?"

"So I can give you a massage."

Laughter burst from my lips, and I smiled. "Well, I've got to give you credit for your persistence. I appreciate the offer, but I'm already comfor—Ow!" My shoulder spasmed again.

Damn it. It was if my body was conspiring against me.

"Don't be stubborn, Riley. You're in pain. We're both losing from this."

His tone—and the fact that he called me Riley instead of Pepper—made me think he was being serious. Still, I was wary about agreeing to receive a massage from *him*. A man who had clearly stated his intentions to pursue me. A man who could trigger an orgasm with a chorus.

I narrowed my brows. "How so?"

"You can't do your job if you're hurt, and if you can't do your job, you can't manage our finances."

Crap. He had a good point. "I'll be fine," I mumbled.

"You said our relationship was going to be strictly professional, and that's what this massage is. Professional. Trust me."

The ache began to worsen again and just looking at his beautiful face and hearing his deep voice was starting another ache of its own—this time between my legs. "Alright," I resigned petulantly, eager to move to a position where I wasn't facing him. "Just don't try anything fu—" Before I could finish, he gripped my legs and deftly flipped me over. The smooth move left me wondering how the hell he pulled it off without hurting me.

Jax came around to my side and the next thing I knew, I felt light pressure through the back of my blouse, long fingers gently exploring the landscape of knotted muscles.

My eyes widened. *Good lord, that feels good.*

From the first touches, it was obvious he knew what he was doing. My body responded to him like clay in a potter's hands. I hated to admit it, but I found myself relaxing, the soreness fading fast.

His thumbs worked at a place in my neck where I'd ached ever since I got whiplash on a Tilt-a-Whirl when I was in high school. Jax may have had his faults—manwhore, arrogant, dangerous, to name a few—but being bad at massages was not one of them.

With one palm on each side of my spine, he folded his fingers together and made a sharp, quick motion. My neck cracked with a loud *snap*.

"Aaaah! Did you just break my neck?!" I cried. I reached to rub at the ache, expecting to feel a bone popping out the side of my neck only to find that my neck now bent more when I flexed it—and it didn't hurt.

"Relax," he said in a low voice that seemed almost intimate. "This is just the beginning. I had to do that to loosen you up."

Finding nothing out of place, and in fact actually feeling much better, I settled my cheek back onto the leather cushion. He resumed kneading my back and shoulders, and it wasn't long before I found my eyes closing and thoughts of the hectic day dissipating by the second.

"You're holding your breath," he said softly as his fingers plied at sensitive muscle. "You need to relax."

I exhaled with control, becoming aware that his hands had moved to my lower back and that I'd been holding my breath ever since they got there. "I am relaxed."

"That's better. Now you are," he said, pushing at a tender spot, making electricity jolt up my spine. It felt amazing and I bit my lower lip to prevent a sound from escaping. "You know . . ." he said softly, "moaning helps."

With my eyes closed and my body feeling like gelatin, I managed a wry smile. "If you think I'm going to moan for you, I wouldn't get your hopes up."

"You will," he said, so casually that it seemed trivial.

"I won't," I responded, mimicking his tone.

He settled into a rhythm, kneading the muscles along my neck and working his way down my back, then starting at my neck again. Slow, languid movements. Soft but firm. Up. And down. Again and again.

"Little harder, right there," I breathed, as I felt Jax's hand drift over a sore spot at the base of my lower back. He lifted the bottom of my blouse slightly and splayed his warm hands over the area, gradually increasing the pressure with the heels of his palms. I found little reason to resist and lacked the energy to as well. With the barrier between his hands and my skin removed, his touches felt twice as good.

"Harder," I insisted softly.

"Patience." He took his time, squeezing his thumb into the ache, steadily increasing the pressure and sending relief flooding through my body.

My fingers dug into the leather cushion. I arched into his palms, feeling the heat of his body spreading into mine. His hands were so big they could almost cover my whole back at once, and I squirmed against them trying to feel their radiating pressure.

I was vaguely aware of his muscular thighs straddling me as he leaned his body into the movements. I writhed beneath his touch, my heartbeat pounding in my ears. I couldn't think of anything but sensation.

I felt something warm near my shoulder and realized it was his breath, hot and hungry and so very close. His mouth lingering inches away from my flushed skin, I trembled with a need that I knew better than to fulfill.

"You smell incredible," he whispered, his mouth close to me, the rasp in his words vibrating through my body, making me shudder with pleasure. Emotions swirled in my head, but the one that dominated was lust. Tornadic, destructive lust. I wanted him.

As his lips brushed against my shoulder, I opened my mouth and released the pent-up energy. The moan that escaped my lips sounded like one I would have right before an orgasm.

Then nothing. The sudden absence of Jax's hands on my skin felt almost like pain.

Still throbbing with need, I twisted at the waist, maddeningly confused. I watched him stand up, pick out a sandwich from the fridge, and walk toward the stairwell, whistling a tune I recognized as one of the songs the band had played at the Wallabee.

He reached the steps and turned back to me, a mischievous glint in his eyes. "That's for New York. See you in Chicago, *Riley*."

Chapter Eight

FIRST STOP: CHICAGO

Half an hour before The Hitchcocks were scheduled to take the stage, I was doing exactly what I was hired to do: making steady progress on paperwork. Only I was in a backstage maintenance room, surrounded by power tools and foul-smelling cleaning supplies. I'd been trying to avoid Jax all day—and so far, I was succeeding.

I'd thought about calling Kristen in the morning to tell her about all the craziness of yesterday with Jax, but she already had so much on her plate with the baby that I decided to call Jen instead. I was relieved to get it off my chest.

Jen had been surprised and sympathetic at first, but then she'd changed her tune. "Typical Riley. Always getting into trouble. I'm not there to hold you back this time, so if you're basically living in close quarters with the rock god, you're pretty much fucked." Jen's lack of faith in me only bolstered my determination to keep Jax at a distance. I'd show her. And Jax.

Jax. Ugh! I put my hands over my face and hung my head in front of the laptop screen. Just remembering how he left me with blue balls last night—or whatever the female equivalent was called—made me furious. And the worst part was I'd been stupid enough to fall for it. Although he'd fixed my sore shoulder, I ended up tossing and turning through the night, and not because the couch cushion felt like it was made out of bamboo.

I was just too aroused to fall asleep.

I'd considered ways of relieving the tension—the privacy of the bathroom being one tempting option—but I was too stubborn. I could picture him smugly imagining me touching myself from the massage he'd given me.

My first reaction had been to retaliate. I'd spent at least a half hour pondering how to get him back, giggling maniacally to myself as I brainstormed ways of getting my hands on Viagra using an old-man disguise. I'd give him balls so blue that a smurf would look at them and say, "Damn, that's blue!"

Then I'd snapped to my senses. That was exactly what he wanted. He wanted me to play games with him. And that's why I made up my mind this morning to stay away from Jax at any cost—even if it meant doing my work seated on a propane tank with my laptop on a rusted oil drum.

Shaking my head of stray thoughts, I took a sip from what was my fourth coffee of the day, and got back to reviewing the files.

The Hitchcocks were skyrocketing in the charts—the newest Billboard chart showed their album *Wild* at number twenty-six and rising. And to think, I'd thought they were just some local act that regularly played at dive bars when I first saw them. Turns out, their impromptu show had been a publicity stunt to drum up media excitement for the tour.

But despite their growing success, I was right to worry about the financial health of the band. Every month, they were spending as much as they were making, sometimes more.

It wasn't sustainable. No wonder the label saddled Hans-Peterson with a two-week temporary stint; they wanted a hatchet man. The Hitchcocks didn't need a kind, gentle money manager. They needed someone to do a hack-and-slash job on the budget so everyone could keep getting paid. Every time I pieced another expense into the band's financial picture, it looked worse.

The Hitchcocks needed budget cuts, but from what? Jax would be the best person to ask, but I didn't want to get sucked into another one of his games.

As I sighed and opened another spreadsheet, a knock interrupted me.

"Come in," I said, turning away from my laptop.

The door swung open, and a man with dark suntanned skin and sunglasses burst in. He sported a blonde ponytail behind a slicked-back hairline that had just started receding. He was attractive for sure, though he had probably been hotter a decade ago. Dressed in a sharp white suit sans tie and with the top button of his pink oxford casually undone, he reminded me of an older, more shopworn version of David Beckham. The sparkling diamonds in his ears and shiny Rolex peeking out from beneath his right cuff made it clear he was rich—or, at least, that he really wanted people to think so.

"Riley, baby," he said with a voice as slick as his hair. "I've been looking all over for you."

"Huh? Sorry, have we met before?"

"Name's Reed." He posed for a second as if to let me drink in his image. "I'm the band manager."

Ah, that explains it. Palmer's dossier had mentioned Reed. Somehow, I'd expected him to look a little more down-to-earth. If this man, with his diamond earrings and expensive suit, was managing the band, it was no wonder they saw nothing wrong with spending their money as fast as they made it. He was the reason this job was such a pain in my ass.

"Riley Hewitt. Nice to meet you," I offered. I shook his hand cordially and he squeezed a little too hard. It was a clear assertion of dominance and I didn't like it. After thinking about the situation for a moment, I realized that it was in Reed's best interest that the band had a high spending budget, precisely because it made his commission look small. That unfortunately made our positions at odds.

He opened his mouth as if to say something, but stopped as he looked around the room. "By the way, what are you doing back here?"

"Uh, just needed a place to focus, that's all."

"Ah, great. You're a go-getter. I like to hear that. Now, listen, Riley, I think we should go over a few things while you're getting started. Is now a good time?"

I sighed, putting my computer in suspend mode. Reed being here right now wasn't ideal, but I needed to talk to him about the budget before the tour went much further. He seemed like a busy man and I had no idea when I would see him again. Besides, it would be good to finally find out a bit more about how the band operated. "It's as good a time as any."

"This your first tour? What a crazy band to start with," he said, not waiting for me to answer the initial question. "What do you think of the band so far?" He leaned forward intently.

"They're . . . not bad." I thought they were—as a whole—extremely talented musicians, but my unfavorable opinion of Jax tainted my overall view.

"Jax isn't bad, you mean," he said, an eyebrow raised.

Oh God. Does he know?

I tried to hide the nervousness in my voice. "He's a good singer," I allowed.

"And?"

I didn't like where this was going. "He's very . . . tall?"

"He's fucking hot, and you know it."

My cheeks heated and I cleared my throat. "Okay?"

Reed shook his head. "You don't get it. With a look like that, Jax could be—correction, *will* be—the biggest cash cow I've ever managed. It's why I've got big plans for the band. Why they needed the big bus."

"About that bus," I said, a note of annoyance creeping into my tone, "Why all the crazy amenities? The convertible modifications alone must have cost a fortune."

"Riley, have you ever heard of GMZ? Perry Hilton? Hawker? How about Humans Magazine?" He started talking with his hands, gesticulating with nearly every word. "The best publicity you can get is the free kind, and that tour bus is the best marketing tool the band has. Hell, the hot tub alone got us a dozen write-ups in gossip rags. The paparazzi eat this shit up."

Even though I didn't read that kind of stuff, it made sense. Magazines and websites didn't cover bands for managing their money well. People wanted excitement, novelty, and luxury—they could get frugality at home. Even so, I couldn't give in that easily. If Reed thought he could sweet-talk me out of doing my job, he'd have to think again.

"You do realize I'm here for a reason, right?" I said. "The Hitchcocks are going to run out of money if I don't fix their finances. I'm only here because if it's not straightened out now, they won't have enough cash on hand for expenses through the end of the tour."

"The label's worried for nothing," he said, shaking his head. "This band is on the cusp of greatness. One, maybe two more hit singles, and they'll have a number one album. And then the money makes itself.

We just have to keep pushing the promotion budget in the short term."

I didn't like the sound of that. "What do you mean by 'pushing'?"

"With an extra ten, maybe fifteen percent add-on to the promo budget—that's stuff like giveaway posters, bumper stickers, spending on social media, getting radio interviews—The Hitchcocks could really shine. After that, money's not a worry. They'll be rolling in it."

"If they don't run out of cash and have to cancel tour stops first."

He waved a hand in the air dismissively. "Don't believe the bluster and bullshit from the label. They won't cook the goose that lays the golden eggs."

I shot him a skeptical look. "They seemed pretty serious when they called my firm, or I wouldn't be here."

"It's their job to worry," he said, seeming totally unfazed. "Budget versus popularity is always a tightrope at this phase. But it's my job to know when to push it."

"And you think now is the time? What makes you so sure?"

He shrugged. "Call it intuition. Call it research, if that makes you feel better. I just know that *that*—" He thumbed over his shoulder. The sound of fans cheering for the arrival of the Hitchcocks on stage dimly resonated through the concrete walls. "—is the kind of star power you see once in a career. Trust me. You don't want to blow this band's chances by nickel and diming every expense."

"I'll keep that in mind."

"Glad to hear it. Now, let's talk cash flow."

For the next hour, we tried to hash out the money issues. Since he knew I had to reduce the budget with or without his involvement, he suggested a few places for budget cuts that would have a minimal impact on promotions and marketing. It wasn't enough to solve all my problems, but it was a start.

When he departed, the room was thankfully much quieter. I sent a quick text to Palmer, telling him that as far as I could see, the Hitchcocks needed cuts fast. Squinting at the laptop screen, I was about to figure out how to do it when the oil drum shook, breaking my concentration.

I scanned the room, not seeing anything that could've caused the shaking. A small earthquake maybe? I looked at the clock on my screen and realized the band should be on a break between sets.

I was diving back into work when a muffled sound permeated the walls. I'd been able to hear scattered rounds of applause through the whole show, but the band wasn't playing at the moment. What was it?

Shaking my head, I focused harder on my work. My fingers flew over the laptop keyboard as I got into a rhythm, inputting the numbers from the tour's receipts to date into a column. Numbers were safe, sterile, and thoroughly unsexy—exactly the opposite of the rock god I was sharing a tour bus with. If I could keep my head in the numbers, I could keep it away from him.

Then the laptop started to vibrate. My styrofoam coffee cup, which was still a quarter full, nearly tipped over before I caught it. The computer jostled to a rhythmic beat like there was a dinosaur stomping around outside. *What the hell is going on out there?* Frustrated that I couldn't get any work done, I stood, opened the door to investigate, and was nearly knocked backwards by a powerful force.

boom-boom-BOOM!

"WE WANT JAX! WE WANT JAX! WE WANT JAX!"
It was the fans!

I'd wanted to avoid Jax but even his fans seemed to be conspiring against me. The craziest part was, they weren't chanting for The Hitchcocks as a band. Just Jax, the rock god.

I entered into the hall. Every step I took brought me closer to the source of the echoing, pulsing sound. The audience now sounded frantic, half-hysterical, and the thumping vibrations in the floor sped up to match. At a spot just offstage, I was finally able to see what was happening. Thousands of audience members, stomping their feet in unison, were making the floor shake in time with their chants.

The lights went down, and the crowd's stomps and chants gave way to keening wails. Just as the audience reached a fever pitch, a chord broke through the screams and the stage lights came up.

Sky, wearing a black and white minidress, started playing the song's bassline, while Chewie kept a beat with his standard stoned-out look. The guitars kicked in next, Kev and Jax facing each other as they riffed. Standing in the multicolored spotlights, Jax had never looked more at ease. His leather pants traced the outline of his muscular legs, and he moved his body sinuously as the audience screamed for more.

I'd seen The Hitchcocks from the crowd before, but here just behind the side curtain, as thousands of people screamed in my direction, I saw for the first time how a performer could feed on the energy of the crowd. Like a wild beast, Jax stalked ferally across the stage as the guitars started playing. He opened his mouth to sing, and the crowd started yelling even louder.

I want to see your fall from grace

I want to see your angel face
smashed to pieces, blown to bits
Your lies can't hurt me any more
I'm not the ones who came before
I'm not your toy, not your boy
I'm still here
I'm still here
I'm still standing
I'm still here

His voice started in growls, low and deep. He stretched his arm out into the crowd, and dozens of hands scrambled to touch his tattoo sleeves. The memory of him massaging my shoulders with those hands unwillingly came flooding back, making my heart race.

From where I stood, I could only see the first few rows—but they seemed at least as hysterical as the crowd in New York. That show had been in a bar packed almost to bursting, a room that could barely contain Jax's seductive energy. Here, the venue was bigger, but Jax's seductive energy still permeated through every square inch. No one was having an orgasm, at least as far as I could see, but the screams were almost deafening.

"He really is incredible," a female voice said nearby. I turned to see a curly-haired venue staff member licking her lips, her eyes locked on Jax's still silhouette.

Sweat dripped from Jax's forehead as five thousand fans roared for more. It was hard to deny the appeal. "Yeah. I guess he is," I said, surprising myself with my response. I'd been trying to avoid him all day and yet here I was, watching him from backstage, mesmerized by his performance.

Jax, stalking across stage, came to a sudden halt at the exact same time the music stopped. He stayed in position for a few moments, still and silent. The lights dimmed, and the crowd's manic cheers trailed to a hush. Almost imperceptibly at first, slow, quiet notes emerged from Kev's guitar. One at a time, then closer together, the notes began to form a haunting, lonely melody, bringing a round of quiet applause from the audience. Jax's arms fell back to his guitar and he pulled his body inward.

A single yellow-orange light glowed warmly on him. His voice dropped almost to a whisper as he sang into the microphone.

The city moon was full
on the night I met you first
we were heading for disaster right away
We wished on falling stars above
but now I know too well
Nothing holds up to the savage light of day

You can't know who I have been
Your love can never be true
We wear masks til our faces fade out
And someday your mask becomes you.

His voice stayed quiet, but with hoarse undertones of restrained urgency that made it seem like he could cry out at any moment. The notes pierced into me, hitting something deep inside my chest. My arms hugged against my torso, tight.

I'd never seen him quite like this. Jax had been intensely seductive, animalistic, strutting around the stage like he owned it. Now, it was like he'd melded with the music. I couldn't deny my physical attraction to him, but now, I was finding myself strangely wanting him even more. He wasn't just a pretty face—or a gorgeous body—or even just an incredible voice. He was a passionate soul.

I couldn't help noticing the effect he had on the crowd here and the one that night at the Wallabee. It was so extraordinary that I decided to put a name to it: The Jax Effect. And, for the first time, I felt myself starting to truly surrender to it in spite of my best efforts.

His voice was pure sex, compressed into its most elemental form, and listening to it made me unable to think of anything else. I craved Jax's strong hands. I ached with need for his lips on mine. I found myself wishing that I could just run onto the stage and kiss him, imagining his powerful arms encircling me, his mouth hungry and eager as our tongues twisted together.

The crowd stood at rapt attention as the chorus approached, silent, completely changed from their frenzy of a few minutes before. The sudden silence was almost a sound in itself. It was like Jax had cast a spell on the entire audience, and no one was immune.

The chorus started, and Jax tilted his head back in pure rock ecstasy. His vocal cords soared into the top of their range, screaming with passionate intensity. Fireworks lit off, one after another, exploding into fiery blossoms behind his taut form. Heat washed over my face. I knew it was from the pyrotechnics, but I wondered how much of it was actually from Jax.

His hands gripped the neck of his guitar roughly, and I couldn't help but remember his strong fingers driving me wild as they pressed into my skin. I had a sudden flash of fantasy: bound in his arms, his fingers stroking my body with the passion and precision of a guitar solo. A massive firework blast fired right behind Jax as he changed keys and went into the song's last chorus.

Breathe, Riley, I told myself as my daydreams took over despite my best intentions. *Just keep breathing*.

As Kev struck the final guitar chord, Jax stood in the bright arena lights like the rock god he was: arms out, eyes closed, face relaxed. I took a deep breath, trying to calm myself down. Butterflies cascaded through my stomach, and I felt my toes curling and clinging to the soles of my flats.

It's just a song, Riley, I tried to tell myself. *It's nothing to get worked up over.* But not everyone could sing the way Jax did. His voice had been so grief-stricken, so forlorn, that it sounded like he was experiencing heartbreak for the first time. I tried focusing on the other members of the band. If I was going to watch the show, I owed it to the band to keep myself from letting the Jax Effect turn me into a brainwashed fangirl.

Focusing on Kev shredding on the guitar, Sky slapping away on the bass, and Chewie rocking the drums made enjoying the rest of the show a little bit easier. By the time the encore was over, I felt like I'd been put through an emotional wringer. The band stood basking in the applause, and I couldn't help reassessing my opinion of Jax.

Maybe I'd misjudged him. Maybe he was a deep human being who didn't only have sex on his mind.

I stepped off to the side, preparing for the band to leave the stage without noticing me back here.

As Kev, Chewie, and Sky began to walk over, Jax lingered, taking the microphone one last time. "I just want to give a final shoutout tonight. This goes out to that special girl out there who goes 'til she's *sore*. Let me tell you something, Pepper: it's your move."

What?!

My hand flew to my open mouth. Blood rushed to my face. I couldn't believe my ears. He was toying with me.

My head shook in disbelief. Before it had just been between the two of us, but now he was involving thousands of people into this tug of war game. All just so he could get into my pants? I began to realize that I couldn't just avoid or ignore Jax anymore. Doing so only escalated the situation. I already had trouble focusing on my work because of him, and if he kept raising the stakes, it'd be damn near impossible.

Hiding behind another curtain, I watched the band come backstage. Chewie and Kev wasted no time getting a groupie apiece, and Sky had not one, but *two* hot guys fawning over her. Jax followed them, but noticeably without any groupies accompanying him. They all went into the green room together, overflowing bottles of champagne in hand. A moment after the door shut behind them, I heard through the door what sounded like a dozen people laughing.

But I wasn't laughing. I was worried. I had to put a stop to Jax's pursuit before things got out of hand.

Chapter Nine

ARRANGEMENTS

The next morning, the pain hit before I even opened my eyes. The muscles all around my back ached from sleeping on the hard-as-a-rock couch. I groaned, turning over onto my side for some relief. Just my luck. First the button-making, now the couch. What else was going to go wrong?

I groggily picked my phone off the floor and looked at the time. Damn it. 6:30 AM. I was hundreds of miles and a time zone away from my New York office, but my body apparently hadn't gotten the memo. I'd slept less than four hours. Was this how it was going to be for the whole two week assignment?

Bleary-eyed and sore, I didn't have the willpower to get up, so I checked for new emails. I was surprised to find I'd gotten one from Palmer in the middle of the night—subject line "HCs Urgent."

> R: Looked at your analysis and agree. HCs budget = fucked. Needs minimum 10% cuts, not gonna be easy in 2 weeks. In recognition, got the higher-ups to approve $20k bonus for on-time completion. Don't say I never did anything for you. Don't fuck this up.
> —P

My breath caught in my throat. *Twenty thousand dollars?* Holy crap. That was almost four full months of salary, enough to pay off the rest of my student loans and still have enough left over for a week of sipping umbrella drinks on a tropical beach. This, alone, could make up for my crummy luck so far. I was so excited I could've kissed my phone.

I stopped just before my lips made contact with the screen. There was one thing that stood between me and the biggest bonus of my career so far, and his name was Jax.

Reducing a budget was already a difficult task, but if Jax wanted to oppose my cuts, he could hold up the process for ages while we tried to hammer out the details. I had to get him on my side, which meant I needed to win him over.

But that was another whole problem in itself. He was trouble. Serious trouble. All he wanted was to play games with me, and it didn't help that I was drawn to him in spite of how much he frustrated me. My strategy had first been to avoid him, and now, more recently, to tell him off. But if I wanted that bonus, it'd mean I'd have to persuade him to be agreeable. *How the hell was I going to pull this off?*

Shaking my head at my new dilemma, I rose from the couch, and a sudden shooting pain traveled up my neck, reminding me of how terribly I slept last night. As I simultaneously yawned and groaned in agony, I figured out how I could relieve these aching muscles.

I pressed my ear up against the stairwell. Light snores greeted me from upstairs, and as I looked around, I couldn't see any of Chewie's telltale clouds of secondhand smoke. *Perfect.* I hadn't had time to sprawl out on my own since I'd gotten on the bus.

I rummaged through my suitcase for my new bikini, taking the tags off the purple-and-green plaid top and solid green bottoms as I went into the bathroom to change. I had packed the bikini in a flash of inspiration, when I thought that we might be stopping by some hotels during the tour.

When I finished changing and came out of the bathroom, I spotted a set of stemmed glasses and three bottles of Dom Perignon next to the staircase, all opened. Two were completely empty, and I could see the bubbles still clinging to the sides of the third. *Last night must have been crazy.*

I looked around at some of the goodies the band had brought back to the bus. Part of me wanted to yell at them because of their wasteful spending—but another part of me was sorry I'd missed it.

I couldn't stand the sight of expensive champagne going to waste, so I fixed myself a mimosa. Drink in hand, I climbed the stairs to the roof deck, and found what I was looking for: the hot tub, warm and inviting in the early morning light.

I slid the cover off the hot tub and dipped a toe in. *Mmm, warm.* As I set my glass on the edge of the tub and lowered my aching body into the water, an involuntary sigh of relief escaped my lips. There, that was much better.

The wind whipped through my hair as the bus rolled smoothly down the highway. I was high above the traffic, so even though I was technically outside, the roof deck still managed to seem almost private. I closed my eyes, feeling like I'd fallen into someone else's dream.

I didn't know how I was going to fix my Jax problem, but between his late-night party schedule and how early I'd woken up, I was sure he'd still be asleep for hours anyway. I could at least enjoy the calm before the inevitable storm.

As I sunk my body lower into the water, the warmth rose up my neck to the bottom of my chin. I turned on the bubbles as the powerful jets started massaging my aching body. I loved the soothing sensation. With each slow breath, I felt my muscles unknotting and my tension easing away.

When I opened my eyes again, all I saw was purple.

The swirling water was rapidly changing color. I realized with horror that the culprit was my own bikini top. "Shit!" I said, standing up as quickly as I could. Was it really too much to ask for a bikini, of all things, not to bleed dye when it hit warm water?

I realized immediately that I had two choices: get out of the tub *now* before any more dye bled in or take my top off. No matter how crazy I'd gotten, toplessness in public had always been a no-go for me, drunk or sober.

I started to get out, but cried out when a back muscle spasmed. If I left the tub now, I'd be sore for the rest of the day, maybe longer. I looked around as a precaution, but didn't see anyone. The water was high enough to cover my chest, and I was pretty sure no one would be able to see me from the road. The coast was clear.

With a sigh, I untied the back of the bikini top and set it on a deck chair just outside the tub. I made sure it was within reach, in case I needed to grab it quickly.

At least it was the top, not the bottom, I thought as I sank back into the tub. The jets were working their magic, and I closed my eyes in relaxation again. Ah, wardrobe malfunction aside, this was the life. The Hitchcocks took rock star luxe to the next level, and it was such foreign territory that I couldn't help but be awed. Officially, I disapproved, but it was impressive in its own way to see what kind of tour bus would satisfy their requirements.

My parents had prided themselves on their frugality, and even my modest weekend warrior lifestyle had earned me a number of well-meaning lectures from mom and dad. I wondered what they'd think if they could see me today, drinking last night's champagne at seven in the morning, topless in a hot tub that belonged to a rock band.

I made a mental note to text them later. I'd have to tell them I was busy with my accounting work in Manhattan, a comforting white lie that would hopefully keep them from calling back until the two-week stint was over.

The wind picked up with a massive gale that made the bus' top deck sway. I held my glass tight, eyes closed, relishing the feel of the currents. The wind slowly died down and I opened my eyes again.

He was standing there on the roof deck.

The bikini top lay in a crumpled heap beside Jax's bare feet, blown halfway across the deck by the wind. His dark eyes were piercing straight into me.

"Eeep!" I squeaked as I quickly turned the bubbles to HIGH and sank into the water, mortified by the situation.

He was dressed in a t-shirt and slate gray shorts that sagged slightly at one side of his hips. His long hair was more than a little tousled like he'd been tossing and turning in bed. This new side of him was surprisingly hot and it only added to my shock.

Does he see the bikini top? Please be no. Please be no. After the stunts he'd already pulled on me, I dreaded him discovering how much of an advantage he could have over me right now.

He nodded at my mimosa. "You start drinking early, I see."

His eyes were on me rather than his feet, which made me think that maybe, just maybe, he didn't see the purple bikini. "You're awake," I said, as if to confirm to myself that this nightmare was really happening. "I thought you'd be sleeping for a long time." I hugged my arms tightly against myself. I was silently praying he'd leave soon so I could get my top back.

"Never got the hang of sleeping," he said casually. His feet shifted slightly as he ran a hand through the sexy mess of his hair, fixing a problem spot.

My heart was pounding in my chest. I swallowed to clear a lump that had developed in my throat. "Okay, well . . . if you don't mind, I'm trying to relax. If you want to talk about counting sheep or something, we can do it later in the day."

He paused for a moment, staring at me with a skeptical look. I kept a firm expression on my face until he eventually shrugged then turned to leave. I watched in anticipation as he got as far as the sundeck entrance, where he stopped.

"You know what," he said, "drinking in the morning does sound like a good idea." He turned back around and walked toward the bar. He inadvertently stepped on my top as he did so, sending a spike of fear through me . . . and then flashed a grin. "I think I'll join you."

My stomach sank. *Goddammit, Jax!* He approached a barstool a few feet away from me and plopped his ridiculously nice ass down on it, making himself comfortable while I stared ruefully at the purple fabric like a child who'd dropped a prized possession down a grate. "Jax, I'm kind of busy right now—"

"So am I," he said with a heart-stopping smile as he poured from two bottles of amber liquid into a cocktail glass with ice cubes in it. "What are you drinking?"

"A mimosa," I said through gritted teeth, "since your band doesn't seem to think good champagne is worth finishing."

He smiled nonchalantly. "Sounds delicious. Mine's a Godfather. Scotch, amaretto. Brando's favorite. Want some?" He took a sip of the drink, never taking his dark eyes off me.

"No," I said, barely concealing my irritation then nodded toward the towel cabinet beside him. My voice lightened. "Hey, can you throw me a towel?"

He looked briefly at the stack of towels. "You've got arms, grab one yourself." He raised the drink back to his lips and took a leisurely sip.

That asshole!

"Why are you up, anyway?" he asked. "I'm usually the only one awake at this hour."

"Yeah, well, makes sense since you're a vampire," I snapped, feeling like I was cornered and running out of options. I focused on keeping my eyes away from the bikini top, no matter how much I was tempted to make sure it didn't blow further away. I had one last resort and that was to keep him distracted. "No need for sleep."

He nodded toward the rising sun with a wry half-smile on his face. "Your theory's got some holes in it."

"No it doesn't. Sun or not, you still suck."

His smile widened. "So why aren't you asleep?" he reiterated, ignoring my barb.

I rolled my eyes and sighed. I sensed that the more I pushed, the more his interest in me grew. "Can't really get a good night's sleep on the couch, at least not yet. Combination of my internal clock and the hard seats."

"You could always sleep in my bed," he said so matter-of-factly that he might as well have been saying, *you could always get a Diet Coke from the fridge.*

"In your dreams," I replied, the memory of the crazy New York concert and Jax's run from an angry mob still fresh in my mind. "I don't get in bed with guys who almost get me killed twice in a week."

The wind picked up again, and the bikini top rolled end over end further away. *Damn it.* Fate was so cruel.

"You're kidding yourself. I know you liked the danger. After all, you're the most badass tour accountant I've ever met."

"Save the lines for someone else." I rolled my eyes again even though a small part of me was delighted by his compliment. Whatever game Jax was playing, it wasn't one I wanted in on. Besides, if we played now, I'd be starting with a handicap of one item of clothing and a whole lot of dignity.

Without warning, he set his drink down, stood up, then walked over to the scrap of purple-and-green cloth. A wave of dread passed over me as he casually bent to pick up the bikini. He looked at it curiously as he dangled it between two fingers.

My eyes widened in horror.

"Did you see this?" he asked, waving the bikini. *Shit! Shit shit shit.*

I was a wreck of negative emotions. "What?" I spluttered.

He tilted his head to the side for a moment, studying it. "One of the groupies must have left it behind."

My pulse leaped. Did he seriously think the top belonged to some other girl, or was he just playing around? I swallowed hard. "Yeah, must have."

"Then there's no reason to keep it on the bus." Jax held the top over the ledge. Clenched in his fist, the bikini strings blew wildly in the wind.

"Don't litter!" The words burst from my mouth hastily, and he cocked a brow. "Uh . . . the last thing the band needs is bad publicity for being a bunch of litterbugs . . . and being fined for littering. Let's just toss it in the trash." It wouldn't be a great place for my swimsuit, but at least my top wouldn't be highway debris.

"The trash?" Jax said, his scarred eyebrow raised. "I've got a better idea."

Reaching into his pocket, he pulled out a silver lighter and struck the flint. I watched with terror as he slowly moved the flame toward the dangling strings.

"*Wait!*"

"I know how you feel about groupies," he said, a flicker of amusement passing over his face. "I'm doing this for you." He brought the flame closer.

"No!" My hand raised desperately.

He paused to look at me oddly. "Why so reluctant? Wait. Don't tell me. You want to do the honors." He gestured for me to get out of the tub and go over to where he was.

"Oh! Uh . . . sure," I said with a smile, realizing the opportunity. "Bring it over here to me. I'll burn the hell out of it."

His eyes twinkled devilishly, making my heart thump hard in my chest. I hated how a simple look from him could have such an effect on me. It was impossible to deny his allure. "Nuh uh," he said wagging his finger.

"Nuh uh, what?" My nerves were on edge.

"How do you ask nicely? You've been unusually rude to me ever since I came up here."

"Ugh." I groaned so hard it sounded like I was about to vomit. Of course he wasn't going to make this easy. He never made *anything* easy. "It's not unusual. I'm acting how I normally act around you. Maybe you're just sensitive."

"I'm waiting . . ." An expression of displeasure marred his beautiful face.

"Fine, fine! 'Please'? There I said it. Happy now?" I hoped he didn't sense the desperation in my tone.

He crossed his large biceps across his chest, refusing to budge. "That the best you can do?"

"*Pretty* please?" I said, forcing my voice to sound sweet.

"See? That wasn't so hard, was it?" He came toward me, holding the bikini in front of him, sending a surge of hope through me. When it was close enough, I reached for it . . . and grabbed nothing. Confused, I tried again—and missed.

"Hey! No fair!" I shouted, realizing he was pulling it away. I grabbed for the top again, this time more forcefully.

"Who said anything about fair?" He took a step back just in time to leave me empty-handed.

I feinted grabbing to the left, then went to the right. Every movement I made was echoed by one of his, keeping the bikini tantalizingly out of reach. *Ugh!*

"I've never been fishing before," he said with a grin. "But I think I'm starting to understand the appeal."

"What kind of game are you playing?" I cried in outrage. A horrible feeling began to settle in my gut.

I'd never seen his sparkling black eyes so intense as he leaned toward me, so close that I could catch his masculine scent. "The kind where everyone wins." His sultry voice sent shivers down my spine, even with hot bubbles swirling around me. He pointed to the water in the tub. "You've been trying to pretend that you're not skinny dipping in my hot tub. You think I wouldn't notice?"

My heart slammed into my chest. "I'm not skinny dipping!"

"Sure. This top belongs to some other girl, not the one trying desperately to keep me from seeing her chest under the water."

"I'm wearing the bottom, that's just the top. Give it back!"

"Nope." He took a step back and smiled.

"Alright, fuck you, Jax. I'll just stay here, then." I sank back into the water and crossed my arms. If he expected me to keep reaching after the top until I fell over or he saw my nipples, he'd have to think again.

"Will you, now?" he said, his eyebrows lifting. "You say so, but I doubt it. That hot tub's pretty warm. You'll either get out or pass out, soon enough. I guess I'll stay here and fix myself another drink while I wait." He moved to the bar, set the bikini down, and started reaching for the bottles again.

"You're really going to just stay here until you see me topless?" I cried in disbelief, aware that I admired his audacity as much as I hated it. "I knew you were an asshole, but I didn't think you were a scumbag!"

"You can have the top back whenever you want it, Riley," he said with a shrug, pouring himself a second drink.

"What's that supposed to mean?" I scoffed. "I already asked you for it!"

A half-smile turned up one corner of Jax's luscious mouth. He sipped, slowly, then said, "You asked, but you didn't offer anything in return."

I glared at him, confused.

He continued, "Usually, when one person has something of value that another person wants, they make an exchange. I give you something you want, and you," he said, looking at me with seductive eyes, "give me something I want."

"You ungrateful bastard!" I cried, splashing him with water from the tub. "I already saved your life. I think giving my bikini top back is the *least* you can do."

Jax looked down at his wet t-shirt. "Not quite, Pepper. I saved you when I helped you onto the band bus, which I didn't have to do. Right now, I'm holding onto your top, which I also don't have to do. If I let it go, it blows out onto Interstate 80—if we're talking about the *least* I could do."

I was mortified. I knew men like Jax didn't always play fair, but I didn't expect him to really hold my bikini hostage. "I can't believe I used to be attracted to you," I said, scowling.

"Believe whatever you want. You're the one topless in the hot tub. If you want this back," he said, gesturing toward the top, "you're going to offer me something. And you know what I want. I'm looking right at it." His eyes directed straight at me sent an unwelcome desire fluttering through my belly.

I inhaled sharply. "Dude, I've told you before, and I don't want to have to tell you again. My job—"

"Yes, I'm sure the people at Hans-Peterson take professionalism very seriously. Are you the same Riley I met Saturday night? Picks locks, dodges security guards?"

"My boss wasn't going to find out I picked a lock. This could get back to him."

"You'd be just as fired if he found out about the night you kissed me and touched my cock. What can they do, fire you twice?"

Fuck. He had me there. At this point, Palmer would probably throw me out onto the streets of

Manhattan if he heard the whole truth. Which made things worse, because the other reasons I didn't want to sleep with Jax were a lot more difficult to talk about than potential HR problems. "But if one of the band members tells them . . ."

"Pepper, I give you my word," he said, reaching out to lift my chin until I was looking directly in his eyes, "I can handle the band. They're not going to tell anyone."

"You can't guarantee—"

"Hold up," he interrupted, putting his finger to my lips. Then he softly brushed it across my bottom lip, sending unwanted tingles of excitement through me. "Here's how this is going to work. You're going to give me a kiss. It's going to last as long as I want it to. After that, you can have your top back."

Wait, a kiss? I thought he'd been referring to sex this whole time. A kiss was already trodden territory between us. I squinted at him. This seemed too easy. "Fine. It's a deal."

"That's not the whole deal," he said, seeming to enjoy correcting me. "You're also going to give me a kiss after every show on this tour."

My nipples hardened at the thought of kissing Jax over and over again for the next two weeks, and I felt my body trying to say "yes" before my brain put the brakes on. "You're asking for too much. One kiss right now. But that's all."

His eyes burned into me, and when he spoke next, his voice was a low growl, "No deal."

"Fine," I said dismissively, feeling vulnerable in more ways than one. "Because I know how this story goes anyway." I'd been playing the scenario out in my head long enough that it was easy to see. "Girl plays games with rock god. Rock god plays until he gets bored. Then he moves on to the next new thing and the girl goes back to her humdrum life."

"Sounds like it's not a bad deal for the girl."

"Spoken like someone who's used to taking advantage of others, not getting taken advantage of himself."

His jaw tightened. "You don't know me, Pepper."

Surprised by his reaction, I realized I must've hit a sore spot. "I know enough to know that you like picking on the young and helpless." I considered myself young at twenty-five.

He waited, his hand clenched around his drink. Clearly, I'd hit close to home.

"And it's not just that," I said, feeling the words tumble out before I'd even thought about them. "You put the dark and dangerous act on harder than any guy I've ever met, and in my experience, most guys who do that are hiding something. Usually something big." *Like a prison record. Or a wife.*

Jax set his drink down on the edge of the hot tub with a loud *thunk*, bending his knees until he was at eye level with me. His dark eyes were pools big enough to drown in and he stared directly at me. "Do you think I'm hiding something?"

I could feel his breath as he spoke. His scent filled my mind, and my eyes ran slowly over his taut, tanned skin. His body was inches from me, draining my resistance, making it impossible to free myself from his gaze.

"Yeah," I said at last. "I do."

He straightened and turned around, shaking his head. "See you around, then."

Shit. Whatever Jax was hiding, it was none of my business, and I didn't want my bikini top to be a casualty of my curiosity. "Wait! Wait, wait, wait. Fine. Let's negotiate."

He turned back around. "I was already negotiating."

"I'll agree to your terms. One kiss after every show, no telling anyone," I said.

"It's a d—"

I cut him off with a raised hand. Letting him get his way without asking for anything in return would make me a pushover. I needed a counter-offer to show him who he was dealing with. "That's not the whole deal. I also want a ten percent reduction in your band expenses. I see how you spend money. I know you can do better."

His brows raised. "I thought you didn't want to mix business and pleasure."

"But I already did," I said. My voice was resolute now. I couldn't show any weakness in front of Jax. "It was an accident, but it happened. I've already taken the risk, professionally. If there's any possibility I could get out of this with my career not just intact, but better off than when I started, I want to take it."

"This is an *unusual* request," he said, a grudging smile spreading across his face. "But that doesn't mean I won't work with it. What's in this for you?"

I held up my chin. "There's a twenty-thousand dollar bonus on the line for me, if I can achieve all budgetary goals for the band within two weeks."

"Ah, I see. So it's purely mercenary," he said smirking. "Well, these budget cuts affect me and the band's shows. So if that's how you want it, Pepper, you're going to have to sweeten the deal. A hand where you had it last time for this kiss, and I'll make your budget cuts."

"Over your pants or under?"

"Under."

"Then no deal."

Jax's kiss was one thing. But his naked, thick cock in front of me again? That would be a surefire way to make a mistake I'd regret later.

"Fine. Over. But they have to be *good* kisses."

I smiled confidently. "Oh, don't worry. They will be." If I could be sure of anything, with someone as hot as Jax, it would be that.

"Do we have a deal?"

His low, throaty rasp was so close to my mouth that I could feel the heat of his breath.

I took a deep breath, feeling more excited than I should. My body was aching with arousal for being so close to him for so long, half-naked. Once my mortification had worn off, the whole situation kind of felt naughty.

"Yes, Jax. We have a deal."

"Then let's seal it."

He looked at me like a lion looking at its prey—and then I felt his lips.

With frantic urgency, Jax's tongue pressed hard against the seam of my eager mouth. It penetrated fiercely as I cried out in surprise. His hands ran down my bare back as his fingers pressed roughly into me, gripping my wet skin tightly, and I moaned against his mouth.

I felt him pulling back slightly, and I followed, unwilling to break our lips apart. I was like an animal in heat, consumed with need, rising from the water inch by inch to keep my tongue tangled with his. He'd said he wanted good kisses, and I intended to show him.

I slid a hand down to his pants, pressing my palm into his crotch. He was already getting hard, the heat from him throbbing through the thin fabric. As I rubbed him gently, he grew even larger. A hungry groan escaped from his mouth, and I slowly moved my hands up his body with a slight twinge of regret. He had negotiated for a hand down there, but he hadn't said for how long. Besides, if we kept this up, I'd end up making some serious life mistakes.

My hands found their way to his velvety hair, fingers caressing his scalp as the kiss grew deeper. His mouth, ravenous but subtle, started an avalanche of pleasure. Each small sensation combined into something much larger, something I couldn't control or even comprehend.

His movements grew sweeter, more lingering and soft. The kiss had begun in lust, but now there was something else there, something new, almost frightening with its gentleness.

Surprised, I pulled away, hearing a loud suction sound as our lips parted.

Our faces inches apart, I saw that his eyes were still closed. He opened them slowly as if waking from a dream. "Are your kisses always this good?"

"Sometimes better," I said, as I stared at him defiantly, daring him to kiss me again.

He opened my palm and dropped the bikini into it. "Then I'd say I got a bargain, and you got ripped off." Smiling to himself, he headed to the stairs.

As I watched him walk away, I tied my top back on and felt a surge of victory; I'd gotten the top back, and I'd even managed to get Jax to agree to an arrangement that could put me one step closer to my bonus. If anyone was ripped off in this exchange, it was him.

But as I toweled off, the negotiation played back in my mind, and I realized with a growing sense of discomfort that he'd gotten me to do exactly what I'd wanted to avoid. I'd started the morning wanting to tell Jax we were through with playing games. But now we had an ongoing agreement—a dangerous game I'd have to replay every time the Hitchcocks took the stage.

Chapter Ten

THE JAX EFFECT

My aching body was feeling a whole lot better by the time I went downstairs and changed back into real clothes. I tried forgetting about what happened with Jax moments ago—his soft lips, his hungry kiss. But it required a lot of effort. I had to remind myself that I had things under control, that all I needed was a little self control, and I could keep him at arm's length. A kiss every now and then wouldn't change anything between us, no matter how much he wanted it to.

After scolding myself and taking a few deep breaths, I was finally able to concentrate on the work that needed to get done. I wanted to have the band's finances in some semblance of order before the next show, so I set up shop with a stack of papers on the first floor, working as the rest of the band eventually woke up.

When afternoon rolled around, I had a pretty good idea of where to start making changes, but I had to discuss the changes with Jax first—a prospect that sounded less than ideal after what had happened in the hot tub. Ideally, a tour accountant could regard band members as co-workers, team members— possibly even friends. But even then, cutting budgets could lead to conflict and drama.

One of the first things I learned at certification training was to make sure the band understands where your friendship ends and your working relationship begins. With Jax, I'd broken the rules in a big way, but I hoped it would have an equally big payoff. If he was willing to make the cuts, my job was about to get a whole lot easier. Of course, that was a big if. I didn't know for sure if Jax meant to keep his end of the bargain, but I was about to find out.

I got up from the couches and steeled myself with a quick lifesaver on my way up the stairs. I wasn't sure I'd need it, but I wanted to be as calm and collected as possible when I approached him.

On one of the second-floor couches, Chewie and Sky were rolling blunts together in the mid-afternoon sun. With marijuana legal in Colorado, they were working their way through the band's stash, and planned to restock in the morning when we arrived in Denver. Knowing how a lot of rock stars liked to party, I was just grateful they were sticking to weed—at least it was cheap.

As I walked past them, holding my breath to avoid a contact high, I heard voices emanating from Jax's room, too quiet to understand. Was he in there with someone?

I tapped at the door, tentatively. "Jax?"

The voices suddenly went silent. He opened the door a crack. "Can it wait?"

"Not really." The sooner the expenses were cut in the budget, the sooner I could notify venues and change vendor requests. "I wanted to get these expenses trimmed before we got into Denver. Want to go downstairs?"

He opened the door wider, and I saw a TV inside the room, paused on a frame from a black-and-white movie. "I've got a better idea. Why don't you come in here?"

"I'm . . . not sure that's a good idea at all."

"Then we can talk some other time. How does next week work for you?" he said, starting to shut the door again.

Oh no you don't. I wedged my arm into the door frame. "No, Jax. This has to happen today. It can't wait."

He sniffed at the air. "Then come in, but close the door. Everything smells like skunk out there."

I noticed the white clouds of pot smoke drifting into his room. Was he trying to get me to play another game? I didn't know, but I didn't want to piss him off by making his room stink. I scooted into the small space, shutting and latching the door behind me.

"So this is the famous Fortress of Solitude," I said, taking a look around. The room was barely wide enough to fit Jax's king-sized bed. I had no idea how they'd gotten the mattress in, but it hugged snugly against two walls. Thick fabric swaths hung from the ceiling, in dark, subdued hues.

Pillows in dark brown, deep purple, and navy blue covered a bed layered thick with dark comforters. A guitar hung next to the wall-mounted flat-screen. The effect was somewhere between gypsy caravan and blanket fort.

He sat on the bed in a gray v-neck, a different shirt than he'd been wearing before, probably because I splashed water on the last one. Jax looked like a Mongol khan in his tent, his golden skin a glistening highlight against the dark fabrics. The room smelled of him—a rich, earthy scent I couldn't get enough of.

Control yourself, I thought, tempted to slap myself again. *Just finish the expense talk, say goodbye, and get out.*

"Since you're already here," Jax's voice broke through my daydreaming and jolted me back to reality, "Want to stay for the movie?" His eyes were glued to the screen.

A couple of hours of being next to him in a room with a locked door? That couldn't possibly be a good idea. "Maybe some other time," I responded nicely. "Right now, we've got more important things to do."

"More important than the greatest film of all time?"

I broke away from my paperwork and looked closely at the screen, but all I saw was two men on a train car. I shrugged. "I don't think I've ever seen it."

"I'll give you a hint. It's from the director so great I named the band after him."

Ah, right, The Hitchcocks. "And here I thought the band name was just an excuse for innuendo," I said, remembering how I'd first mistaken the band's shorthand for its real name.

His eyebrow scar moved almost imperceptibly upward, and the corners of his mouth turned up. "You should know by now," he said, each syllable making my heart beat faster, "that I don't need an excuse for innuendo."

I had to steer the conversation back to safety. "You know, I've never seen one. A Hitchcock movie, I mean."

"Not even *Psycho*? *The Birds*?"

"Nope," I said grinning. "Guess our tastes are incompatible. Ready to talk business now?"

"Exactly the opposite. I'm ready for you to watch," he said, but he wasn't smiling back. "You need to know what you're missing." I tried to interrupt, but he continued, "If you don't watch *Strangers on a Train*, I won't talk expenses with you and that's final."

I felt myself bristling. "Hey! You promised in the hot tub you'd make the expense cuts."

"That's true. But I didn't promise I'd make them in the middle of my favorite movie. Now, are you staying or going?"

"Just so we're clear, if I stay for the movie, we can talk expenses right now. No bullshit, no tricks."

He nodded once. "No bullshit. No tricks."

I sighed. It didn't seem likely, but it would be far easier to talk to him now and watch the movie than to try to catch him later when he could come up with some other excuse to be "unavailable." I also kind of found myself almost looking forward to a break from work. "Oh, what the hell," I said.

As soon as I plopped onto the bed with my laptop, my eyes went wide. The mattress was the exact kind I liked best—supportive, but with enough pillowy softness at the very top to keep it from feeling like a board. Given what I slept on last night, I couldn't help letting out a soft, comfortable sigh.

Jax's dark eyes twinkled. "I knew I was good, but I didn't know I was *that* good."

"Get over yourself." I shot him a wry smile. "It's this bed."

"Strange," he said, scratching his chin in mock mystification. "It's never had that effect on me."

"It's definitely the bed, and not you," I reiterated, not wanting to feed his ego. "At least it doesn't plant fake female fans in the audience to come on cue."

"There aren't any planted fans," he said with amusement. "It's real."

"Really?" I rolled my eyes. "Let me guess, the Jax Effect at work."

He rubbed his thumb against his chin, smirking. "The Jax Effect." He laughed, sending a tingle of warmth suffusing through me. It was the first time I'd heard him laugh. It displayed a warm, human side of him I hadn't seen before in our interactions. "I like it. Sounds like an album title."

I started laughing. "Maybe we'd better talk about those budget cuts," I said. Even though Jax was playing nice for now, I couldn't let this conversation get too far off track.

A dark cloud passed over his face and just like that his voice became cold and pure business. "What's my easiest route to keeping the label off my back about money?"

I knew that I'd messed up. The brief glimpse of the warmer side of Jax had disappeared so quickly that I wasn't even sure if it was real. But then again, talking business was exactly what I wanted to do. If he wanted to keep things professional, that suited me just fine. "I've noticed one of the most expensive discretionary spending items you have is pyrotechnics. It's literally burning up your money."

He looked skeptical. "Pyro's an important part of a good rock show. It's something that separates us from bands that aren't doing as well, and bands that aren't willing to go the extra mile."

"I'm not talking about getting rid of all of the pyrotechnics," I said hastily. "But I don't think you understand the kind of financial trouble you could be in."

"Explain it to me then." His response seemed like he was genuinely interested.

Does he really not know? I'd heard band members were often kept in the dark about finances, but I'd never seen it in person. "So, to start with, your spending money isn't really yours," I told him. "It comes from the label, and it's an advance on your future album sales."

"I know that much."

"Well, you're selling a lot of albums right now, but you only make a small percentage from each one. Every show you put on, every firework blast you set off, is coming out of that percentage."

He looked mildly annoyed. "So we wait for the money to come back to us through the tour receipts and merch table. No band really makes their money on album sales. That's why we have accountants, to keep the cash flowing."

"But that's exactly what I'm trying to tell you," I said. "You're spending so much that your tour will be lucky to break even. Look at this page, here."

Jax squinted at the columns of numbers. "What am I supposed to be looking at?"

"This means that right now, given how much you've brought in and how much has gone out . . ." I thought for a moment about how to best express the band's financial situation. "You can think of your concert budget for today's show as coming out of your album sales from next week. But if you keep going at this rate, soon, all of next week's money will be spent. You'll be spending more and more in advance, a month, then two—"

"And then we're playing low-budget shows in dive bars just to avoid bankruptcy."

"Exactly."

He stared at the wall, seeming lost in thought for a moment. "Fine," he said at last. "We'll cut the huge pyro scenes from 'Glass Brick' and 'Find Your Way.' Those songs are probably off the set list once we've got new material, anyway."

I looked down at my detailed budgets. The cuts would reduce the pyro spending by forty percent, which put The Hitchcocks one step closer to solvency and me one step closer to a huge bonus. "Thanks," I said. "This is a step in the right direction."

He let out a low grunt that I assumed meant approval, or something close to it. I got the feeling from his reaction that I'd be better off not pushing him into cutting more—at least, not yet. I also knew that once I got the momentum moving in the right direction, the rest of the cuts would get easier.

"So we're done?" he asked. "Because I have a movie I'd really like to get back to. I've held up my end of the bargain."

Well, that's that. I was surprised at how smoothly it had gone, though now I'd have to watch the rest of the movie with him. I hoped there wasn't much left. "Don't bother starting it over again. I'll figure it out."

He pressed the remote, and the movie started scrambling until he pressed it again and opening credits started playing. "I'm not having you start a Hitchcock movie halfway through. It wouldn't make any sense."

I felt a sudden twinge from him ignoring what I'd said. But still, I felt oddly curious about watching his favorite movie. Since I'd gotten Jax to agree to cuts I thought I'd have to fight for, I was even a little bit ahead of schedule. *It could be worse—at least the mattress is comfortable.*

Within a few minutes, I could see why he wanted to start over. It wouldn't have made any sense if I'd missed the first part. The two strangers on a train from the title each had someone they wanted dead. The problem was, the first suspects for any murder are the people closest to the victim—neither of them could get away with committing the murders they wanted.

But, one of them reasoned, what if two people who didn't know each other at all traded murders? Then, the victim's attacker would be totally unknown to them, and the person who actually arranged the murder could also arrange to be somewhere with witnesses at the time of the murder's commission. The perfect alibi meant it was the perfect crime.

At least, that was the plan. Since it was a movie, everything started to go wrong right away: an alibi didn't work, one of the men had a flashback and almost killed a second person, and the police were always hot on their heels. I was surprised to find such an old movie so entertaining.

"You're pretty clever," Jax said. "Think you could pull it off?"

I blinked and looked at him curiously. "I'm sorry, what?"

"The murder plot."

I shrugged nonchalantly. "Yeah, sure, easy."

His scarred eyebrow shot up. "Easy?"

"They'd never even find a body."

"Okay . . ." he said with uncertainty.

I was amused by his reaction. I put my hands behind my neck and laid flat on the bed, getting comfortable. "It's not that hard," I said coolly. "You start by destroying identity evidence for the victim. Use a hammer on the teeth and the face, torch the fingerprints. Crush as much skeleton as possible, cut the body up into small parts and put the parts in plastic bags full of bleach, bury them in the middle of the night in graves as deep as possible, and clean up with more bleach. Or just use sulfuric acid to dissolve them so you can trickle them down the drain a bit at a time."

His nose wrinkled. "Jesus. Where the hell did you learn all that?"

"Nowhere that crazy. TV shows and a little bored Googling . . ."

He shook his head. "I've got to be more careful about pissing you off. I didn't realize the guy you maced got off easy."

"Yeah, I bet you didn't know you dodged a bullet when you gave me my bikini top back," I said, an over-the-top gruff look on my face. "I already had a plan to make sure they'd never find you."

He smirked. "And you say that *I* lay the dark and dangerous act on thick."

I couldn't help but smile back—television show knowledge aside, I didn't make a very convincing tough guy, and I knew it. "So how about you? Think you could get away with murder?"

"Sure," he said, laying down next to me. I suddenly felt like we were on a picnic blanket, watching the stars—except that there was only the fabric-covered ceiling above us. "Know where I can find a willing stranger?"

"Well, my next couple of weeks are booked up, but I can probably squeeze in a quick kill after that," I deadpanned. "But too bad we're not strangers anymore."

"Getting to know one another isn't so bad. I'm learning that you're not against watching horror films."

I chuckled. I thought about some of the worst horror movies I'd sat through with my exes. "Actually, I usually hate them."

"Oh?"

"Yeah, a lot of them are just about chopping people up. Plus, if you're a woman who isn't a virgin, good luck making it to the end of the movie. Gives me nightmares." I shuddered, imagining what would happen to me if I was put into one of those movies.

Jax put his arms behind his head. "You know, Hitchcock said he wrote his films so he could get rid of his nightmares."

"Then he's kind of a jerk, right? He makes movies to get rid of his nightmares, but then he ends up giving them to everyone else."

He laughed. "Not quite. In nightmares, bad things happen for no reason. It's the way we feel when we're out of control in our lives, like we can't do anything."

I looked toward the screen. "And like everything that could go wrong is about to."

"Right. But Hitchcock beats other horror directors by turning a nightmare into a fantasy, all by giving order to it. When you're done watching, his characters make sense."

I nodded at Jax, musing the information as I soaked in the sight of him in bed next to me. I noticed his muscles bulged through the thin grey t-shirt, and I found my eyes idly tracing his shoulder's curve.

"So no scary movies," he said. "Should I download *Sleepless in Seattle* for next time?"

"Ugh, gag me." My face contorted with mock disgust. "Screw that boy-meets-girl, boy-marries-girl stuff. Who cares? They're always so boring." It was only after I'd answered that I realized I'd gone along with the idea that there'd *be* a next time.

He raised a brow. "No scary movies, no romcoms. Well, Riley, what *do* you like?"

I grinned. "Action movies! The more over-the-top, the better. *Kill Bill* is my favorite, but I'll watch basically anything with a crazy revenge plot and a lot of broken glass."

"Revenge?" I thought Jax would laugh, but he didn't. "Seems like that could be terrifying, too."

"But action movies really are fantasy. The bad guy almost always gets what's coming to him, and the good guy's basically magic," I said. "It's my personal favorite brand of escapism."

"I'll bring something with more explosions next time." He grabbed the remote and hit pause just when it was getting to the good part.

"Hey! Why'd you stop the movie?"

"I know you're not a horror fan now, so I'm surprised you've stuck it out so long. But I think I've tortured you enough. You can go ahead and leave if you want."

"Are you kidding? You can't just tease me with the first half of the movie then stop it when I'm getting into it. We gotta finish this." I reached over and pushed play on the remote.

He smiled. "Whatever you say."

As the movie continued, I felt my body relaxing and realized it was the first time I'd ever been truly comfortable around Jax. Was there more to him than bullshit? We'd just had a conversation that felt natural and, given the situation, almost normal. We were laying next to each other, but I didn't feel pressured or anxious—just at peace.

If I could just keep this moment, just like this, I thought with a yawn as I nestled into the pillow. I closed my eyes, trying to lock the memory into my mind.

When I opened my eyes again, it was dark outside, and the TV screen in front of me was black. *Shit!* I'd fallen asleep in the middle the movie. In his *bed*, quite possibly the least appropriate place on the entire bus—or the world—for me to be. But then I remembered our conversation. We'd gotten so personal. How had it happened? Where was Jax?

Disoriented, I propped myself up on my elbows and looked back. He was there, wide awake, scribbling into a notebook.

"Oh god, I'm such an asshole," I started. "The bed was so comfortable, and I've been so tired—"

"It doesn't matter," he said. "But we have to talk about something serious. You're tired during the day. More than tired. Practically falling over."

I didn't want him to think I was sleeping on the job. "I'll get used to sleeping on the couches," I said quickly. "It won't keep interfering with—"

"No. I don't care about that," he said. His hand squeezed my shoulder. The gesture was oddly reassuring—I had to admit, I was starting to like this kinder, gentler Jax. "I care about you getting enough sleep. The couches clearly aren't working out."

"I'm only here for two weeks," I said. "I don't need anything special." I was here to salvage the band's finances, not cost them even more.

He scratched his chin. "Hmm. Did you try the foldouts up in the hallway?"

"Yeah. They're harder than the couch." I groaned. "Seems impossible, I know."

"Too bad we don't have room for another bed." He seemed lost in thought for a moment. "Well, then. It looks like you're going to be sleeping right here."

The mattress was comfortable, but not enough to make me completely lose my mind. "I'm going to be doing *what*? I think you misunderstood what it meant for me to watch a movie with you."

He laughed briefly. "Riley, it's not what you're thinking. It's a big bed. I barely sleep as it is. If you can relax in it . . . well, I'm just glad someone can."

"Seems kind of convenient. Was this your plan all along?"

He looked at me with a puzzled expression. "You really don't trust people, do you?"

"I only trust people who give me good reasons to trust them," I said. "You've done nothing but play games with me since the day I got here. Since *before* the day I got here, if I count the groupies." I twirled my hair and imitated their vapid looks.

"So you think it was my plan to, what, lure you up here and force you to sleep with me, using the power of the Jax Effect?"

"Sounds very Hitchcockian." I knew it wasn't fair, but when had Jax ever played fair?

He winced at the jab, sending a momentary pang of guilt through me. "Listen to me. I didn't bring you up here. I didn't make you sleep here. How could this be my plan when it depended on what you'd do?"

I knew he was right, but I was stubborn. "Right. Next you'll probably tell me that you sleep naked," I said. "You always just keep pushing it."

His face slumped slightly. "We've played a lot of games. But I'm not a monster, and I'm not playing tonight. You've made your position clear. Our deal from earlier still stands, one kiss after every concert, but there will be no sex in this room—and that's a promise."

"I'm supposed to believe that?"

"I'll sleep on the floor. Will that fix it?"

"Well, what about the band?"

"What about them?"

"I can't have your band thinking that I'm having sex with you when I'm the tour accountant."

"Relax, Riley. Even though the tour bus is the biggest one we could find, everyone knows that it's cramped in here and we have to share. Kev and Chewie sleep in the same room and nobody thinks they're having sex in there."

I looked at his face. Was this a trick? He didn't seem like he was being sly or dishonest. Just the same, the band called the room his Fortress of Solitude for a reason. From what I'd gathered, he almost never let people inside. Now he wanted me to sleep here? Even in my daydreams, I only ended up in

Jax's room for sex. Moving into his space didn't figure into my fantasies.

"Jax, I don't want to say no," I said cautiously, "and I don't want you to sleep on the floor."

"Then just say yes. It's an easy word. Three letters, one syllable." He studied my skeptical expression. "I swear to you, nothing will happen in this bed, except that you'll finally get a good night's sleep."

I looked at the bedding around us. "Fine," I agreed. Sighing, I flopped backwards on the intensely comfortable bed. "But get out some pillows, because they're going between us."

He reached down to a corner of the bed and pulled up a body pillow that was nearly as long as he was tall. "Think this will do?"

I looked at the pillow and crinkled my nose. "Promise me you don't use this for anything gross."

He shook his head, smirking, and strands of his long dark hair fell across his face. "Hadn't even occurred to me until now."

I looked into his eyes. "If I sleep here, we're *only* sleeping okay? No games."

He didn't say a word. He just sat up and slid a thick, downy blanket up over my legs. I hadn't been tucked into bed in a long time, but when Jax did it, I felt somehow safe, protected. I couldn't say no to that—and I didn't want to.

"I wish your bed wasn't so damned comfortable . . ." I said softly, my words fading as sleepiness took over.

A dim light overhead turned off with a gentle *click*.

"Good night, Riley," he said turning over on his side of the bed.

I clutched my pillow close as the room went black, realizing that Jax's earthy scent lingered on it. In the pitch dark, I buried my face deeper and fell asleep to the soft, steady sound of his breath.

Chapter Eleven

THE MILE-HIGH CITY

The faintest hint of sunlight woke me up the next morning. The bed had done its job—I didn't ache the way I had when I'd woken up on the couch. Feeling well-rested and alert, I rolled out of Jax's bed while he continued sleeping. I admired him laying there for a moment. He looked so peaceful. It was almost hard to believe I was looking at the same man who'd taken my bikini hostage yesterday morning.

I smirked and shook my head. I hadn't really expected him to make a move on me last night, but I was somewhat surprised that he didn't so much as put his arm over the pillow wall we had between us—or at least, I hadn't noticed if he did.

I quietly slipped out of his room, went through my morning routine, and then grudgingly spent the rest of the day drowning myself in work in order to avoid thinking about my evolving feelings for Jax. Work provided a momentary distraction, but the second I stopped, my mind immediately went back to thinking about him. The only trouble was, I didn't know what to think about him anymore. When I'd first met him, I'd thought he was only about rocking out and getting his rocks off. But after seeing a more down-to-earth side of him yesterday, I began to suspect he wasn't just a sexy Siren who needed a backstage orgy to have a good time. He might even be someone I could actually fall for.

It didn't help that my physical attraction to him hadn't lessened since we'd first met. If anything, it had grown, and now that I was sleeping in his bed, a part of me was afraid of what might happen if I let my self-control slip, even for a moment. Ever since that massage he'd given me, I'd been more than a little sexually frustrated, throwing myself into work to try to keep myself distracted. It helped a bit.

Hours passed as I worked. We'd been halfway through Nebraska when I started, and by the time I paid any attention to the passing scenery, the flat plains had given way to rolling foothills—we were well into Colorado. The bus had made stops here and there for the band to get legal pot, but I didn't pay too much attention, since I didn't intend to smoke on the job.

Cramped from sitting on the second-floor couch all day, I was stretching out my arms and legs when I heard footsteps bounding up the stairwell.

One by one, Chewie, Sky, and Kev filed through, their arms loaded with brown bags. From the Christmas-morning looks on their faces, I could tell they were eager to unwrap their presents.

"Oh man, Riles, you totally missed out," Chewie said, lifting up his shades to look at me. "We've got enough stash to last a lifetime."

"Or just a typical day in your life," Sky said, jokingly slapping him across the chest.

I smiled. "Sounds like it was a blast." Returning to the budget tables on my laptop, I couldn't help but feel a little jealous. I would've loved to check out the shops, just to see what they were like and say I'd been in them, but unfortunately, work came before fun.

While Kev rummaged around in the fridge grabbing bottles of beers, Sky slid a record from its cover and placed it on the stereo system. She handed the album cover to Chewie, who plopped down on the couch opposite me and immediately went to work breaking up a variety of weed strains on the album cover and then rolling it all up into a blunt.

"Time to hotbox this whole floor with the dankest nugs the fine state of Colorado has to offer," Chewie said as he lit up the blunt and puffed on it.

I reluctantly turned down a beer from Kev since I wasn't quite done with my work yet, and I scrambled to finish my lingering tasks as the room quickly filled with a murky marijuana haze and the bombastic rock of the Black Keys. I looked up at them. "Can you guys do me a favor and give me any receipts you have if you're using band funds? It'll make my job a lot easier."

"No sweat, Riley, consider it done," Sky replied sweetly.

Chewie held up a blunt that was as thick as a magic marker. "You know that smoking some of this sticky icky will make your job a whole lot easier too, right?"

I laughed at the generous offer. "Thanks, but maybe some other time. You guys can roll papers down here, but I gotta unroll spreadsheets upstairs."

"Suit yourself, more for us," Chewie said. He had a big cheesy grin as he puffed away.

I shut my laptop and headed to the sundeck. Opening the door, I was greeted by the shining sun and a cool breeze—just the type of fresh air and silence I was hoping for.

"Just can't get enough of me, can you?"

The deep, flirtatious voice caught me by surprise. I turned and saw Jax standing where the side-railing met the bar. Wearing a black v-neck and black jeans, he looked unusually relaxed in the middle of the day, slouching against the bar with a drink in one hand. The band had a show tonight and from what I'd noticed, Jax would be in a serious mood on show nights, while the rest of the band would be already in party-mode.

"Yeah, right," I said coolly, used to deflecting his teasing by now. "You wish."

"Yet you're here. And I'm here."

"It's a coincidence. Your bandmates were smoking up a storm and I just came up here to get some fresh air."

"Ah, yeah. That sounds like them." He nodded slightly and took a long sip.

"Sure you don't want to join in the fun with them?" I asked.

He finished his drink, looked down into his ice-filled glass, and shook his head faintly. "Not really in the mood right now."

Jax seemed off his usual game. I wondered if he came up here to be alone.

"Do you want me to leave?" I asked, taking a step toward the door.

He waved away my question and rattled the cubes in his glass. "Want a drink? I'll fix you one."

I'd planned to get work done, but sensing a rare vulnerability in Jax, I decided that work could wait. I shrugged. "Sure, why not? I'll have whatever you're having."

His expression lightened. "It's pretty strong. You sure you can handle it?"

I smiled. "I know I can."

I left my laptop on the table and went to lean back against the bar next to Jax as he fixed two drinks, pouring them into matching glass tumblers.

He handed me one of the glasses filled with amber liquid. "A Godfather for the lady."

"Thank you, Mr. Corleone," I replied, holding up the glass to toast him.

"My pleasure," he said. He clinked his glass against mine, smiled, and took a drink.

It smelled like pure rubbing alcohol, but I bravely took a sip, only to almost spit it right back out. I liked a strong drink, but he must've liked his as stiff as a board. The liquid burned my throat the whole way down, but it left a surprisingly sweet and pleasant aftertaste in my mouth. The drink reminded me of Jax's kiss—dangerous, but worth it.

"Impressive," he said before taking the glass from me with a smile, "but it's alright, I'll make you a mojito. You don't need to finish it."

I took it back from him with a smile of my own. "It actually tastes pretty good. I can see why you like it." I had to admit that he was being kind of sweet, and I thought maybe I wasn't giving him enough credit. Underneath the bad boy veneer, there were layers of humor and warmth—maybe even kindness. "Hey Jax," I said, "thanks for letting me sleep in your bed last night. I really haven't slept that well since I got on the bus."

"I'm just glad you were able to get some rest. Maybe you won't be so cranky next time I hit on you."

I nudged my shoulder into his, and it felt like nudging a brick wall. "Yeah, right. A few nice gestures go a long way, but the final verdict's still out on you."

"What I'm hearing is you're keeping an open mind," he said, raising his brows at me.

"And what I'm hearing is you're actually listening to me, for once."

"Wouldn't keep your hopes up on that one," he said with a wink.

I was really starting to like this side of him: playful, but without the games. I took another sip of my drink, but this time it didn't burn as much. "You know, you were sure out cold this morning."

"Oh, yeah . . ." he replied. His smile faded, and his gaze slowly drifted off into the distance.

"I thought you said you never slept."

He took a sip of his Godfather without looking at me. "I do. Just not a lot."

I studied him as an unspoken tension hung in the air. I wasn't sure if I'd said something offensive. I guess he really didn't get a lot of sleep, and I briefly wondered if it wasn't because of something more than insomnia.

Jax pulled out a joint from his t-shirt's front pocket. "You mind? I know you said you wanted some fresh air."

A minute ago I might've minded, but I saw it as an opportunity to ease the lingering tension that had arisen between us. "No, by all means, go right ahead."

He slipped the joint between his lips, sparked it up with a silver zippo lighter, and puffed on it a few times, causing the burning tip to sizzle and smoke. Pinching the joint between two fingers, he held it out to me. "Want to hit it?"

I half-smiled and shook my head lightly. "No thanks. I've smoked a few times before, but it doesn't do much for me. Wouldn't want you to waste it."

"If you say so," he said. He put the joint up to his lips and inhaled as he looked me up and down.

Judging from the way his bandmates went through weed like bags of M&Ms, I'd always assumed he did too, but this was the first time I actually saw him doing it.

"Do you always come up here to smoke?" I asked, idly swirling my drink.

He nodded slightly and exhaled toward the horizon. "Most of the time. The band likes smoking together and playing around. It's a social thing for them."

From what I've seen of my friends, pot-smoking always happened in groups. I studied his expression. "Isn't it always a social thing?"

"It can be," he said then puffed again and shrugged. "It can also just help you clear your mind. Block out some thoughts, you know?"

"What kind of thoughts?"

"Bullshit ones," he said casually.

Jax was being unusually open with me. I wanted to know more about him, but I was afraid of asking things that would make him uncomfortable. I smiled and nudged his arm in an attempt to lighten the mood. "Oh really? Before last night I would've thought you were bullshit central."

He let out a small laugh. "Yeah, okay, I deserved that."

I lifted my brow. I'd given him a playful opening to sling something back at me, but I was surprised when he didn't seize the opportunity.

"So you agree?" I asked.

"What can I say?" he said coolly. "I like to have my fun, I can't deny that. But don't pretend that you don't like it too."

I wondered if I was ready to admit that in spite of his games being stressful, they were also kind of fun. I could feel we'd grown closer over the past two days, but despite our increasing intimacy—the kiss, me sleeping in his bed—I wasn't ready to tell him that a part of me enjoyed his games.

I took another sip of my Godfather, which tasted better with every gulp. "No, you're right, I like having fun," I said as a general statement. "You know I can let loose. But that's only on vacation or on the weekends. Most of the time I live a normal, professional life like everyone else. The real world has consequences, so unfortunately, not everyone can live like a rock star."

He cocked his head. "You think I don't live in the real world?"

"Well, you do, but your real world is different from mine."

"How so?"

I narrowed my brows, confused that he didn't see the difference between being an accountant and being a rock star. "You've got countless adoring fans fawning over your every word. Some even come by your voice alone. You've got groupies. You can drink and smoke pot at work. Your whole life is one big rock concert."

After a few seconds, he raked his fingers back through his dark, windblown hair. "It wasn't always this way, you know."

"Oh?"

"I used to skip school, get into fights," he said before taking a long drag on the joint. "Surprising huh?"

"You getting into trouble at school? Never would've pictured that," I said jokingly.

He smiled and exhaled. "That's when I picked up a guitar. Don't know who came up with the idea first, but Sky and I decided to start a rock band. Back then we thought if we were going to be in a rock band, there's certain things that we just *had* to do first. Like doing a lot of drugs, partying 'til dawn, trashing hotel rooms, rocking out, and all that crazy stuff."

I'd partied hard in my day—especially back in college—but I was pretty sure none of it compared to any of the crazy stuff he'd done.

"I've always wondered what it would be like to be on stage with all the glitz, glamour, and groupies," I said as I motioned with my glass to the extravagance dripping from every inch of the bus. "You're living the dream."

He shrugged. "Sure, all those things are nice perks, but that's not why I play music."

I tilted my head, curious. "Is that so? Then why do you do it?"

He gave a wry grin. "Why not? It makes me feel good."

"Feel good?" I asked. I'd been half-expecting him to say something deep and philosophical, but what he said seemed fairly mundane.

He nodded. "Yeah. When you think about it, that's really all that matters. Feeling good." He turned his gaze to me. "You know, to be able to forget about the shit from the past, stop worrying about the future and just feel good in the moment."

His words resonated in their simplicity. When I wasn't working, I was always partying. The partying helped me forget about working—and the crappy parts of my past.

"Maybe you have a point," I replied.

"Maybe you and I aren't that different after all," he said with a smirk.

"Hey, that doesn't mean I'm agreeing that being a rock star and being an accountant are the same thing," I said playfully.

"Yeah they might be different, but we all want the same thing, no matter how we go about it," he said before his tone became serious again. "Whether you're a rock star or an accountant, some people are fueled by a drive to experience more pleasure. Others are just trying to avoid pain. But we all do it for the same reason: to feel good."

"I never thought about it that way," I said, pondering the implications. "Which one fuels you?"

He took a long drag. "Pain," he said quietly. He turned to me and held up the joint, his onyx eyes focused on the burning end. "That's what this is for."

I couldn't help but stare at the joint's simmering orange tip reflected in his haunted eyes. As magnetic as his charm was, his pain was just as palpable. Overwhelmed with empathy, my own painful past tried resurfacing in my mind, and I struggled to push it back down into its dark, hidden corner. I could tell that he was also hiding his own personal issues, no doubt fighting against them just like I had to fight against my own.

I reached out, plucked the joint from his hand, and brought it to my lips. He watched me as I inhaled, held in the warm smoke for a second, and then exhaled. Neither of us said anything—but then again, there was nothing else to say.

We passed the joint back and forth in silence, smoking it down to a burnt nub while we watched the sun sink behind the mountains, casting a long shadow all the way across the sundeck.

Chapter Twelve

PYROTECHNICS

As soon as we finished the joint, Jax said he needed his usual uninterrupted alone time to mentally prepare himself for the show, and he left to get ready. I stayed up on the sundeck for a little while finishing the drink he made me and reveling in my first-time high. I felt so mellowed out, enjoying the gorgeous evening as a radiant purple and orange sunset disappeared behind the city's skyline.

After sharing that connection with Jax, I was even more confused about him than I was when I woke up in his bed. I had to admit that he was giving me plenty of reasons to not only trust him, but also fall for him, and yet I still worried that I'd only end up getting used if I gave in to his seductive charms.

Once we were outside the venue, I flashed my credentials to security and headed inside. The crowd's buzz was escalating as rapidly as I was sobering up. Having caught up on most of my work during the day, I had a bit more leisure time to enjoy the show.

As I was about to peek out from behind the red crushed velvet curtain to look at the crowded auditorium, a soft tap on my shoulder surprised me. "Excuse me."

I spun around to find a squat bald man in a white button-up shirt and black tie with shiny badge on his chest. "Yes?"

He cleared his throat. "Sorry to bother you, but are you Riley Hewitt?"

I froze, the thought of weed racing through my mind before I remembered that it was legal in Colorado. "Yes, that's me."

"Hi, I'm Jim Rairden, Denver County Fire Marshal," he said holding out his hand. "I was told by your pyrotechnician that you're in charge of all band expenditures."

"Yes, I am," I said as I shook his hand. "Can I help you with something?"

"Well, I was just inspecting the pyrotechnics for tonight's show and it looks like you're going to have to sign up for an additional ballistics policy. I'm afraid it's gonna run upwards of ten thousand dollars to cover the deductible."

"Ten thousand?" I inhaled sharply. *Holy shit!* Even with the cuts Jax agreed to, we didn't have an extra ten thousand dollars just lying around. "Wait a second, all the proper permits have been acquired. Plus, according to the pricing table I was reviewing earlier, none of the permits are priced at anything more than a few hundred dollars."

The Fire Marshal flipped through a stack of papers on a clipboard. "This isn't about permits. It's about insurance for the 'Monster Inferno Fountain.' That's still classified as an experimental pyro device and it requires a special ballistics policy."

I eyed him skeptically. We didn't have to deal with a Fire Marshal in Chicago, and this guy was pitching some expensive stuff. I wasn't sure exactly which one was the "Monster Inferno Fountain," but I was sure that the band wasn't introducing any new devices for this show.

I raised an eyebrow and said, "We have an insurance policy *and* we just used this in Chicago the other day."

"Chicago doesn't have millions of acres of pristine national forest nearby," he said somberly. "Wildfires are the most dangerous part of our summers here. In response, the city council passed a strict fire safety ordinance to ensure that bands have the proper amount of fire insurance liability to cover pyro displays of that magnitude. And your policy doesn't quite cover the full liability for that particular pyro."

Great. Just great. Jax had just told me that he didn't want any interruptions while he prepped for tonight's show. I checked my watch. We'd be cutting it close even if I didn't run to ask him, which meant I had to make a decision. Since Jax had already agreed to trim some of the pyro, what was one more? He might not like the move, but we really didn't have the cash to cover this expensive policy. And after all, this was a rock show, not a fireworks display.

I crossed my arms and said firmly, "That's okay, we'll cut it and not get the insurance."

"Alright, please inform your pyrotechnician then. Have a good evening and enjoy your stay here in Denver." He shook my hand, smiled, and walked away.

I exhaled, realizing it was a good thing I handled this issue. We really dodged a bullet. I could only imagine what would happen if he had talked to one of the other band members. Chances are, Chewie would've ended up buying ghost insurance on top of the ballistics policy.

After disappointing the band's pyrotechnician with the bad news about the Inferno Fountain, I went back to the sidestage. I was actually eager to see the performance today. Things between Jax and me had progressed from adversarial to friendly since the last show, so I didn't feel the need to avoid him by hiding in a maintenance room. Even though there weren't any seats around, standing sure beat sitting on a propane tank.

Once again, I peeked out to get a good look at the crowd. The people were now packed in tight, and the crowd's size was more impressive than the one in Chicago. I immediately noticed that the majority of them were women. *No big surprise there*. Scanning the faces of the raver girls dressed in pure neon, the staid bespectacled librarians, the bubbly and tanned sorority sisters, and the businesswomen still wearing work clothes, I wondered with annoyance which one Jax might bring on stage in order to give her a mind-blowing, aural orgasm.

The thought of Jax making women orgasm caused me to unexpectedly relive the passionate kiss I'd had with him. The thought that I'd have to give him another one after this show sent goosebumps across my skin. It was getting frustrating—thinking about him, having these feelings for him. I had to constantly remind myself of the professional as well as emotional risks involved with sleeping with Jax. But my god, would it finally ease the near-constant ache between my thighs since I'd started the tour.

A palpable intensity filled the room. Every person in the auditorium was fully attuned to the stage, all of them in fervent anticipation to see the Hitchcocks. To see *Jax*. And I couldn't blame them. When I checked earlier today, the band's album had already crashed into the top twenty, reaching number nineteen. The Hitchcocks were rising stars, and Jax was their burning hot core.

All of a sudden, Chewie, Kev, and Sky hurried past me onto the stage as the crowd started clapping. I watched them with keen interest, loving this up-close view of the band gearing up to start the show.

"Trying to keep an eye on me, Pepper?"

I nearly leapt out of my shoes as Jax's familiar voice whispered in my ear. I'd been so intent on watching the band set-up that I'd let him get the jump on me.

Knowing who it was, I didn't bother turning to face him, but I also didn't move away. "Somebody needs to make sure you stay out of trouble."

"And you think you're up to the task?" he said, his warm breath tickling my ear.

His mischievous tone was a far cry from his earlier mood, and I wondered if our conversation had anything to do with it.

I turned my head slightly, looking at his searing grin through the corner of my eye. "How hard can it be?"

"It can be very hard," he said, his voice a velvety rasp. "But I trust you." He shot me a quick wink that made my heart flutter.

As he left me to take the stage, I got a whiff of his raw, earthy scent, and my brain scrambled. It seemed like no matter what I did, we were continuing to grow closer. The sexual tension building between us was starting to drive me crazy, and I wondered if he felt the same way.

The lights dimmed as Jax sauntered out onto the stage and the audience erupted into crazed cheers and hoarse shouts. Those lucky enough to be in the front row were frantically grasping at his leather-clad legs. The fans were screaming their faces off.

Jax positioned himself in the center-stage spotlight and The Hitchcocks exploded into a sonic surge that echoed off the far walls and reverberated through the concert hall. A rumbling bassline poured from Sky's fingers and Chewie's rapid-fire snare drove a steady beat as Kev's guitar riffs built an intricate melody on top of it all.

But it was Jax—always Jax—who stole the show, growling into the mic and prowling the stage like a predator stalking its prey. His fluid movements and mesmerizing lyrics hypnotized the audience and they collectively followed his every step, gesture, and word. I couldn't even begin to fathom what it must've felt like to have thousands of reverent fans idolizing me and worshiping my every word, but Jax drank it all up and thrived on it.

The band played almost exactly the same songs they had at the first show, but they gave the audience exactly what they came to see: a wild rock 'n' roll spectacle that left them breathless. This time I was more familiar with the set list and the show's overall arc, so I was almost able to anticipate what song was going to come next. My eyes never left Jax's writhing torso and gyrating hips. Without realizing I had been doing it, I found myself moving my hips in unison with his seductive movements, and I quickly stopped it. Thankfully no one was around to see my momentary lapse of self-control.

After cycling through more songs, the band launched into a catchy one that got me all riled up. It was quickly becoming my favorite one. I sang along to the parts I knew and tapped my hand against my hip to keep the beat. Trying to learn all the song's words, I focused in on Jax's lips curving and twisting as he sang the lyrics. I had the sudden desire to run my tongue over his lips, and I licked my own, anticipating our scheduled kiss after this show.

Jax turned his head my way as the song moved into the bridge. When he noticed me singing along, he locked eyes with me and we synced our singing.

I won't bend my knees
and I won't beg you please

'Cuz I know we can't ever be together.
But it's times like these,
I just can't feed my needs
And I don't know if I can last forever.

Only time will tell
If we can end this hell,
Oh the hell with time
I wanna make you mine.
Only time will tell
When we can end this hell,
Oh the hell with time
I'm gonna make you mine.

Singing those words together as we gazed into each other's eyes sent a chill coursing through my body. He turned back to face the crowd, swung his boot up on an amp, and continued belting out the lyrics, reaching out to his fans reaching out to him, his fingers just inches from theirs.

I felt a momentary concern. Had he been singing those words *with* me or *to* me? And did he think I was singing them back to him?

Toward the end of the set, the entire room was riding close to a musical pinnacle. The band had been building up the whole show to the final climactic crescendo, getting the audience—including myself— more and more amped up with song after song of euphonic foreplay. Cymbals crashed in thundering metallic clangs and the guitars hurled harmonies in cascading waves of reverb. Strobelights flickered wildly while bright white flashes detonated and sent sparks flying across the stage. The intensity of the show had me so excited that my pounding heart felt like the kick pedal from the bass drum was smashing directly into my chest.

Jax moved his hands from his guitar to grip the microphone on its stand as he howled out the verses, his left foot stomping along to Chewie's drumming and his guitar hanging around his neck. Still gripping the microphone with one hand, Jax's other hand shot up above his head signaling for the band to immediately pause the high-octane song as he belted out a sustained note. His rich baritone voice reverberated in my ears sending tingles through me.

Standing in the spotlight maintaining the deep note, Jax kept his hand up above his head as beads of sweat dripped down his cheekbones. He was holding the note so long, I swear he must've had an extra set of lungs buried under all those muscles and tattoos.

Sustaining the note, he glanced back over his shoulder, his eyes darting around the stage. The rest of the band exchanged baffled looks with him, shrugging and shaking their heads. With his arm still awkwardly held above his head, I could hear the note start to strain against his vocal chords. His face turned red, then dark red, and then a deep shade of purple. It looked like his head was about to explode, but he kept singing.

Something was very off.

I held my breath in suspense. The faces in the crowd slowly shifted from wide-eyed euphoria to scrunched confusion as second after tense second passed.

All of a sudden, the pyrotechnician sprinted out onto the stage. Jax mercifully cut off the note and covered the mic with his hand. The two exchanged a few quick words, both of them pointing at all the pyrotech devices strategically strapped down around the stage. Jax shook his head and took a deep breath as the pyrotech ran off the stage.

"Sorry," Jax said into the microphone. "Our dumbass pyrotech fucked up the show. But don't worry, Denver, a little fuck-up won't stop us from rocking you!"

Shit, the pyros! My hand flew to cover my gaping mouth as queasiness filled my stomach. He must've been waiting on the Monster Inferno Fountain as a cue the entire time.

The band collected themselves and broke into the next song. The crowd went berserk, seemingly unaffected by the mishap.

I wiped my forehead, relieved that my decision to cut the pyro didn't ruin the show. But then I caught a look at Jax. He had an unmistakable scowl on his face that told me he was seething about the communication breakdown.

***

Wringing my fingers, I paced anxiously up and down the long, narrow hallway that led to the green rooms. The show had ended a half hour ago to a roaring applause, but Jax's expression hadn't changed since the pyro mishap. In fact, he looked even more pissed when I saw him leave the stage.

I knew I had to talk to him to take responsibility for the accident, but I wanted to wait for the right time—or was that just my sense of anxiety talking? Exhaling deeply, I finally decided to talk to him now and clear up any misunderstandings. Better to get it all out in the open than to wait for him to cool down and risk the issue festering.

I rapped my knuckles against the door.

"I'm not talking to anybody right now." Jax's voice boomed through the door, brusque and guttural, confirming my worry that he was still in a bad mood.

Nervous, I cleared my throat. "Jax, it's me."

There was a shuffle and the door pulled inward. Jax's statuesque silhouette filled the doorway. He was shirtless but still wore his smooth leather pants; they fit so well that they looked like they were made just for him. A hard expression on his face softened when our eyes met.

"Riley," he said, his voice gentler. "Sorry about that. I didn't know it was you." He sighed, looking worn from agitation. "What's up?"

I caught a glance behind him and saw that the room was a mess. Concert outfits were strewn along the floor and there was a broken guitar among them, the strings flexed in curls. It wasn't the typical neatness Jax preferred. Had he done all of that?

"Jax, I . . . um, wanted to talk to you about something."

He studied my expression, the lines on his forehead deepening with concern. He touched his warm hand to my cheek. "What's wrong?"

I took a deep breath. "I wanted to apologize for what happened with the pyro . . . I'm the one who cut it."

His hand brushing my cheek stilled. His brows turned to steep lines. "What did you say?"

"I cut the pyro, Jax. I'm sorry."

He pulled away as if I'd burned him. He then closed his eyes and pinched the bridge of his nose. "You need to leave."

"Jax, I—"

"Stop." Pointing down the hallway, he looked me directly in the eyes. "Go wait for me on the bus. We're going to talk about this," he said, his voice barely concealing his anger. Then he slammed the door in my face.

I stood there, stunned. I had the urge to bang on the door and scream at him for treating me like a child, but I resisted the urge. Just barely. His tone shocked me and hurt me, making my throat constrict and my eyes sting.

Blinking rapidly, I backed away from the door and hurried out of the venue, trying to make sense of what just happened. As I hurried back to the bus, I thought about how in just a few hours we went from being closer than we'd ever been to being infuriated with each other.

Chapter Thirteen

HEATED

I sat on the first floor couch with my arms folded across my chest and my flats tapping the ground impatiently. Everyone else was out partying but not me—I was caught playing Jax's waiting game. I felt ridiculous, stupid even, like I was back in kindergarten and Mrs. Elswick put me into timeout for saying a bad word I'd heard from three older girls. It'd been well over an hour since Jax slammed a door in my face. How long was he going to make me wait for him? If anything, *he* was the one acting like a kid.

Groaning in frustration, I went upstairs to get some air on the sundeck. I took a seat at the bar and poured myself a glass of whiskey, hoping to calm my nerves.

It was midway through my second round when Jax suddenly appeared from the stairwell, his expression serious. He'd put on a shirt that matched his black leather pants since I last saw him. As always, he looked too gorgeous. No matter how much I wanted to avoid him, push him away, or be mad at him, I couldn't help the part of me that was attracted to him.

I set my glass down and felt my emotions well to the surface. I stood and pointed angrily at him. "You made me wait almost two hours for you! I told you, I was sorry. I thought we were past these petty games!"

"Sit down," he commanded, pointing to the barstool I'd risen from. "The time for games is fucking over. You crossed the line when you messed up my goddamn show! I knew I shouldn't have trusted you."

His voice shook me. I was scared at first but then I realized he was yelling at me for something that wasn't entirely my fault. I stayed right where I was. "I did what I had to do! You're the one who's acting like a damn princess!"

He approached me, shaking his head as if I didn't get it. "You asked me to make cuts, and I did. Now you're making cuts behind my back..." He snatched my drink from the counter and pounded away the remaining contents. "All for that fucking bonus," he said, slamming the glass down so that the ice cubes rattled.

"What are you talking about?" I asked, taken aback. "That's not the way it is—"

His eyes blazed. "I let you sleep in my bed. I let you talk me into trusting you. You said you wanted to keep things professional between us, but here you've been fucking with me this whole time."

Oh god, that's what he thinks? I could hear it simmering beneath the surface, in his voice and in his words—the tension between us that had been building over the past couple of days as we'd gotten closer.

He grabbed my arm, firmly enough to be intimidating. "Tell me, what was going through your head when you made the cut, huh? Did you trick the pyrotech too?"

My eyes stung. I threw his arm off me. "Damn it, Jax!" I cried, unable to stop a tear from falling down my cheek as I faced him. "The fire marshall came to talk to me! I had to make a choice."

"What?" he said, his volume still elevated.

I wiped my cheek with the back of my hand. "He said we had to either cut the Monster Inferno or pay an extra ten grand for ballistics insurance."

The fire in his eyes waned. His brows furrowed. "The fuck?"

"There wasn't time to check with you! I had to make a decision. And I did."

He put his hand to his head and exhaled in a rush. "God . . . Why didn't you tell me? I could've changed the cues if I'd known."

"I told the pyrotech, I thought he was going to tell you!"

His hand covered his eyes and he shook his head. "Fuck."

"I know," I said softly. "I'm sorry."

"Jesus . . ." he said shaking his head lightly. "Ten grand for insurance? Really?"

"Yeah."

An uncomfortable silence passed between us that seemed to last an eternity. We'd apparently cleared up the miscommunication, but the damage had been done. It was obvious that the unspoken tension between us was becoming a problem—not just for me, but for him as well. It'd be easier for the both of us if we could end whatever this weird thing was between us and start over as professionals.

"Jax, I've been thinking—"

Strong arms wrapped around my body, pulling me into his Jax's chest. My train of thoughts faltered. I could only think about how good it felt to be embraced in his arms. I could feel his warmth cocooning me, his beating chest pressed against my tear-stained cheek. It felt right, like the first thing in years that made sense in my chaotic life.

He released the hug and looked down at me.

"What was that for?" I asked, surprised.

His dark eyes were gentle as they stared into mine. "I'm sorry for blaming you."

I blushed. "Thanks," I said, meaning it.

He tilted his head and touched his lips tenderly to mine. Caught off guard, it took a second before I remembered that I owed him a post-show kiss. I began to reciprocate, pressing my lips softly against his. It was nearly the opposite of the lust-driven kiss we'd had last time. This one was almost scary in its intimacy.

He gently pulled away. When I opened my eyes, he was looking at me, smiling. "I figured we could use it to smooth things over."

I nodded dreamily, my mind still lingering on Jax's undeniably luscious lips.

He put his arm around my shoulder and exhaled deeply. "Everyone's gone to the afterparty. It's been a long day for me, but you go on ahead. I'm going to the hot tub."

I sighed heavily, equally exhausted. "I think I'm just going to chill out as well. I'm wiped. Not really in the mood to party."

"So come with me. Who needs a party when you have eighty-nine jets?""

I glanced at the hot tub. I could practically hear the bubbles calling my name after such a long, emotionally-draining day. "Sounds like just what the doctor ordered."

I returned to the sundeck dressed in my bikini. I'd run it under warm water this time, checking to make sure it didn't bleed color, and thankfully it didn't.

I saw Jax leaning back in the hot tub, head resting on the edge with a wet hand towel folded over his eyes. A drink—a double, from the looks of it—sat on the ledge of the tub next to him.

Although we'd made up, I couldn't help feeling that there were still big problems between us. There was that pesky sexual tension, there was our growing intimacy, and there was my fear of getting hurt. Our make-up kiss had left me feeling even more confused and frustrated about all those things.

I went to the bar to make myself a rum and coke. I was a bit concerned about sharing the hot tub with him, knowing what happened the last time one of us was in it, but seeing him relaxed—possibly even asleep—put me at ease.

I quietly slipped into the hot tub, careful not to disturb him. I looked over his long, leonine body as I sipped on my drink, admiring the curves and edges of his bare torso. His chest was rising and falling in a slow rhythm, the dark lines of his tattoos making intricate swirls on his skin.

As I sighed and leaned back in relaxation myself, I heard his arm lift from the edge and dip into the water. I watched as his hand moved down to his trunks.

What's he doing?

It was hard to see through the bubbles, but his motions looked suspicious. His forearm was flexed, and it was going up and down in short movements. *No way.* He couldn't be . . .

His mouth opened and a soft groan escaped his lips.

Oh my god! I quickly stood and splashed water at him. "What are you doing?!"

He sat up, pulling the towel from his eyes. "What the fuck?" he said, looking groggy. "What's going on?"

I turned the dial to lower the jets and pointed sternly toward his crotch. "What were you doing down there?"

His brows narrowed. "Nothing. I'm trying to relax. What are you getting so worked up for?"

"You were jerking off, weren't you? I cast an accusatory eye toward his trunks.

His eyes widened. "Seriously? That's what you thought?" he said defensively. "I was just adjusting a wedge in my trunks. The jets were pushing into it."

"Yeah, sure you were."

He looked at me skeptically. "Wow. Are you really freaking out over a guy masturbating? I guess I don't know you as well as I thought." He reached down to his trunks again and this time I was able to clearly see how he was adjusting the wedge caused by the jets.

"Oh puh-lease," I said, splashing a bit of water at him before I sat back down. "I'm not a prude, if that's what you're suggesting. I was just caught off guard, that's all."

He leaned back with his hands behind his head, looking amused. "I just have that kind of effect on you, don't I?"

My chest tightened. The confidence with which he said those words hit a sensitive spot. Since day one of this tour, I'd been trying hard to conceal how much he actually affected me. I wasn't certain how much he actually believed I'd fallen for him, and how much was just arrogant confidence, but I sure as hell wasn't going to admit it.

"You *so* don't have an effect on me," I replied, flashing a smug smile and leaning back in relaxation with my hands behind my head like he did. "At least . . . not anymore."

His brow lifted. "Not anymore?"

"Nope."

He grinned. "Didn't figure you for a liar."

Damn it. I didn't like how accurate his read on me was. I couldn't let Jax believe he had me figured out. It was time to bring out the big guns.

I took a deep breath. "You know . . . I probably shouldn't tell you this, because I know it'll hurt your ego."

His eyes narrowed. "Tell me what?"

"Well, I hate to say it, but I've seen you so often, now, that I've gotten used to you," I said as I idly put my hand against a jet stream, feeling the water massage against my palm. The jet felt good at first, but as I adapted to the sensation, it quickly lost its soothing effect.

"I don't think so," he said waving his hand dismissively. "You have the same feelings for me as you did that night we first met. Probably more."

I shook my head lightly. "Nope. You know, they say absence makes the heart grow fonder. But what they forget to say is: abundance makes the heart grow indifferent. And in this case, it only took about a week."

His mouth curved in displeasure. "I don't believe you."

"But that's exactly the problem, Jax. It doesn't matter what you believe. Facts are facts." I took a sip of my drink and vocalized my pleasure when I found it tasted better than I expected. "I imagine when you first brought me onto the bus, you thought we'd be honeymooning in Pound Town by now. But all you get is a pre-planned, negotiated kiss every now and then. You must be disappointed."

He blinked rapidly for a moment. "Let's not forget that you're sleeping in my bed."

"Keyword is 'sleeping'. And that's all we're doing. You might even call it 'friends without benefits'."

He held up his hand like a stop sign. "Let me get this straight," he said in a serious tone. "You're saying you've 'friend-zoned' me?"

I was surprised he even knew the term. I couldn't imagine a man as desirable as him had been put into the friend-zone often—maybe not ever.

I smiled. "First time?"

He sighed, clearly agitated. For a moment, he seemed to be thinking of something to say, but instead he shook his head and reached for his drink. The fact that I was able to make him speechless emboldened me.

"Don't get me wrong," I added, munching on an ice cube. "I think you've still got the Jax Effect. It just doesn't work on me anymore. I'm immune to it."

"You're beginning to annoy me with your lies," he said. There was a small trace of uncertainty in his voice that I honed in on. He was playing it cool, but I sensed that he cared about me much more than he was willing to admit.

"In fact, maybe it's the other way around," I continued, "I'm the one who has the effect on you."

"On me?" He shifted slightly. "You're hot, I'll give you that. But I think you've been drinking too much. You're getting carried away here."

"We both know it's more than that. You've been sweeter to me than you want to admit. The way you kissed me a few minutes ago? I imagine it's a first for you, going out of your way to please a girl." I flashed him a wide smile. "You might even call it the Riley Effect." With my hand, I motioned a whip then snapped it, making the appropriate sound with my mouth.

"That's it," he grunted, "get out of my hot tub." He pointed toward the sundeck entrance. "I wanted to relax, but you're here stirring up trouble."

"So you're admitting it?" I replied, my heart beginning to beat faster.

"I'm not admitting shit," he said, raising his voice. His eyes pierced me, a dark warning that sent a flood of excitement through my body.

"You're not denying it. So that must be an admission."

"You're pushing it, Pepper," he warned.

I knew I was crossing the line, but I couldn't stop. Not now. Not after everything he put me through since we first met. Not after the mind-blowing kisses we'd had.

"What? Your buttons? Welcome to my world."

He bolted to his feet in the hot tub. "You want to see an effect?" he growled. "Then see it." He reached into his trunks and whipped out his cock. He started stroking himself in a leisurely rhythm, his member quickly turning into an impressive erection in front of me.

I shot to my feet, appalled. "Fuck! I knew it! You were lying earlier."

He shook his head, continuing to stroke himself. "You gave me this idea," he said, smiling. "And it was a good one."

I angrily put my hands on my hips, preparing to get out. "You're unbelievable."

"Guess I do have an effect on you after all," he said smugly. His hand stopped, and he tucked himself back in his trunks as he collapsed back into the hot tub. He pointed to the cabinet on the side with a grin on his face. "Hand me a towel before you leave, would you?"

I had one foot out of the tub when I realized that Jax was just doing this to make me leave. I reached over for a towel and threw it at him before sitting back down in the water with my arms folded across my chest.

"What are you doing?" he asked, setting the towel aside.

I stared at him defiantly. "I'm not letting you kick me out of the hot tub."

"Are you serious? I told you to leave."

"Of course I'm serious. You can't tell me what to do."

His jaw tightened. "You know what I'm gonna do if you stay. You can't stop me."

I could see right through him. He was only saying it to jar me enough to leave—he didn't really mean it. I knew I had him pinned as a sweet guy beneath that bad boy veneer. I'd seen it in the small ways he cared about me. I'd felt it in his lips. He wasn't going to do it because he knew it would upset me.

"Go ahead," I replied. "I'm calling you on your bluff."

His eyes blazed with the same intensity as they had during our argument over the pyro. "I'm not bluffing, Pepper."

I nodded at his elbows resting on the edge. "Then what are you waiting for? Show me."

"I will," he growled.

I watched in amazement as he yanked his trunks down and his still-erect cock sprung from its confines. The bulbous tip peeked above the surface of the water as he began to stroke himself.

My pulse leaped. Eyes wide, I sucked in a sharp breath.

He responded with a knowing smile. "Better leave," he purred darkly. "You don't want your boss to find out about this."

Unable to look away, I continued watching him, watching as he stroked up and down slowly. My heart beat faster as my nipples tightened against my bikini. I couldn't leave, I told myself. I couldn't let him kick me out. I couldn't let him win.

I swallowed and lifted my eyes to meet his. "I'm not telling him. And neither are you."

His jaw tightened. The pace of his hand increased as his gaze moved to my chest. "You think I'm thinking about you while I do this?" he grunted, staring so hard at my bikini that he could've burned a hole in it. "I'm not."

"Oh, you're thinking about me." I stared back, mesmerized by the head of his cock roiling the surface of the water. My thighs pressed together as a dull throbbing began to form between them. The water seemed to be getting hotter, and combined with the alcohol I'd been drinking, it was getting harder to think straight.

He shook his head. "I'm thinking about those twins from before."

My heart skipped, remembering the groupies he'd compared me to. He was clearly trying to rankle me—and as much as I hated to admit it, it was working. "No, you're not."

"I've been thinking about them for a while," he said through gritted teeth, his strokes getting longer and faster. "Next time I'm in New York—"

"You're lying," I shot, the heat of the water and the fire in my body making me touchy.

"The truth hurts, huh?"

"Shut up."

His scorching gaze was fixed to my body, turning me on unbelievably. I could see it in his eyes, in the way he was stroking himself. He was imagining himself inside me.

"I'm gonna give it to them. Rough. Hard." His voice was strained, a raspy snarl barely concealing his desire. "I've wanted to do it ever since I saw them. All this time. All this fucking time."

My breaths came shallow. I could feel it billowing inside me: anger and lust violently clashing together, melding into a destructive torrent of carnal desire.

"You'll be thinking of me, tonight," he growled. "Thinking 'til you're blue."

"You're so frustrating." The words tumbled softly out of my mouth. With Jax pleasuring himself right in front of me and me being already half-naked, the pent-up sexual energy I'd suppressed over the past week was growing dangerously strong, threatening to burst.

"We could end this, Riley," he offered. "I know exactly how you're feeling—you're suffering. Let's cut the bullshit and end this torture for the both of us."

I was vaguely aware of my body shifting so that the jets began to hit against my inner thigh. My aching desire was screaming to be satisfied. Blood was pounding in my ears. It was taking all my strength not to rip off my top and bottom and jump onto his lap.

"No," I said stubbornly.

He licked his lips. "I'm gonna enjoy it. Making you sexually frustrated. All that tension. No release."

The way his tongue brushed against his lips and the way he teased me with his words ignited the yearning inside me like gasoline poured onto a flame. My fingers curled against the acrylic seat, my need for relief so strong it was physically painful. "So what?" I replied, my voice coming weak. "You think I'll have sex with you?"

"It'll keep building," he bit out. "Your stubbornness will force you to give in to me. I couldn't have planned it better myself."

I swallowed hard as the inescapability of his words sank in. "You think you have it all worked out, don't you?" I struggled.

He began to stroke himself from the base of his penis to the swollen tip, showing me how deep he was imagining himself plunging into me. The visual was so intense I could almost feel it, his hard length burrowing inch-by-inch into sensitive, nerve-laden flesh. My toes curled painfully. My heart was beating so fast I could hardly breathe. One by one cracks were spreading throughout the walls I'd built to contain my desire. I'd wanted to prove I could resist. To Jax. To Jen. And most of all, to myself. But I couldn't hold it back any longer. With a final shaky breath, I let it all crumble.

"Then watch me destroy your plans," I said.

I slipped my hand into my bathing suit and pressed my fingers to my clit, tending to the ache that threatened to consume me.

"No. Stop." His fiery eyes became dark.

I shook my head, my breaths coming back and fast, pleasure coursing through my veins in powerful bursts.

His lust-filled eyes were frantic. "Stop it, Riley," he snarled. His fist tightened around his cock and his strokes took on a feverish pace.

His warnings spurred me. I bucked my hips into my fingers defiantly. My fingers quickened their pace, rubbing wild circles, shooting bolts of desire through my tense body. I watched as Jax's movements grew frenetic, thrashing the water more fiercely than the jets around us. The sight of him losing control sent me reeling. I felt myself sliding from my seat, sinking deeper into the hot tub until my knees knocked against his.

"Now you're thinking about me," I panted, my vision getting blurry and my head barely above the water.

He stared at my gyrating hips with half-lidded eyes, a painful expression marring his gorgeous face. "You think that affects me?" he bit out, his voice hoarse with lust.

"You think you affect *me*?" I growled through gnashed teeth, my own voice dripping with desire. I closed my eyes, drinking in the sounds of Jax's pleasure.

Armed with the image of his long, thick cock, I plunged my fingers inside myself. "Oh god," I moaned, unable to help myself.

"Fuck," he cried. I could hear him sucking in air behind clenched teeth. "Fuck, that's beautiful."

His knees pressing against mine widened, spreading me as he spread himself. I opened my eyes to gaze at him and saw he was sinking deeper into the hot tub like me. The tortured expression on his face looked like he was teetering on the edge of agony and bliss.

Suddenly, Jax scrambled to his feet, rising out of the water with his rigid member in hand. Droplets of water fell from the lines of his cut pelvis as he reached frantically for the towel nearby, held it in front of the tip of his penis, and turned around. The sight of his perky ass clenching as he climaxed sent me tumbling over the edge. I came in a flurry, my cries of ecstasy melding with Jax's. My eyelids lowered over the sight of him hunched forward, his butt sporadically flexing as his orgasm sputtered to its eventual end.

Darkness enveloped me, time seemed to stand still as aftershocks seized my boneless body. When I finally opened my eyes, his trunks were back on, and he was standing there gazing down at me. I saw something in his eyes. I'd expected it to be the scorching desire I'd grown accustomed to, but that look was gone, replaced by something wholly different, something grave in nature. I couldn't recognize it. Remorse? Disgust? All I knew was something had dramatically changed between us.

Without a word, he got out, dried himself off, and left in a hurry.

I remained in the hot tub with bubbles swirling around me. The afterglow of the orgasm wore off quickly—quicker than I ever imagined it could—and I hugged my knees into my chest. I felt confused and vulnerable. Used.

I tried adjusting the dial on the hot tub, but no matter how far I turned it, the water felt cold.

Chapter Fourteen

SHOOTING STAR

The next night I was in the auditorium of The Palms Casino Resort. We'd gotten to Las Vegas, the city referred to as the "Miracle in the Desert". But the only miracle I was thinking about was how one minute Jax and I had been pleasuring ourselves in front of one another, and the next minute he was treating me like a stranger.

I'd woken up completely alone, and Jax had proceeded to ignore me all day, managing to stay out of sight whenever I tried looking for him. It wasn't my first time being shut out by a guy, but it still stung. I'd been wary of him hurting me, so I wasn't completely surprised, but it still hurt more than I thought it would.

I didn't know why he'd done it. He probably thought his conquest was over—or maybe he didn't respect me anymore after I'd touched myself in front of him. It didn't really matter, though: it still pissed me off either way. *Whatever*, I thought. I had to remind myself that I just wanted to get done with this tour, get my bonus, and then peace out for a real vacation.

The concert was already in progress. This time, as I watched Jax from backstage, a faint, jealous gnaw tugged at me every time he reached out to the crowd. I'd been right in the first place. We weren't from the same worlds. For him, my world was boring, and for me, his was unreachable.

The noise from the crowd was deafening, but the applause made my stomach knot with tension. It was possible that Jax was just getting too famous for me to keep his interest.

"Stop thinking like this," I scolded myself, realizing how it hard was to break bad habits.

Just out of view of the audience, I nervously tapped my foot along to the Hitchcocks' greatest hits, hoping for the set to end so I'd finally be able to corner Jax and talk to him about giving me the cold shoulder. I wanted answers . . . even if the truth hurt.

While the final song's drum solo crescendoed, Jax walked toward a shrieking brunette in the front row while taking a swig from a water bottle, then poured the rest of the water onto himself.

With a practiced motion, he grabbed his white shirt from the bottom hem and pulled it up over his head, holding it above him with both hands. He twisted it and water streamed from the shirt, drenching the brunette below, who shrieked with orgasmic glee.

My hands tensed into fists. I couldn't help but feel used. With a sea of gorgeous women at Jax's beck and call every night, it'd only be a matter of time before I had to see him go backstage with one. Why had he led me on? I found myself looking over the women in the front row with a sense of jealous fatalism. If it happened—correction, *when* it happened—what would my replacement look like?

The crowd's roar registered dimly, but it wasn't until Chewie came backstage, hand up for a high five, that I realized the set was over. "Now *that's* what I call a show!" he said, his half-yell jolting me back to reality. "Rye, have you ever *seen* a crowd so crazy? I guess that's Vegas, baby!"

Kev followed right behind him, gripping the neck of his guitar, beaming brightly. Sky ran over from behind Kev and gave a big hug to Chewie—and then one to me. "Rileeey!" Sky squealed. "Tell me you saw that last set. Tell me you saw how incredible it was."

Releasing from the hug, I forced a grin. "Yeah," I said. "Pretty incredible." The band walked into the dressing rooms, and I looked back to the auditorium, my fake smile gone.

Jax bowed deeply and walked offstage, catching sight of me and smiling like nothing was wrong. I turned away. It was bad enough to lead me on and ignore me—now he wanted to get on my good side? The whiplash was just too much.

His hand, unexpected but surprisingly gentle, squeezed my shoulder softly. I whirled back around.

"What?!" I asked, my jealousy and anger bubbling to the surface.

Jax's dark eyes opened wide. He looked surprised, even worried. "Hey, relax," he said. "I just wanted to know if you're ready for the encore."

"Yeah, sure," I said with a scoff. The audience showed no sign of quieting down—whether or not I was ready, they certainly were. "Ready as I'll ever be."

Jax reached behind him and grabbed a brown rectangle thing from a shelf. "Good. Because you're coming with us." He thrust the metal object into my hands, and as I looked down, I realized it was a cowbell. "You said you wondered what it was like to be on stage? Now's your chance."

I glanced in horror at the cowbell, then back to Jax, my eyebrows raised with disbelief. "You've got to be kidding. What am I supposed to do with this?"

His face erupted in a broad grin. "You're supposed to bang the hell out of it."

I gave a wry grin. "Yeah, right. I've been to this show a few times now, remember? There's no cowbell in the encore."

"There will be tonight. Thanks to you." He looked dead serious.

The thought of getting to play as a rock star for a few minutes was thrilling, but suddenly, the magnitude of the crowd noise struck me, and I felt a wave of dizziness as I thought about making a fool of myself in front of an audience of thousands.

Shaking my head, I held the cowbell at arm's length, trying to hand it back to Jax. "No. Hell no. I can't play any instruments."

Jax crossed his arms in front of his chest. "Maybe so, but I'm not going back on stage for the encore— not unless you're coming with."

"I can't believe you're trying to pull a trick like this *during a show*," I said, gritting my teeth.

Scattered shouts pierced the applause: "ENCORE!" "BRING JAX BACK!"

He lifted his eyebrow at me and tilted his head toward the crowd noise. "What trick? Let's go. Your public is waiting."

As the crowd's calls for an encore got louder, Kev, Chewie and Sky emerged from the dressing room, now in their crazy silver-and-gold finale costumes. Sky spotted the cowbell in my hand instantly, and her face lit up. "Oh my god!" she said, her eyes wide. "You're coming with us?"

"Nope," I said, directing an exaggerated grimace toward the cowbell. "No sense of rhythm. Believe me, you don't want me out there."

Jax laughed. "It's a bell, just ring it," he said. "If you fuck it up, who cares? It's the encore, everyone's going nuts. No one will notice."

Was this some kind of a trick? "Don't toy with me like this," I said to Jax. "I'm not going to make an ass out of myself on stage in front of thousands of people just so you can have a laugh."

Jax wrinkled his eyebrows. "Toy with you?" He said, shaking his head. "I just wanted to show you a taste of what being a rocker is really like."

I narrowed my eyes at him. Was he telling the truth? Or was he playing another game? Turning to Chewie and Sky for help, I was dismayed to find Chewie already nodding vigorously with Jax.

"It's just like he says, Rye," Chewie said. "No one cares about the encore. Besides, what happens in Vegas . . . "

In the auditorium, the screams of the audience were becoming heated. Kev said, "I don't want to be a drag, but we have to get on stage, or people are going to start thinking the show's over."

I studied Jax's face again. His eyes looked completely different than they did when he left me in the hot tub last night. I saw no insincerity, no guile—if he was trying to play a game, I had no idea what it could be. I sighed. "Fine, I'll go. But remember: if they hate it, this was *your* idea."

He smiled. "Deal." Grabbing my hand, he walked on stage and pulled me along behind. I didn't know what to expect, but I knew that with my musical incompetence, it was sure to be a disaster. I'd try to stay as invisible as possible—at least then I couldn't screw it up for the band.

As we walked past the curtain, I could barely see at all.

After spending the entire show in the darkness of backstage, the spotlights were so blindingly bright that they hurt my eyes. *How do they do this every night?*

Then Sky's bassline started, funky and deep, and the audience, which I could barely see through the glare, roared in ecstasy. My eyes still adjusting, I tentatively rang the cowbell.

I heard nothing but the noisy crowd.

Just before the first verse started, Jax looked over at me and smirked. When he saw me tapping the cowbell lightly, he just shook his head with a half-smile, then started singing.

My eyes narrowed. If he didn't like my playing, it was his fault I was out here in the first place. I shook the cowbell again, harder. This time, I could hear the metallic clank over the crowd . . . but barely.

The encore number always got the crowd to sing along. As their voices swelled for the chorus, I realized they probably couldn't hear the bell, either. The crowd was so excited that they'd have cheered for—and sung along with—a mariachi band, as long as Jax had been out in front.

And if *that* was the case, it meant I could at least have fun without worrying about making a fool out of myself.

I started pounding on the bell every third beat out of four: one-two-THREE-four, one-two-THREE-four. I didn't keep time perfectly, but I didn't need to. I turned toward Jax as I pounded away, and he caught my eye. Instead of avoiding me, he came over and bumped the side of his hip against mine, mid-verse.

My hips started swinging with the beat, tapping against Jax's rhythmically, and I realized that like the rest of the band, I was jamming with the music. Sky, riffing on her bass, walked closer to me, then knelt down with the bass and played like she was worshipping the cowbell. I laughed.

Bolstered by her strong backing vocals, I started to sing out with the chorus. As the song built to its final climax, Jax went to the front of the stage, high-fiving crowd members. The next time he looked back to me, I was doing exactly what he'd told me: banging the hell out of the cowbell. When he smiled, I smiled back—and I had one more thing I wanted to do.

Following his lead, I walked downstage and reached out a hand to the first audience member I could. I felt first one palm shaking mine, then another, then another. It seemed like the mass of people went on forever, a dark tangle of bodies that went back as far as I could see. No one seemed to care that I wasn't part of the band. They just wanted to touch a person who was on the stage, to bridge the gap between the show and its stars.

Just for tonight, I was one of those stars. And it was all because of Jax.

The final guitar chord went off, and with it, a pyro blast exploded from both sides of the stage. I felt radiating warmth from the firework against my face for a fraction of a second, and then the audience burst into its biggest round of applause of the night.

"Thank you, Las Vegas, and good night!" Jax shouted into the microphone.

The lights went down—and I realized that for the first time all night, I didn't want the show to end.

Under the dim lights, I turned to see Sky, Chewie and Kev walking off the stage, probably heading to the green room. As the curtain fell in front of the stage separating us from the audience, I started to follow them toward the wings. I felt exhilarated, but a voice in the back of my head wouldn't be quiet. Why had Jax given me the chance to play the cowbell? He was being hot and cold in a way I hadn't seen before, and I couldn't put my finger on what was going on.

"Stop. Trust me. Don't step away." The low, sensuous voice was unmistakably Jax's, his mouth so close that I could feel his breath. A familiar heated feeling of arousal was starting to build in between my legs.

My back stiffened at the unexpected brush of his lips against my ear, and I stopped in my tracks. "What's going on?" I asked, trying to make my voice loud enough for him to hear me. The noise of the audience leaving the auditorium was just on the other side of the curtain.

"Stand still," he commanded, and I felt his body press up against me from behind. Then I felt a wisp of soft cloth on my face, and my vision went black. "In a minute, when I tell you to, you're going to hold my hand and follow me."

A blindfold? "Promise me this isn't turning into a Hitchcock movie," I said, trying to keep both my nervousness and my arousal out of my voice.

"It's a surprise," he said, each word sending an involuntary thrill through my spine. "A good one. Just trust me. I want to show you some more of the rock star life."

I wanted desperately to look into his eyes, to see whether he was telling the truth or just playing another game. But with the blindfold over my eyes, all I had was his voice. *Trust me*, he said.

In the blackness, I reached my hand out and felt Jax's strong fingers clasp around it.

Chapter Fifteen

SURPRISE

My heart beat fast. Blood rushed through my veins. My feet were moving as if they had a mind of their own. Sounds of cards shuffling, chips clanging, women cheering, and men groaning reverberated in my ears. There was the faint smell of cigars and martinis in the air. A small splash hit my arm. A drink? A new sound started. It was a bell ringing as if a woodpecker was attacking it, followed by clanking metal and then an elderly woman screaming like her hair was on fire. Applause broke out.

I briefly wondered what the sight must've looked like—me in a blindfold being tugged along by the hottest rocker in the world across what I imagined was a casino floor. It'd be a disaster if the image got back to Hans-Peterson, but it was hard to take that possibility seriously when I was so excited. Besides, I knew how the saying went—what happened in Vegas, stayed in Vegas.

I gripped Jax's hand tighter as he pulled me forward, carefully guiding my blind self past moving bodies and up steps. I didn't know what he had planned to show me, but I couldn't wait.

A ding, then our feet stopped. He stood beside me, hugging me by the waist close to him. I couldn't be sure but it felt like there were people standing around us. Before I could process the situation, another ding, and we were on the move again.

Moments later, I heard the soft click of a door closing behind me, then felt the velvety cloth slip away from my eyes . . .

. . . And realized that even with the blindfold off, I couldn't see a thing. Wherever we were, it was pitch black.

"Jax, what is this?"

"That's the surprise," he responded. "Take a step forward."

Careful to avoid bumping into anything in the darkness, I tentatively put my right foot in front of me.

"WELCOME, JAX TRENTON!" a cold, steely voice suddenly boomed from overhead.

Startled, I jumped. "Fuck!" I gasped.

The voice continued as the lights went up: "WE HOPE YOU ENJOY YOUR SKY VILLA STAY."

I began to relax when I realized it was just an automatic voice greeting that they had at high end hotel rooms. We must've been in one of the suites.

"Oh my god, Jax, you could've at least warned me," I said, feeling suddenly embarrassed.

He smiled and guided me a few steps forward with his hand at my back.

A light turned on, and when my eyes adjusted a few seconds later, I saw that we were in a hallway. At the end of it was a room with a sleek leather couch and a bar. I'd read about giant, sprawling Vegas hotel rooms, but I'd never gotten to see one in person.

"The real perks of being a rock star come after the show is over," Jax said, gesturing toward the end of the hall.

I studied his face. His delighted expression contrasted sharply with the last image I had of him in the hot tub last night. What happened to the stormy, walled-off rock star? A discomforting thought nagged at the back of my mind when I reflected on the events of last night until now. Had I been wrong about Jax? Maybe *I* was the one with the problem. Not him. It was possible that I'd been acting crazy and paranoid, seeing bad things in Jax that weren't actually there.

My brows furrowed slightly. "You're being really nice tonight," I said, a note of skepticism creeping into my voice.

He raised a brow. "Am I? Let's just say I've got a party planned later tonight, so I'm in a good mood. You're invited of course." He smiled, and when I gave him a puzzled look in response, he exhaled as if he was weary to spell out something totally obvious. "You mentioned before that you wanted to see what being a rock star is like, so I figured I'd show you."

A finger on my chin, I thought back to when we shared a smoke together on the sundeck. "Actually, I said that I have to live a normal, professional life most of the time, so I can't live like a rock star."

"But tonight you can." His eyes seemed to twinkle. "Go on," he continued, "check it out. I want to see your reaction, the robot voice was just the beginning."

With a smile to show my appreciation, I set my concerns aside, and let curiosity and excitement take over. I got to the end of the hall and found myself in a huge sunken living room. Each direction I looked made my eyes open wider, as I realized how big the suite really was. At one end of the room was a bar stocked with expensive, imported bottles, while on the other end, a projection TV idly played an image of a live aquarium on the wall. In between there was a huge kitchen, hallways leading off to what looked like a bathroom and two bedrooms, and the rest of the living room was covered in floor-to-ceiling curtained windows. Just the living room was bigger than my entire apartment in New York.

My jaw dropped in wonder. "This is one hell of a hotel room, Jax."

He looked at me curiously. "You're a success at one of the biggest accounting firms in New York," he said. "I pictured you having a loft a lot like this, all steel and black."

"Is that what you think of me?" I said with a laugh. "I live in a tiny place I can barely afford. For a steel loft, I'd need to either make partner or rob a bank."

"Well, if you need to study bank robbery, I've got that covered, too." He pointed to the living room's coffee table.

On it was a stack of DVDs, all action classics: *Die Hard*, *Rambo: First Blood*, *Reservoir Dogs* . . . and right on top, in a place where I'd be sure to see it, *Kill Bill*.

I smiled at Jax. "My favorite. You remembered."

"I did."

I thought about how he'd been sweet earlier by asking me to play cowbell during the show's encore even when I didn't want to at first. I ended up having a blast with the entire band. "Want to watch it with the band?" I asked.

"Yeah," he said. He looked down at the floor momentarily. "We can. Whenever you want. But don't you want a tour of the room, first? You've barely looked around."

He was right—I did barely look around. As excited as I was about the suite, it also made me worried. I didn't want to tell him the reason—every time I saw another room, I felt a little more sick at how much the room must be putting The Hitchcocks over budget. I'd worked hard to keep the band's budget tight, and I knew every line item. There wasn't one for a fantasy suite party. I hoped Palmer didn't get wind of it. *Goodbye, bonus. Hello, help wanted ads.*

"What's behind the windows?" I asked, trying to shake the feeling of impending doom. I knew it was probably far too late to get a refund, and since we were already here, I might as well enjoy what the suite had to offer. I hoped that whatever party Jax had planned, it was worth it.

Jax picked up a small, black remote control. "A view," he said. "But let's wait until we're on our way upstairs—the view's better from up there."

"Upstairs?"

Jax turned his head and gestured with his chin, and my eyes followed to see.

Oh my god.

"A glass elevator?" I said, startled. "But Jax, that's not where we came in." I walked closer to the elevator. It seemed impossible, but there it was, extending up to the floor above—an elevator *inside* the hotel room. It would have made me giddy, if I hadn't already been so worried about the band's budget.

"I know," he replied. "Maybe you should get in."

I pressed a button, and the elevator doors opened. The two of us stepped into the glass-walled enclosure, and I saw two buttons marked "1" and "2." Biting my lip, I pressed the "2," and watched as the doors closed around us.

Jax, waiting at the back of the elevator, had a remote in his hand. "Want to press the button?" he asked. I was confused, but pressed it anyway.

As soon as I did, the window curtains began to part, revealing a view of The Strip that made it clear we were high above most of the other hotels in town. I gasped. "Jax, it's . . ."

"Wait for it," he said, his voice barely containing his excitement.

As the curtains pulled back further, I saw it: a giant T-shaped swimming pool, just off the living room area, that projected out beyond the edge of the hotel and over the street outside.

My eyes opened wide, and I felt my hand tightening its grip against the elevator railing as the doors slid open to the second level.

"Holy *fuck*," I said, my voice barely above a whisper. A two-story suite with a private pool? I didn't even want to estimate the cost. It made me almost sick to think about, and Jax's eager face made me feel incredibly guilty. He'd wanted to show me the rock star lifestyle, but all I could think about was cold hard cash.

He stepped off the elevator, and I followed behind, feeling anxiety churn my stomach. "You can let the running tally go," he said. "I can hear the cash register going off in your head every time you see a new room."

I grimaced. Had I been making myself that obvious? "You'd just better not tell me that all the money I cut from the budget is being spent here."

"What, on this suite? No," he said, walking over toward one of the walls. "Come over here, check these pictures out."

I picked up my pace to catch up with him, but not before catching a glimpse of another bedroom and a full dance floor. This place was more insane than my friend Kristen's place—and her husband was a billionaire.

Then, looking at the wall, I saw the pictures. Photographs of politicians, musicians, and actors, from Kanye to Clinton, speckled the wall. All of them were posing in the hotel room where we were standing—even Hugh Hefner was in on the action, standing in front of the incredible pool.

My eyes traced over the A-list icons in the photos. "You're telling me this room, with all these celebrity guests, isn't going to put us over budget?"

"The room's free for main stage performers," Jax explained. "Welcome to the big leagues, they said. I wanted to show it to you. I thought you might like it."

Free. I exhaled in relief—that meant I could start enjoying the amenities, instead of trying to figure out what they'd cost.

"You thought right," I reassured Jax, happy that it was the truth. ". . . Hey, I've got an idea. Let's get a photo of the Hitchcocks later. We can give it to the hotel so they can add it to their collection."

"Yeah, imagine a photo with Sky right about *there*," he said, pointing to an empty spot on the wall next to Miley Cyrus' portrait, "Just so she could flip off Miley."

I giggled. "Yeah, and right here, Chewie would—"

BZZZ! The doorbell to the room cut me off before I could finish my sentence.

"We'd better get that," Jax said, walking toward the elevator.

"Is it the rest of the band?" I asked as we got back in. "Or the party guests?"

A hint of a smile played on his face. "Let's go downstairs and find out."

When he opened the door, I expected to see Chewie, Sky, and Kev bounding in. Instead, a veritable army of room service waiters pushed a procession of carts through the entrance hallway and into the living area. There were enough covered dishes on their trays to cater a small banquet.

"Where shall we serve the food?" One of the waiters asked, his voice soft and melodious, with an understated French accent.

"That won't be necessary," Jax said, hastily, then dug into his pocket and stuck a green wad of bills into the waiter's hand. "I can serve it myself."

"Yes, *monsieur*," the waiter said, giving a small, deferential bow before leaving along with the rest of the room service staff.

Once the last white uniform was gone from the suite, Jax spread his arms out toward the room service carts. "Pick anything you like," he said.

I took a quick look under a couple of plates: one had a sushi roll, beautifully plated. The next was covered in a thick slab of chocolate cake. It didn't look like party food—but it did look delicious, especially since I'd barely eaten all day because I'd been worried about Jax avoiding me. Add in the intense cowbell-playing, and I was practically dying for a bite.

"There's enough to feed an army here," I said, puzzled, as I set the covers back down. "Why all the food? Are the roadies coming to the party, too?"

"Well, I figured we didn't have to eat like we were on the road," Jax called back to me as he walked to the bar. "You've been eating like a bird on the tour bus," he continued, changing the subject. "Maybe now you can find something you'll enjoy."

I blushed, embarrassed. "I eat," I said quickly. "It's just, when I'm stressed and working, sometimes I forget. And sometimes I'm not hungry. But it's sweet of you to notice."

"Mmhmm. But tonight, you're not working. So relax." He started looking over the bar. This time, I couldn't tell what he was making. Judging by the strangely shaped bottles he was picking—and the blender he got out from beneath the bar—I could tell it wasn't his usual Godfather. He looked back up from the bottles to where I was standing. "Go ahead, pick something good."

I lifted the lids one by one. The first covered dish held a thick burger, while the one next to it had scallops. There was a lot of food, but none of it was as exciting as the room itself. When I lifted the tenth cover and found a fruit plate, I shrugged. "Close enough," I said, bringing the melon and grapes back to the bar and taking a seat on a stool.

Jax was busy adding ingredients to the blender. "What's that?" I asked as I popped a grape into my mouth, watching the liquids blend together.

He poured syrupy, light amber liquid from the blender into two champagne flutes. "It's your drink," he said, then popped a cork on a bottle of sparkling wine and topped each glass with its bubbly contents. "I call it . . . The Riley."

He invented a cocktail for me? "Well, it's a good name. What's in it?"

"Plum puree, champagne . . . and black pepper vodka," he said. "Like I said, it's *your* drink."

I eyed the amber liquid curiously. The drink, the private tour, none of it made sense. Why was he acting so nice? And how could he be so sure I'd like the drink he'd made? With the pepper and dry champagne, it looked nothing like the usual, cloyingly sweet cocktails most guys assumed girls preferred.

It was also something I might have ordered if I'd seen it on a menu—and he'd made it after knowing me for only a little while. But how had he guessed my favorite fruit?

"I get the pepper," I replied, "And the champagne, for the hot tub. But what about the plum?"

"Did you forget that night I gave you the back massage? You were eating a plum then."

I felt my cheeks getting hot. "Oh, right. I'd almost forgotten."

His eyes crinkled as he handed the drink across the bar and lifted his own glass. "To Vegas," he said, his scarred eyebrow arched as if the toast were a question.

"To Vegas," I said, lifting my glass and clinking it to his.

Unsure what to expect from the flavor combination, I sipped the drink tentatively. As soon as it hit my tastebuds, I realized Jax was an even better bartender than I'd given him credit for. The sparkling bubbles hit first, followed by a peppery, fruity burst of flavor that felt edgy and dark, but still refreshing.

It was incredible—a drink I'd have expected to pay way too much for at a bar. I sipped smoothly. "Mmhmm," I said, underplaying how much I liked it. "It's interesting."

Setting the drink down, I reached for the plate of fruit. Jax grabbed the plate and took it away.

"Hey, I wasn't finished!" I cried.

He looked at me skeptically. "You were going to eat melon and grapes with that drink?"

"Is that a crime?"

Walking to the food carts with the half-eaten fruit plate, he called back to me. "Not exactly. But I think you could do better. Let me try."

"What do you mean, do better?"

He lifted covers from dishes, one at a time, but shook his head or gave a half-frown to each one. "No, not quite . . ." he muttered at the carts, then raised his head and looked at me. "Don't you think it's better to find food that goes together with your drink?"

Shaking my head, I smiled at him. "I'm not even sure what that's supposed to mean," I said. "I've had wine pairings before, but it's not magical. It's just the food and the drink. They taste how they taste."

Jax's eye lingered a while on one of the dishes, and he set it off to one side of a cart. "Maybe you just haven't had the right pairing," he said, continuing his search through the feast. "When it's right, what you're eating and what you're drinking don't just taste how they taste—they taste better. It's like melody and harmony."

After looking at the last cart, he stacked three of the covered dishes in his arms and brought them to the bar, setting them side by side.

"What did you bring?" I asked.

Jax walked back to the cart and came back with a napkin and fork.

"Only good things," he said, setting the fork next to me from behind.

I reached for one of the dishes and started to lift the cover, but Jax's hand stretched over mine and pressed it back down. "No," he said, then softened his voice. "Relax. You're going to let me serve you—and no peeking at the dishes, unless you want the blindfold back on. Understand?"

"Okay . . ." I said, unsure what to think, especially after he'd mentioned the blindfold again. A hint of nervous anticipation crept into my voice as I took my hand off the dish. He tied a napkin around my neck, and the sudden brush of his fingers against my skin made my heart race.

A half-smile played on Jax's face. "Drink," he insisted, "and then try this first."

He moved the leftmost dish to my place and uncovered it. Three pieces of creamy looking cheese and a few almonds stood on the plate.

After a sip of the drink he'd made for me, I took a small piece of cheese and an almond and put them in my mouth together. The cheese had a mild, sweet flavor, with a hint of something that almost tasted like maple, while the almonds gave it a smoky crunch.

"Mm," I said, my mouth still half-full. "That's good. Really tasty."

He eyed me as I finished the bite of cheese, nodding as I swallowed. "But not as good as this." He replaced the cheese plate with another dish.

Beneath the cover, I saw something I couldn't figure out. Four wrinkly, thick shell things surrounded some kind of meat. My nose wrinkled slightly, and I sipped at my drink to hide my reaction. "Jax, is this brains, or something?"

He gave me a devilish look. "No. And don't tell me you're not brave enough to try it."

I stabbed my fork into one of the wrinkled shells. "Watch me," I said with a laugh, and took a bite.

The bite exploded into my mouth, intensely flavored. The shells themselves were toothsome and rich, with a hint of garlic, while the meat filling them was smooth and almost buttery. "Wow," I said, grabbing another bite. "This one's even better."

"I'm just glad I could get you eating. It's morel mushrooms stuffed with foie gras."

"It's incredible," I said as I picked up another forkful. "By the way, how do you know all of this about food?"

He smiled and shrugged. "Comes with being a rock star."

I swallowed my delicious bite, a little confused by his answer but too focused on the food to care. "Whatever you have under that last cover, save it for Chewie, Sky or Kev. It couldn't possibly be better than this."

"You have to at least try it. I saved the best for last."

"Fine, then," I agreed. "One bite."

The dish in the center was a little larger than the others, and when he took the cover off, I smelled something, an earthy scent that reminded me somehow of Jax. I saw a sliced duck breast spread into a fan shape, its crackling skin crusted with pepper. A richly-colored sauce—red wine of some sort, I assumed—was drizzled over the top.

"Oh *wow*," I breathed. "That's almost too beautiful to eat."

"You'll have to tell me if it tastes as good as it looks," he said. "But drink first."

I set my fork down and nursed the fruity, peppery drink, closing my eyes to enjoy the bubbles on my tongue. When I finished a few sips, I realized that Jax had picked up my fork and was cutting a piece of the duck breast.

"Did you want some?" I asked.

"This is for you," he said, lifting the fork to my mouth. "Open."

I opened my mouth slightly, and felt the fork gently push past my lips. I bit down, and the fork slid back away, leaving the crisp duck skin and juicy meat on my tongue. The earthy smell was stronger, now, and I tasted it in the dish, something unfathomably deep and complex, dark and pungent. The sauce, sweet and savory in equal parts, kept the earthy taste from dominating.

"Duck with peppercorns, port reduction, and black truffles," Jax said, before I even had to ask.

The truffles must have smelled like him, I realized.

The pepperiness of the duck was echoed in my drink, and I realized I wanted another sip. When I took one, I saw for the first time what Jax meant. The drink and the food both tasted better together than they would have on their own. They almost sparked off each other, bringing new flavor combinations into my mouth that shifted and changed, but never clashed.

I took another bite of the duck breast, and let out a soft moan. "Mmmmm. . ."

Jax's eyebrow cocked higher. "Sounds like you want more than dessert."

I blushed and took the napkin away from my neck. I didn't have time for an innuendo war with Jax—I knew where those led, and the last thing I wanted was for the band to see the two of us lip-locked. And come to think of it why wasn't Jax concerned they'd see him serving me?

"Uh, so when's everyone getting here, anyway? The food's getting cold."

Jax finished making his own Riley and sipped it for the first time. He gave a half-smile, as if to say *not bad*. "The rest of the band's probably gambling or hanging out in their own free suites. They weren't invited anyway."

"Huh? Then who'd you invite?" The room suddenly felt a whole lot warmer, and I took a large swig of plum and champagne.

One of his eyebrows flicked upward, and a smile spread over his face.

"Just you, Riley."

Chapter Sixteen

DESSERT

My hand flew to my mouth, and I almost spat the drink all over the bar.

Taking a hard swallow, I set the glass down and narrowed my eyes at Jax. "You must think I'm really naive, if you thought I'd fall for this."

"Fall for what?" He had the nerve to laugh.

"The cowbell. The blindfold. The food, the drink . . ." I tallied them up on my fingers, my voice rising. "The whole thing was a setup. You didn't want to show me the rock star lifestyle, you just wanted to get in my pants!"

Jax's smile faded, and his eyes lost some of their luster. "Hold on," he said, reaching out to touch my arm. "I didn't realize you were being serious. Yes, I planned tonight."

I brushed his hand away and glared at him coldly. "At least you admit it."

"And yes," he added, giving my body a head-to-toe stare that made me feel suddenly naked, "I'd be happy to spend tonight fucking you. But this isn't a game like you're thinking. It's not a conquest."

I crossed my arms over my chest. "It sure looks a lot like one from here."

His mouth twisted, and he squeezed both my shoulders. "Dammit, Riley," he said. "I'm doing this because I *like* you. Because I care about you."

I rolled my eyes, but my heart started beating faster. "Yeah? Then why were you ignoring me all day?"

He looked taken aback. "Ignoring you? Is that really what this is about?"

"In the hot tub, you looked at me with disgust and left me without saying a word after we . . . after what we did."

"What? No . . . no." His expression looked pained. "Riley, I'd never look at you with disgust. You're gorgeous."

"Then what was it?"

"Something changed," he said, momentarily averting his gaze. "I don't know. When I was looking at you, I felt . . ." His eyes softened, and he shifted, seeming uncomfortable with what he wanted to express. After a pause he said, "I felt I had to do this." He gestured to the room around us. "It took some effort to get all this done, Riley. I had to arrange it quickly, and I couldn't exactly do it with you in the room."

I stared at him for a moment before the realization hit me like a ton of bricks. Jax had put a lot of energy into planning tonight—he'd been doing exactly the opposite of ignoring me, and I hadn't been able to see it because I'd been so worried about the way he'd treated me before the show.

Which meant I'd been the jerk, not him.

I took another look at the lavish room and the food before me. Suddenly, it didn't seem like a game. It seemed like he'd tried to make a fantasy come to life. Given different circumstances, an act like this would have made me throw my panties onto the nearest lampshade but things between Jax and me were complicated.

"Jax, I—this is . . . incredible. Really, it is. The room, all of it, it's amazing," I said softly. "But it doesn't change things between us. We're still not having sex."

He brought a hand to my hair and brushed a strand away from my face. The soft touch of his fingers sent a warm shiver through me. "It changes one thing," he said. "I haven't forgotten what you said when you agreed to sleep in my bed—that we wouldn't have sex there. Well . . . we're not there, now."

It was hard to even think with his hand in my hair and his beautiful face so close. I knew I should've moved away, but I didn't. "There's something you have to understand, Jax," I protested. "Masturbation is one thing. That's just us getting out our sexual frustrations. But sex, real sex, is something else entirely. Sex changes things."

His dark eyes burned into mine, sending a flutter into my stomach. "So you're going to miss out on the best fuck of either of our lives, just because you're afraid of change."

The offer was tempting—especially coming from Jax's full, luscious lips. But after the talks we'd had, the connection I'd felt with Jax in his room, becoming fuck buddies would almost seem like a step backwards.

"I'm not opposed to casual sex," I said, averting my eyes from his gaze. "But things aren't casual between us. Not any more."

He slid a finger underneath my chin and gently moved it upward, forcing me to look at his face again. "Listen to me carefully, Riley," he said. "Casual sex is what I have with groupies. It's something I haven't done in a while."

"But what ab—"

"Let me finish." His voice was rough. "Whether you say yes or no tonight, there won't be any groupies—not as long as you're around. Since the moment I saw you, I've wanted you. No one else."

I stared at him, wide-eyed and confused. Could he mean it? I felt a tremble of arousal start in my body, something I couldn't control or conceal. "You mean, since the tour started, you haven't . . . "

"No," he said, his voice low and dark-tinged. "Not once."

For a manwhore like Jax to ignore the groupies at the crazy shows we'd been to . . . it was one hell of a compliment, if it was true. My mouth felt dry, and it was hard to even speak. Desire, more intense than I'd ever felt, pulsed through my veins.

"I don't know what to say," I whispered, afraid to give voice to the burning, raging need I felt in my core.

"Then don't say anything," he said hoarsely. "Give me that after-show kiss you owe me."

My eyes closed and my lips turned upward waiting for his kiss. I felt his mouth just inches from mine . . .

And then felt his lips move to my neck, hovering a fraction of an inch above my skin. His hot breath sent flutters of aching sensation through me, and I yearned for the feel of his lips on my body. I heard a soft sigh, heavy with desire, and only realized a moment later that the sound had come from my own mouth.

I felt Jax's hand against my bare back, beneath my shirt, and gasped as I felt him unhook my bra. He took his mouth away from my neck and brought his hands to my collar, unbuttoning the front of my shirt. I stopped his hand with mine. "Wait," I said, breathless. "What happened to the kiss?"

"You didn't say *where* I could kiss you," he said, trailing his index finger along my side. "I'm still trying to make up my mind." He gently took my hand away, undid the buttons, and slid the shirt off my torso. Already unhooked, the bra fell from my shoulders onto the floor.

I brought my hands to my breasts to cover myself by instinct, but Jax shook his head and firmly drew them away, leaving me exposed. Bending down until his face was inches from my chest, he turned his eyes upward to look at me.

My nipples stood erect, almost painful with arousal as Jax's open mouth moved toward one. His open mouth lingered just above my nipple, almost touching—but not quite. I sucked in air as the aching need between my legs reached a fever pitch.

"Mmm. Tempting," he said. "But maybe . . ."

I felt the soft caress of his fingers on my back, and then there was a sound. *My zipper!* Before I could say anything, I felt a firm tug, and my skirt fell to my ankles, along with my underwear.

I realized suddenly that I was totally naked in front of him—even though he still had all his clothes on. He dropped to his knees, his mouth inches from my thighs, and my eyes grew wide. He looked up and down my body with a ravenous hunger that frightened me even as it turned me on.

"What are you—"

He brought his mouth to my inner thigh, then slowly moved it upward. "I think I've made my decision," he said, his hands caressing my thighs as he looked up at me.

I realized what he meant instantly, and my hand slid down in front of me, embarrassed. "No, Jax, you can't," I said, hurriedly. "I haven't showered all day."

His scarred eyebrow raised, and a half-smirk grew on his face. Closing his eyes, he brought his face between my thighs and inhaled deeply. "Good. Better. I like you this way."

I felt a flush spreading through my body and then I felt his lips, pressing against the softness between my thighs. A pang of arousal radiated through my skin as his tongue stroked against me, and I felt myself shudder with lust.

Then he took his mouth away and stood up, licking his lips. "I think I made the right decision about where to kiss you," he purred. Wild with desire, I moaned in a wordless reply.

"Lay down on the bed, Riley," he said, but I felt frozen to the floor, shivering at the absence of his lips.

Did he think that's all it would take? I looked at the round bed, lit softly in the bedroom a few yards away. "We're not going to—"

He shook his head. Holding my upper arms, he took a step forward, making me take one backwards, toward the bed. His voice more forceful, he commanded, "Lay down on the bed. You got to eat what you wanted. Now it's my turn."

The urgency in his voice made the wetness between my thighs even more intense, but I still felt the faint tug of embarrassment holding me back. "I've never had a guy start out with this before," I whispered nervously to him as he walked me back toward the immense round bed.

"Even better. Don't deny that you want it. I can *feel* it." He stopped stepping forward for a moment and brought a hand down to the cleft between my thighs, then drew his finger through, making me gasp.

When he pulled it away, it was slick and glistening. "You can't deny it. Not when you're dripping wet for me."

The bed was only a few feet behind us, now, and I looked up into Jax's eyes, crazy with need. "I do want it," I breathed. "I want your mouth."

"Good," he said, beads of sweat forming on his sun-kissed forehead. "Now, lay down."

I lowered myself onto the bed and closed my eyes. Jax's hands pushed my thighs apart with a surprising gentleness, and I felt his tongue press against my slit slowly, almost tenderly.

"Jax," I moaned, "that's incredible." His mouth trailed in a line that sent shocks of pure pleasure all the way to my fingers and toes.

"You're perfect, Riley," he murmured. "So beautiful and pink . . . and so wet for my touch."

I whimpered, and his mouth probed more hungrily, his tongue smooth, circling ever-tighter, focused at the center of my desire.

My hands clutched at the plush red bedspread beneath us, and Jax slid his tongue to the side, licking and nuzzling until I felt like I would melt. Tiny, teasing motions drew out my sensation, sending urgent flutters rippling to my fingers and toes.

"Your mouth . . . God, Jax, what are you *doing*?" I moaned, my entire body trembling at the tortuous brush of his lips.

"My voice is my instrument." He spoke against my skin, each murmured syllable a deep vibration that made my back arch with pleasure. "Knowing how to use my mouth is my job."

My clit throbbed as his tongue swirled against it, each movement more intricate than the last. Shaking, I felt my body clench, craving release.

"Please, Jax," I gasped, straining toward his mouth, "I need more, please, give me more . . ."

The velvety heat of his tongue pierced into me, and my hands clutched his dark hair as I cried out. Crazed with desire, my hands fisted in his hair, pulling it as he went deeper, harder.

As I cried out, he drew his tongue back to my clit, pushing against it with a raw, primitive rhythm. Each new sensation brought me closer to the carnal chaos I craved.

His lips held my clit, moving quickly. The trembling, head to toe, was unbearable now, Jax's tongue pushing me over the edge, my face contorting with wild, animal need . . .

Yes. Now. Jax, please, now, yes, yes yes YES . . .

Climax—intense, explosive, primal—seized my quaking body and didn't let go.

Thrashing against the bed, unable to control the spasms coursing through every nerve, I clung to his hair and screamed Jax's name.

Chapter Seventeen

DEEP

His tongue lapped slowly against me as the shaking subsided. When I finally let go of his hair, he crawled into the bed next to me and laid down. I turned to face him and saw that he looked utterly contented.

"Jesus, Jax." I turned to him, still feeling aftershocks pulsating through my body. "That was the best head I've ever gotten."

His mouth spread into a blissful smile. "Let me try again. I'll see if I can do better."

I laughed. "Is this part of the rock 'n' roll lifestyle, too?"

"For you? You'd better believe it," he said, his eyes teasing wickedly.

I'd never seen him look so at ease. My gaze slid over his long, lean torso, and a wave of sudden warmth bolted through my body, centered where Jax's tongue had been. Even clothed, he was like a statue—lean, muscled, all sinew and strength. Then, as my eyes crept lower, I noticed his erection, long, thick and so hard it threatened to burst from his pants. "And what's that a part of?" I asked as I looked, my eyebrow playfully raised.

Jax smirked. "That's part of having an irresistible redhead in my bed."

The heat between my legs intensified, but I realized I hadn't prepared for a night like this—in any way at all. "You're making me wish I had my purse," I said ruefully.

"But you do have your purse." He propped himself up on an elbow. "I had it brought up from the bus during the concert. Check your bedside table."

He brought my purse? "You thought of everything," I said, surprised.

His burning eyes searched over me. "All I think about is you." His tone was so low and intimate that I blushed and turned away to look in the table drawers.

My bag was in the top one, and I rooted through it with nimble fingers, searching for something I'd never expected to use during the tour.

"There we go," I said triumphantly, pinching the foil square between my fingers.

Did he see what I grabbed? I looked back toward Jax, but he was facing away, taking off his shirt. His muscles looked incredible under the golden glow of the fantasy suite bedroom. It was like I'd found a Greek god, lounging in the improbably oversized round bed. Then again, maybe he looked even better. The Greek gods never knew what tight denim could do for a guy's perfectly tight ass.

I couldn't help it—I licked my lips.

He looked over toward me, and his eyebrow lifted with recognition as he saw the condom wrapper. "Give that to me." He reached out for the packet, but I held it out of reach.

"Not a chance," I said, opening the wrapper as I nodded toward his dark-washed jeans. "Just take those off."

"I thought you didn't want to fuck," he teased, his eyes gleaming as he peeled the tight denim off his body.

"You changed my mind," I said, trailing a finger along his taut abs. Tracing slowly with my fingertip, I drew a line downward, past the perfect triangle of his pelvis, and ending only when I reached the tip of his cock.

He sucked in his breath, and his thick cock throbbed in front of me. I smiled—I'd learned a few tricks about how to make a guy remember his first time with me, and if Jax and I were going to do this, I wanted it to be totally unforgettable. Putting the condom between my thumb and forefinger, I rolled it slowly over him, feeling myself get wetter by the moment. Jax moved as if he thought he'd climb on top of me, but I stopped him.

"No," I said, looking down at him as my fingers stroked idly along his cock. "It's your turn to lay back and let me work my instrument."

He looked for a moment like he would object, but then shook his head with a short, staccato laugh. "Fuck. How can I say no to that?"

I'd wanted to do this for so long—I ached to feel him inside me, and I couldn't hold back any more. As he lay down on his back, I straddled him and lowered myself gently, feeling myself stretch to fit him inside me.

He was big—massively thick, enough that it almost hurt as I buried him deeper into me. I cried out as his length slid further, but I couldn't stop. I didn't want to.

I just wanted more.

I rocked against him, feeling myself pulsing around his thick erection, every inch sending shocks of sensation all the way to my fingertips. My hips moved faster, more urgently, and I felt Jax's palms clenching around them. "Slow," he gasped, his strong hands holding my body still even as I tried to keep up the same frantic pace. "God, Riley, please go slow."

"Too intense for you?" I said, my voice breathless as I pressed myself against him harder, taking him deeper into me than before.

"No, I just want to feel you—all of you." His body rose, impaling me on his cock until I almost screamed.

"God, yes," I cried, quickening my rhythm. "Just like that, Jax."

"I want you to feel me, Riley," he said, forcing my hips down until shudders of ecstasy ran through me. "Every inch, to the hilt. I want you filled with me, more than you've ever been filled in your life."

Jax's cock had felt intense when I'd ridden him fast, but his new, slower rhythm sent fiery, raw need flaming into every part of me. His raw, languid strokes made me inhale sharply with every thrust, and I writhed over him, my hands gripping against his thighs as my spine arched backwards. "Oh my god, Jax, it's almost too much."

"But only *almost*," he said with another thrust that caught me by surprise. I screamed, and immediately covered my mouth so no one else in the hotel would hear me.

Jax smiled and sat up in a fluid motion. Suddenly we were sitting, face to face, with his cock so deep inside me that all I could do was writhe and moan. "Don't cover that gorgeous mouth, Riley," he said, taking my hands away. "I want to hear you. Let it out."

Wrapping my legs around his torso, I looked into his eyes. The heat of his body was consuming me from inside, but his face was surprisingly tender. "Oh god," I said. "Jax, you're so deep in me, it almost hurts."

He stroked my cheek in time with slow thrusts. "Relax. Keep your eyes open, Riley."

Struggling against myself, I felt another climax fighting to the surface. I gripped the skin of Jax's back, my nails digging into flesh. His face was beaded with sweat, and I could feel his breath, hot and hoarse, with every thrust.

As he rammed harder and harder, I stopped caring if anyone heard me. Screaming out at the top of my lungs with each thrust, I felt my body clenching, reaching, blending with his body until I didn't know whether the ragged breaths I heard were mine or his.

"God, Riley, yes, that's it," Jax rasped. "Just like that, so tight around me . . . I think I'm going to . . ."

"Yes!" I grabbed his hair as I felt his body start to spasm, and my orgasm pushed upwards into me, dragging us into feral, primitive sensation, our cries mingling and echoing from the suite walls as he pumped, again and again, into my hungry wetness.

Closing my eyes, I crumpled onto Jax's sweat dampened chest, my breath shaking.

Holy fuck. Flickers of pleasure lingered as I pressed my cheek against his skin, sending cresting waves through my body.

As I listened to his heartbeat, erratic and fast, a flash of post-orgasmic sobriety suddenly made me self-conscious. *What did we just do?*

I'd given Jax what he wanted but what if that was a mistake? If I was just a conquest, he'd won. I was conquered. *Is this where he tells me it was all just a game?*

He spoke softly, his baritone resonating through my body. "I've been wanting to feel that since the first night I saw you at my show."

I searched his dark eyes. When I saw in them the same look I'd seen in the hot tub last night, I realized that I'd been wrong all this time. It hadn't been disgust or remorse that I'd seen; it had been a look of sober realization that in the struggle to fight your feelings for someone, you could end up falling harder than you ever could've expected. I knew how he felt because his eyes and my eyes were meeting, knowing, reflecting—it was like we could see into each other for the first time.

I shivered, still trying to catch my breath, and felt Jax's fingers running through my sweat-damp hair. If I'd known it would be like this after, I couldn't help thinking we'd have done this sooner. Or if I'd known it would be that good *during* . . .

We stared at each other for a long moment, my fingertip tracing the outlines of his muscles as he looked down at me. *I hope this isn't where it gets awkward.* "So, what now?" I asked tentatively.

"Now this." Smiling softly at me, he ran a hand down my cheek and neck. I closed my eyes, and felt his lips over mine again, sweeter and gentler than I'd ever felt them before.

I didn't know exactly what he meant by it, but I could tell something had changed between us. There was a spark I'd never felt before, a pull between us that went deeper than even a few hours ago.

Sex changes things, I'd told Jax. This time, at least so far, it looked like they'd changed for the better.

I bowed my head to kiss his chest, just above his heart. "Thank you for tonight," I said, a blissful smile spreading across my face as I realized just how perfect the surprise "party" had been after all.

"The night's not over, yet," he said, wiping his forehead with a hand. "But I think we should both go cool down—how about it?" He nodded toward the cantilevered pool.

I frowned, wishing I'd been better prepared. "I'd go in, but I didn't bring a swimsuit."

He moved to the side of the bed and stood up, then looked down at me with his scarred eyebrow arched. "Who said anything about swimsuits?" he asked, giving me a frank, appraising stare. "I want you just the way you are."

The way he said it made my heart skip a beat, but the pool hung thirty stories above the city streets, well over the edge of the hotel. "Won't people be able to see us?"

"That's the wrong question in Vegas, Riley," he said. "The real question is—will anyone care?"

I couldn't resist looking him over as he stood there, next to the bed. His bedhead made him even sexier, and his erection was still as hard and thick as when I'd first noticed it.

"Come over here," he said, beckoning me with his eyes. "We're not letting that pool go to waste."

I got off the bed and approached him, my body still aching from his thrusts. Tilting my head up, I kissed his lips, softly at first, then slipped my tongue past them.

His mouth moved against mine, hungrily sucking at my tongue, and I felt his hands move, cupping my upper thighs. Effortlessly, he lifted me from the floor, and I found myself wrapping my legs around him instinctively.

"Perfect," he said, carrying me toward the pool with my legs tangled around his waist. With each step, he kissed, trailing little lines with his mouth down my shoulders and neck as I clung with arms and legs around his strong torso.

We passed through the door. The night air was cool and dry as Jax stepped into the moonlit water. The view was breathtaking: all the lights of the Las Vegas Strip, and the city sprawling out gaudily for miles in every direction, just beyond the blue, transparent pool edge. The water flowed up around Jax's legs, then his thighs, and then his ass.

As he stepped further in, I felt the warm water flowing around us, the currents rippling gently against my skin. Then, like a burst of light, I felt Jax's cock nestling against my cleft, slowly easing its way inside me.

He looked at me, an unasked question in his eyes.

"Yes," I breathed. "Oh, Jax, please, yes."

The next time I screamed, it was into the Las Vegas night sky.

Chapter Eighteen

ALONG FOR THE RIDE

I jolted awake the following morning to an image of my own body floating above me, splayed naked over silk sheets. For a second, I thought I'd really died from an orgasm and my departing spirit was now looking down at my corpse. But then I realized I was looking into a gigantic mirror mounted above the bed, and I breathed a sigh of relief.

Propping myself up on my elbows, I saw Jax sliding on a pair of black jeans at the foot of the huge hotel bed. I fell back into the soft bed as everything from last night suddenly came flooding back to me, leaving me feeling satisfied and happy.

I stretched out and watched my naked, well-fucked body twist in the mirror above the bed. Sitting up, I tried taming my crazy bedhead as he watched me with a warm smile.

"You don't have to fix your hair. I like it like that, all wild and unruly. It suits you," Jax said, giving me a sexy smirk. "So we've all got the day off today. I'm guessing the rest of the band's probably off gambling away their per diem." He sat down on the edge of the bed and slid on his black boots.

I pouted prettily. "You're leaving already?"

"I've got a surprise for you." He stood up and pulled a black tank top over his head, covering the tight contours of his muscular torso, but leaving his tattooed sleeves exposed.

I perked up. "Another surprise? What is it?"

"You know better than to ask by now." His smile widened and he winked at me. "I had the hotel bring up some clean clothes for you. They're on the dresser next to some breakfast. I'd stay to enjoy it with you, but I need to go downstairs. Meet me in front of the hotel in twenty minutes."

"You're killing me with these surprises." I playfully tossed a big fluffy pillow at him.

He caught it with one hand and looked at me with a palpable hunger in his eyes. "And you're killing me just lying there in bed. I'm a second away from ripping off my clothes and jumping back in with you."

"I wouldn't mind that," I said, my pulse quickening, "but I guess it wouldn't be a surprise."

"Exactly." He leaned over the bed and kissed me softly on the forehead before disappearing out the door.

His kiss was comforting, but the absurdly large bedroom suddenly felt a lot emptier. I showered and slipped on the blue jeans and breezy checkered shirt Jax had laid out for me. The jeans fit perfectly and despite the top being a tad too tight I was surprised by how well he knew what kind of clothing to have the hotel send up. After munching on some fruit and a bagel from one of the many left-over trays, I headed downstairs to wait for Jax.

As I walked through the hotel's lobby, the noise was nowhere near as loud as I remembered it the night before, when I'd been blindfolded.

The concert—and everything that had happened after—I still couldn't believe I'd been on stage during the Hitchcock's show. And then my night in the suite with Jax was . . . more than magical.

Wandering through a maze of flashing slot machines, I idly wondered what he had in store for me today. The past few days had left me buzzing with excitement—all of it was like nothing I'd ever experienced before. It wasn't just the rock star lifestyle he was treating me to, either.

Jax's string of pleasant surprises was completely new to me. The only kinds of surprises I ever received from guys in the past were the bad kind—the collect call at 3:00 A.M. begging me to bail him out of jail, the break-up that comes without any warning, the accidental text that was meant for the other girl.

With Jax, things seemed different. Even though I still had some lingering concerns where things were headed with us, I could tell it was going to be a wild ride, one that I didn't think I could get off of even if I wanted to.

Outside the hotel, as I eagerly awaited Jax's arrival beneath the sweltering afternoon sun, a jet-black motorcycle came rumbling down the street. The biker pulled into the hotel's curved driveway riding what looked to be a classic bike.

I'd had fantasies of being a badass biker chick, but owning a vehicle in Manhattan—even something as compact as a motorcycle—was a hassle I could do without. I enviously eyed its rider in his dark cowboy hat, wishing it was me on the bike instead of him.

When he parked, I squinted through my sunglasses and realized that it was Jax. Of course. It wasn't entirely surprising that a bad boy like him would ride a motorcycle.

"I didn't know you rode a motorcycle," I said excitedly, as I hurried over to the thrumming bike. I lifted my sunglasses to get a better look at him and I bit my bottom lip. "Or that you'd look so hot doing it."

"Must be this desert heat." Jax smiled and tipped his hat to me, the sun casting a shadow from the brim across his chiseled features.

"A cowboy hat, huh?"

"Like it?"

"Hmmm . . . " I said, tapping my chin and taking my time with it. "It's cute but I'm not sure if it fits with your usual style."

Jax gave me a wink. "Thing is—I'm adaptable. Rock 'N' Roll sex symbol. Cowboy sex symbol. Biker sex symbol. It's all the same to me."

I laughed, and Jax revved the bike a few times, the roar sending a thrill down my spine. I ran my hand along the shiny black machine rumbling between his legs. "Okay, Mr. Sex Symbol, where'd this come from?"

"Been hauling it around in the trailer attached to the roadie bus." He revved it again and I admired the powerful roar of its engine emanating from its sleek design. "This is my vintage Vincent Black Shadow. It's pretty old but it's a classic. You're lucky today because sometimes it has trouble starting. It must be behaving extra well just for you." Jax gave me a wink.

"Looks like a high-speed Fortress of Solitude," I said with a nod.

He grinned. "I do usually ride by myself, but today's going to be different."

"How so?"

"Because today you're coming with me." He patted the cushion behind him in a welcoming manner.

"Really?" I hopped on, excitedly draping my arms around his neck and kissing his cheek. "I've always wanted to ride one!"

"Your first time?" He twisted his head back to face me. "I'm shocked. Given your taste for trouble, I figured you'd ridden before."

"I've just never had the chance." I wrapped my arms around his waist and squeezed firmly.

"Until now." He reached into a side compartment and pulled out a helmet. "Here, put this on."

I reluctantly took the unwieldy helmet. "You get the cool cowboy hat and I get the frumpy helmet?"

"I don't want you bumping that pretty head of yours," he said, sliding his hands over the arm I still had wrapped around him.

His warm touch reminded me of what he did for me after I'd been sore from making buttons for the band. "But you already made me bump my head. On the fridge shelf before you gave me that massage," I said, pinching his sides playfully.

He reacted only slightly to the pinching then pulled my free hand up to his mouth and kissed it. "Ah, you're right. Sorry about that."

"Besides, what's the point of riding on your motorcycle if I can't feel the wind in my hair?" I dropped the helmet in his lap. "I know you want me to be safe, but you know I'm not going to put that on."

He laughed and returned the helmet back to the side compartment. "Promise me you'll hold on tight then."

"Now *that*, I can do." I embraced him with both my arms and hugged his body close to mine as he revved the engine.

We pulled away from the hotel, the vibrations of the bike beneath me making me giddy, and before long we hit the highway.

The speed immediately sent a surge of adrenaline through my body and I could see why Jax loved riding. Jax masterfully swerved and wove around the slower cars, not letting anything slow us down. I gripped him tighter, running my hands across his ridged abs, slightly disappointed there had to be a layer of clothing separating us. As the wind blew through my hair, I briefly closed my eyes, and I could feel my heart racing from the thrill. The rush from the combination of being on the bike, clinging ahold of Jax, and the overall sensation of the new experience was exhilarating. But I wanted more.

Seeing a long stretch of open road before us, I shouted to him, "Push it faster!"

Jax turned his head and shouted back, "Give me your hand."

I tentatively let one hand go and reached forward. He wrapped my hand around the throttle and the vibration sent tingles shooting up my arm. I rested my chin on his firm shoulder to get a good view of the highway, which shimmered in the distance.

"Now, slowly twist it."

With his steady hand over mine, I twisted the throttle and the bike thrusted forward. I screamed with excitement at the top of my lungs. Even though having control over this dangerous machine filled me with a sense of wild abandon, I still squeezed my other arm around Jax's waist for safety.

After a few more exhilarating miles down the highway, I gave control of the throttle back to Jax. As fun as it was, my arm was tired and numb from the rumbling of the machine.

Jax took us down the highway a few more miles before he turned onto a dirt road in the middle of the desert. He parked close to a set of small wooden buildings that looked deserted. We got off the bike and my legs felt all wobbly, like I just spent hours on an elliptical machine, but Jax steadied me.

"Where are we?" I asked. Aside from the cluster of deserted-looking buildings, there was nothing for miles except cacti, shrubs, wildflowers, and tumbleweeds. I was still pumped from the ride, but the more I looked around, the more this desolate spot spooked me. "Did you bring me to a ghost town?"

"Don't tell me you're afraid of a few ghosts now." Jax grabbed my hand, which was still tingling from holding the throttle, and we headed toward the buildings.

"I don't think my pepper spray is going to work on them."

"Yeah, you're right, that probably won't work. Don't worry though, Chewie trained me in hand-to-ghost combat."

"Hand-to-ghost combat?" I said, arching an eyebrow. "Is there anything you can't fight?"

He looked into my eyes and his smile made my heart flutter. "Maybe." He squeezed my hand. "Come on, I want to show you something."

We approached the largest of the buildings, a big wooden structure with red paint long since faded away into an almost translucent pink. When we were only a few feet away, a resounding crash clanged from inside of the building. Startled, I clutched onto Jax's arm.

A man with a weathered face wearing a red checkered shirt and brown cowboy hat appeared from the building leading an all-white horse that looked like a unicorn missing her horn.

"Surprise," Jax said turning to me and gesturing to what I now realized was an old stable. "It's a Wild West horseback ride."

"Horseback riding?" I asked, eyes wide. "Now you're just messing with me. First you've got a cowboy hat and now we're going horseback riding? Are you the same Jax that rocks out on stage in front of millions of fans?"

He grinned and shrugged. "It's not too different from riding a motorcycle. Riding a horse offers more freedom to explore the wilderness and the unknown.

You know, get in touch with nature. I figured you'd like it too."

"I do. I mean, I really like the gesture," I said with a nervous smile, "but . . ."

"You're not scared, are you? Don't tell me badass Riley can ride a motorcycle without a helmet, but can't handle a little horse." Jax watched me, an amused look on his face.

I watched the stableboy lead the prancing white horse in a circle. "Horses are different. I'm used to cab seats, not saddles. I don't know how I feel about getting on something with a mind of its own. They're cool and everything, but I'm a city girl, born and raised."

"If you don't want to try it, we can always cancel and do something else," Jax said, watching for my response.

I looked over at the horse, which stood over a foot taller than me, and I rubbed the back of my neck. A quick glance back at Jax's reassuring face steeled my nerves enough to convince me that I could do this. I knew I could trust him. "No, it's fine. Since I've already ridden a motorcycle for the first time today, might as well get horseback riding out of way at the same time, right?"

"There's the Pepper I know." He grinned.

We quickly signed the waivers that the stableboy handed us and returned them to him

"Looks like that's all settled, I'll wrangle up the other horse," the stableboy said as he hustled back into the stables.

"Come on," Jax said, putting his arm around me affectionately. "I'll help you up onto the horse."

We walked a few steps over to the horse and he pointed to a piece of leather protruding up from the front of the saddle. "Now just grab hold of the horn here, and then put your foot in the stirrup down there. And then, as you pull yourself up, swing your leg around."

"Nice horsey," I said as I cautiously approached the horse.

"Just remember—if you stay calm, she'll stay calm. If you get agitated, she'll get agitated." Jax held the reins of the horse. I grabbed the horn and slipped my foot into the stirrup, but I had a hard time swinging my leg up and across the saddle. I struggled for a few seconds until he put his hand on my butt and boosted me up.

With his assistance, I swung my leg up and over the horse and planted myself in the saddle. "I love your hands-on approach."

"It's the only way to teach a feisty girl like you," he replied with a wicked smile that made my insides melt. "So for today's first lesson in horseback riding, you'll need to make sure you're comfortable and stable in the saddle."

"Yes sir, Mr. Trenton." I situated myself in the saddle while Jax held onto the reins. "Is there a seatbelt or something I should put on?"

"No, no seatbelt." He laughed and handed me the reins. "You're just going to have to hold on really tight to these."

As Jax showed me how to properly sit a saddle and control the horse, the stableboy returned, yanking the reins on a menacing midnight black horse that brayed and bucked violently.

"I'm real sorry, folks," the stableboy said, shaking his head. "I know y'all had a reservation, but goshdarnit, I must've made some sort of mistake 'cause this bronc's the only horse I've got left. He's not as bad-tempered as he looks, he's just throwing a bit of a tantrum today. If y'all want your money back, I understand . . ."

"That bronc doesn't look too rowdy." Jax waved him closer. "I'll take a crack at him."

The stableboy eyed Jax cautiously. "You sure about this? Now you ain't gonna sue us if something goes wrong, are ya?"

"Don't worry," Jax said, "I know a thing or two about horses."

"Suit yourself. As long as as y'all signed the waivers," the stableboy said, shrugging.

Great. *That* was encouraging.

"You can't be serious, Jax," I said, trying to talk some sense into him. "That horse is legitimately dangerous."

He gave me a quick wink and took the reins from the stableboy's outstretched hands. Jax smoothed his hand along the horse's neck and whispered something in its ear. The horse quit jerking a little and seemed to settle down slightly as Jax grabbed ahold of the saddle and leapt up onto it in a swift, fluid motion that astonished me. But even with Jax straddling the horse's back, the stallion still bucked wildly.

"Jax, are you sure you'll be able to handle him?"

"No, but that's never stopped me before." He gritted his teeth and gripped the reins, trying to gain control over the unruly animal.

Jax's horse suddenly reared up onto its two hind legs, leaving its front two hooves dangling high up in the air. Shadowed by the sun, the horse held the pose and I watched with bated breath, worried that Jax was going to tumble off backwards. But he held on tight, and I exhaled a sigh of relief as the horse finally dropped back down onto all four hooves.

After a few tense seconds, Jax succeeded in getting the horse to walk around in a small circle, but I could see it was still giving him fits. As Jax steered his horse closer to mine, it unexpectedly calmed down and started sniffing and nuzzling my whinnying mare.

Jax smiled and rubbed his horse's glossy black mane. "Looks like he found what was getting him all riled up."

I reached out to my horse, echoing Jax's actions. "Or maybe this girl here was just able to tame him."

"Is that how you see it?" He flashed a sly grin at me. "You know, it feels weird being on a horse with no name. Horses all have their own personalities and quirks so they usually have their own crazy names too. Some famous racehorses were named Oliver Klozoff or Hoof Hearted or Cunning Stunt. We should name ours before we get started."

I laughed at the names. "Okay, you first."

"I've got one in mind already. This bronc's name should be All Riled Up."

"Maybe it's just in his nature to be dark and dangerous. Kinda like someone I know."

He patted his horse and smiled at me, his dark eyes glittering under the shadow of his cowboy hat. "He's not so bad. Just needs to break out of some old habits."

"Mmhm," I replied. Jax's horse came over to mine and started nuzzling his head against my horse. It gave me an idea. "I think I'm going to name her Stud Tamer."

Jax cocked his head to the side, his scarred brow raised high. "That little horse of yours does seem to have an effect on mine. But 'tame' is a strong word."

"I don't think so. I think this little one has already tamed that wild stud."

He nodded slightly and eyed me skeptically, but then smiled and said, "All Riled Up and Stud Tamer it is. Now that that's settled, it's high time we hit the trail. Come on, let's giddyup."

We both gently tapped our heels against our horses and they started slowly walking down the dusty trail. It was large enough for four to five people to ride side by side, but we rode right next to each other. Despite my non-stop jostling in the saddle, it felt wonderful to spend time away from the tour bus and I was delighted that Jax surprised me with this unexpected diversion. From day one, I suspected that this rock tour was going to be far from normal, but I never thought it'd include a horseback riding trip.

A few yards into the trail, our horses stopped and started nuzzling close together again, so I reached out, snatched away Jax's cowboy hat, and placed it snugly on my own head.

He narrowed his eyes at me and I was half-expecting him to steal it back. "Looks better on you than it does on me."

"Thanks, pardner," I said, tipping the hat at him while he laughed at my cheesy cowboy voice.

We rode at a leisurely pace that left my mind room to wander, and I couldn't stop thinking about how Jax knew so much about horses. "So have you always been a horse whisperer?"

He lifted his scarred brow. "I'm not all spotlights and leather pants you know."

"I'm surprised you're not wearing leather chaps, to be honest," I said with a giggle as I imagined him wearing them—and nothing else.

Jax laughed. "I'll be sure to wear them for next time."

"Come on, seriously, how do you know so much about horses?"

"I used to work as a stablehand for a little while, before I met Sky and the rest of the band, back when I was just trying to survive."

"*You?* Working in the stables?"

Jax smiled at me. "What? You can't picture it?"

"I don't know, I guess it's hard to think of you being comfortable in any place other than on a stage."

He shrugged, a thoughtful frown on his face, before he turned away. "Yeah, I guess I did a lot of things before I ever got on stage."

Whatever he had done in the past, it didn't seem like he was too eager to talk about it.

"So . . . what other types of lessons do you have in store for my first horseback riding class?" I said, trying to steer the conversation away from dangerous territory. Jax had been so thoughtful to plan this surprise for me that I didn't want to ruin the mood even though I was still curious about his past.

A slow smile returned to Jax's face and he set his horse into motion. "Come on, let's keep riding, I'll show you."

As we started back down the trail, he explained how to gently squeeze my heels to get the horse up to gentle trot and then to a rapid gallop. We rode past prickly cacti and patches of wildflowers at a comfortable pace while I marveled at the ease with which he now controlled All Riled Up. As for myself, I was getting used to Stud Tamer, but still struggled sometimes with getting her to do what I wanted.

The ride was peaceful and tranquil underneath a cloudless sky that stretched on forever. It was a complete contrast to the rock 'n' roll world I associated with Jax. A world that revolved around the dark, crowded venues with music so loud you can barely hear yourself think. Even outdoor music festivals were suffused with drunks and advertisements everywhere you look. But out here, there was nothing other than silent nature, and I could see how he'd be able to appreciate this.

We rode in silence down the trail, with only the quiet murmur of nature around us, neither of us wanting to spoil the mood.

After we had been riding for almost an hour, we neared a small formation of rocks. Without warning, my horse came to an abrupt standstill that sent me shooting forward.

"Shit!" I instinctively grabbed ahold of her thick mane and luckily stopped myself from flying head first into the desert sand. Slightly dazed, I sat back in the saddle and tapped my heels to get her moving, but her hooves were glued to the ground.

Jax was riding a bit ahead of me, and I was grateful he didn't see me almost get tossed, but I could not get the horse to budge. "Jax, I think something's wrong with my horse."

He twisted to look back at me and immediately spun his horse around to come trotting over to me. "Whatever you do, don't look down."

Naturally, I looked down.

A coil that almost blended into the sandy dirt sat in the middle of the trail. One end of the coil suddenly sprung up and started shaking like a possessed maraca. I nearly jumped out of the saddle when I realized the coil was a rattlesnake.

"Jax?" I heard my heart pounding in my ears and felt beads of sweat dripping down my forehead. "Um, Jax? What should I do?"

"Don't do a thing. Just stay on your horse. I'll take care of this."

The snake's rattling got louder and faster. My horse neighed and took a step back. I yanked my feet from the stirrups and bent my knees up to my chest, fearful that the snake would strike at any second.

Jax came riding up and quickly dismounted his horse. He picked up a long stick and started prodding the snake away from me. I thought he was going to use the stick to fling it away, but instead he pressed his boot down on the snake's head. And then, without any hesitation, he reached under his boot and plucked up the rattlesnake by the neck.

With my heart still pounding, I sat there in disbelief as he nonchalantly held up the long snake in the air and seemed to admire the brown and gold diamond pattern in its scales.

"What the hell are you doing?" I cried, pointing at the snake, "That thing is poisonous!"

He looked at me with a mischievous grin. "This design would be great for a pair of high heels."

"Screw the heels. Get rid of it before you get bitten!"

He shrugged and flung it toward some yucca plants as if the deadly snake was nothing but a plastic frisbee. He then walked over and cupped my clammy hand in his palms. "Are you okay?"

A few deep breaths coupled with his steady hands calmed down my heart rate. "I'm good, thanks," I said, as I unsnapped the top two buttons on my shirt, trying to cool off from the mix of the adrenaline rush and the hot sun. "But let's get away from this snakepit ASAP. I may be badass Riley, but not when everything out here is trying to kill us."

"Sounds good with me, let's get out of here," Jax said. He leapt back up onto his horse, scanning the area before pointing to a spot about one hundred yards away. "Come on, I'll race you to those rocks."

I might have been out of my element, but I wasn't going to roll over without a fight. "I don't think All

Riled Up stands a chance against Stud Tamer," I teased.

He looked at me, his dark eyes pools of dangerous intensity. "Don't forget Riley, I never back down from a challenge."

"How can I forget? But I'm warning you, get ready to eat my dust."

Jax smirked. "You're on. I'll count it off. One, two, three, forward!"

I tapped my heels a little harder than before and was shocked when Stud Tamer exploded into a gallop. The forward momentum jerked my head back and I grabbed the hat to keep it from falling off.

Somehow, I burst into an early lead, but when I looked to the side, I saw that Jax caught up. Hunched forward, leaning in close to All Riled Up's mane, Jax raced his horse hard and began inching ahead. I squeezed my heels and sore legs tighter against my horse and felt her pick up speed. We were locked in a dead heat.

Bouncing up and down in the saddle like a ragdoll, I struggled to maintain my composure. I clung to the leather reins so tightly they burned against my palms. My ears were roaring with the sound of the horses' hooves clopping on the dry desert ground.

In the final stretch, with the rock formation rapidly approaching, I tried to keep my eyes firmly on the finish line but I chanced a glance at Jax. He rode with his eyes fixed on me instead of paying attention to what was ahead of him. At the final second, I pulled ahead and barely eked out the victory.

He tugged on his reins and I did the same, slowing down our horses so they were walking next to each other. I was happy about my win, but it quickly dawned on me that there was no way Jax would've lost to a first-timer like me. "You let me win!"

He raised his scarred brow. "Did I?"

"I might be a quick learner, but you're an expert horse whisperer and it looked like you were taking it easy on me."

His sexy smile lit up his ebony eyes. "Guess I got distracted by the scenery."

I pumped my fist. "Well a win's a win."

"I think we both won." He looked at me again the same way he had been during the race, and I realized his eyes were looking straight at my chest.

"No wonder." I shoved his shoulder playfully.

Jax just grinned at me.

After we walked our horses slowly on the trail for a few more minutes, Jax surveyed our surroundings and stopped his horse. "This seems like a good place to give these two a breather."

He slid off his horse first. I followed his lead, sliding off with relative ease, before handing him the reins. Although I was thoroughly enjoying my first horseback riding trip, I was relieved to get my feet back onto solid ground.

As he tied up the horses to a lone tree, I took a second to drink up the awesome scenery. The setting sun splashed orange and purple colors across a rock archway. A couple jackrabbits scurried past some cacti while a coyote howled from somewhere unseen. The howl sent a chill along my spine, but I was certain that Jax would keep me safe.

I took off the cowboy hat and combed my fingers through my hair. "Jax this place is absolutely stunning. When did you find the time to plan all of this?"

"I was inspired while you were sleeping," he called from behind me.

I turned around to see what he was doing. Jax walked towards me, holding a handful of lavender, white, and golden wildflowers. He must've picked them from the fields around us while I was admiring the scenery.

"Oh! These are beautiful," I said, unable to stop my smile. "That's sweet of you." I held out my hands for the flowers, but instead of handing them to me, he brought them up to my head and slipped the stems into my hair.

"They're as much for you as they are for me," he said, taking a small step back to admire his handiwork.

My cheeks heated. I looked at his warm eyes, slightly embarrassed by how I was unable to stop smiling. "Thank you."

"Come on." He grabbed my hand and led me over to a boulder. "Let's enjoy the sunset."

As we sat on the boulder facing the setting sun, he slung a heavy arm around my shoulder and pulled me close to him. I leaned into him, inhaling his rich, manly aroma—which was becoming all too familiar to me now but I knew I'd never tire of it. My hand found his and our fingers intertwined. I thought about last night and today, and how he must've went to great lengths to plan all of this out, and I realized how unbelievably sweet Jax was being to me.

Just as the sun was sinking behind the distant mountains, I planted a peck on Jax's cheek. He wrapped me up with both of his arms and hugged me tight as we watched the sun bathe the sky and desert with shimmering tangerine tints all across the darkening blue hues.

Chapter Nineteen

RETURN OF THE LIVING DEAD

The zombie's ghoulish face peered into my eyes, and its decaying hands reached toward my face. A hiss emerged from the back of her throat: "*Braaaaaaaaaiiiinnssssssss . . .*"

I laughed, giving an appreciative nod to the makeup artist airbrushing final touches onto the fingers. "This video's going to be amazing," I said.

Our bus driver, Bernie, had driven through the night so that we could arrive on time to the Los Angeles soundstage where the Hitchcocks were scheduled to shoot their new video.

When we'd left the casinos behind, we realized we didn't want what happened in Vegas to stay there—the pillow wall between us came down between us in Jax's bed. We still stuck to the "no sex on the bus" rule, though. After the huge suite we enjoyed in Vegas, the cramped quarters of the bus bedroom seemed almost claustrophobically small, and I didn't exactly want to advertise what was going on between Jax and me to the rest of the band. If any of them had noticed the amount of time we'd spent together in Vegas, none of them mentioned anything.

The zombie's face broke out into a smile—which would have been terrifying, if she hadn't had such a friendly voice. "I've got to take a picture of this for my kids." She glanced toward a smartphone on the makeup table. "Would you mind?"

"Not at all." Picking up the phone, I tried to find the right angle to capture her at her most undead.

Once we'd gotten to L.A., the band spent most of the morning setting up for the shoot, while I caught up on some work. Every time I took a break, though, I couldn't resist catching a glimpse of the preparations for the video. Like any Hitchcock production, I was expecting a healthy amount of spectacle, but I guess I didn't quite expect this.

Just as I started to snap the picture, Jax leaned into the frame, giving the zombie a mock-terrified face. I laughed, and he went back toward his own makeup chair. I had to hand it to Jax, he knew how to make something as stressful as a video shoot seem fun for everyone. The food and drink had been flowing freely all afternoon, and it felt good to meet the extras and hang out around an actual Los Angeles soundstage.

I didn't know if it was in spite of being so far from home, or because of it but I was feeling better than I had in ages. I hadn't needed to reach for my lifesavers in days, and I couldn't remember the last time that had been true. Jax made everything seem a little bit easier. Being here in Los Angeles felt strangely uncomplicated—I felt, in some ways, freer than I'd felt in my whole life.

A voice I didn't recognize, with a thick Boston accent, ripped into my thoughts. "Hey, strawberry, whatcha dreamin' about?"

I turned around to see a short, bearded man with half a dozen earrings. It was the first time I'd seen him in person, but I didn't need an introduction: Torrence Henderson, the director. He'd shot the video for half a dozen number one hits, among them Lady Dada's last single, and his distinctive celebrity photos had shown up in every glossy-paged fashion mag in the business. Henderson was a perpetual red carpet fixture, and designers lived and died by which shows he watched at Fashion Week.

"Excuse me?" I said, not sure what he wanted from me.

He reached out to the ends of my hair and held it in his fingers. "Nevermind. What dye is this? It's beautiful."

I felt my face getting hot. "No dye."

"Natural. I like that. Gorgeous," he said, looking me up and down in a way that was starting to make me uncomfortable. "Do you have any questions about your costume? I assume you're next up for makeup."

Oh. He wasn't being inappropriate, he just thought I was there to be on camera. "I'm not an actress, you must be—"

"Crazy to hide a model under all that zombie makeup? I agree," he said, giving an exaggerated shrug and sigh. "But this video is high-concept, you understand? If it helps, you can think about all those actresses that won awards for playing ugly. Nicole. Charlize. Halle . . ."

I shook my head and cut him off. "This is all very flattering, but you've got the wrong girl. I'm not here to be in the video." I hadn't acted since flubbing half my lines in my middle school's production of *A Midsummer Night's Dream*—and I wasn't about to try again with Jax's career on the line.

"Then what the hell are you doing on my set?" In spite of the words, he didn't sound angry, just confused.

"I'm here with J—" I started, then quickly corrected myself and extended my hand. "Excuse me. I'm Riley Hewitt, tour accountant for The Hitchcocks."

His brow wrinkled. "You don't look like any accountant I've ever seen."

I gave my best glam pose, my hands framing my face. "All the accountants look like this where I work," I said in a vampy voice, then broke into a grin.

"Then let me tell you, I've been doing my taxes with the wrong people," he said. "Listen, really, sweetheart, we could use a few more extras for the crowd scene. You sure you don't want to be in a video?"

"I'm more of a behind-the-scenes kind of girl."

"But hear me out, I've got this perfect part. See, the zombie nurse that comes after the band will have this giant syringe, and you'll be in a nurse's uniform . . ." He grabbed a costume, still on its hanger, from one of the racks. I could only imagine what Palmer would say if he saw me spending company time wearing a skin-tight nurse's uniform in a rock video.

"Uh huh." I pinched at the fabric of the costume's micro-mini latex skirt. "And what artistic statement is this making, exactly?"

"Darling, it's all about the nature of fame."

"Fame?" Under different circumstances, I might have told him off about the "sweetheart" and "darling" treatment, but I didn't want to piss off The Hitchcocks' director right before he shot their video.

"When a band like The Hitchcocks gets big, their fame locks them inside themselves," he said, suddenly much more animated, talking a mile a minute. It was like I'd turned his dial up to eleven. "They'll start in straitjackets, each band member in a different cell, but even when they escape their cells, the zombies try to keep them from succeeding. You know, the critics, the fame leeches . . ."

Just what I want Jax to think of me as, I thought. *A fame leech and a nurse with a face like a rotted corpse coming after him with a giant syringe.*

I gave an excuse that I had to make an important call in a quiet area, and as I was making my exit, I heard my name being called, somewhere behind me. "Riley?" I looked around, but couldn't see the source of the voice. Louder, this time: "Riley, hey, is that you?"

I looked through the crowd of extras and saw a figure pushing through them. Tall, fair-skinned . . .

My stomach dropped to the floor.

No. It can't be him. Not here. Not like this, not right now.

"Riley? It really is you, holy shit!" He came closer, running a hand through his auburn hair. "How have you been? What are you doing in L.A.?" I caught a flash of gleaming white teeth hiding between his lips as he drew them into a fake smile.

"Connor." The name came out flatly in spite of my shock, and I felt my arms pull up against my chest numbly. "Why are you here?"

He smiled wider."Here as in Los Angeles, or here as in this studio?"

I want to know if you're following me around, I thought, but I kept my voice under control. "Either. Both."

He laughed. "You know, I could ask you the same thing."

I narrowed my eyes. "You first."

"Well, let's start with the city. I moved here for work." He spoke with the slick syllables of Southern California, any trace of his old New York accent long since gone. "As to your second question, I'm here shooting a commercial for my firm on the next soundstage over. I saw your hair and wondered if it was you."

At least he's not following me. I looked back over to the set and realized Jax and the band were setting up on the soundstage. The last thing I needed was for Jax to meet Connor. Jax may have had his secrets, but this was one part of my past that *I* wasn't ready share with *him*, which meant I needed to finish our conversation without starting a scene. Forcing my voice into politeness, I said, "It's been a while. Are you still in law?"

"You got it. McDonald & Ritter. Entertainment law. Mostly films, a little music too. So are you acting now?"

"Accounting."

Connor was trying to make conversation, but I didn't want to engage.

"You mean you stuck with accounting even after we broke up?" His tone, subtly arrogant, made me feel about three inches tall. I gritted my teeth. "I thought you were only in that major so we could take classes together."

"My *parents* were both accountants. I didn't do it because of you." I didn't want to let him get to me, but I couldn't let that one go. "And now it's what I'm going to get back to doing. Have a nice life."

Connor's face clouded over. "Hey, Rye, don't be like that," he said. "Look, I know things didn't end well between us. And I'm sorry for that. I just—I saw you over here and I couldn't let things stand the way they'd been. It's been a long time, Rye-Rye."

I looked at him, unwilling to believe what I was hearing. It was the first time I'd ever heard him make what sounded like a sincere apology. "Yeah. It has," I said, my voice softer than before.

"What have you been up to, anyway?"

I let myself relax a little. If Connor wanted to make small talk and pretend we didn't have a past, fine. "Working. Mostly in New York," I said, letting pride inflect my sentences. "I have a great job in the financial district, but this week I'm out here on business."

"New York." Connor's eyebrows lifted, and he shook his head. "I was happy to get out of that rat race. Hell, even L.A. is relaxed by comparison. At my first internship in New York, three of us woke up at four-thirty every morning to see who could get coffee to the senior partners soonest."

I couldn't help feeling a little secret delight—I'd been able to stay and thrive in the city that had been too much for him. "I guess some people just can't hack it in Manhattan," I said, smiling smugly.

I expected him to be pissed off, but he just laughed. "There's that Riley smile I like to see," he said. "And the attitude. I missed that."

"It's been missing for a reason."

"I know." He stepped toward me, his voice soft. "It's just, you know, I've been thinking about you a lot, lately."

"No. Not interested." I took a step backwards, looking down to make sure I wouldn't trip on any of the cords around the soundstage. Jax and the rest of the band were in straitjackets, and the director filmed them as they writhed on set—I was just glad Jax wasn't looking in my direction.

"There's something I've been meaning to tell you. Something I've been working on, and you deserve to know about it."

I crossed my arms tighter. "Look, whatever it is, I don't want to know. It was nice seeing you, Connor."

"I found out after we broke up that I'm a sex addict," he blurted, loud enough that I looked around to make sure no one had heard.

A sex addict? What the hell does that have to do with anything? "No, you're not, Connor," I said, my voice rising angrily. "You're a self-centered, manipulative liar."

He lifted his hands in a gesture of surrender. "Hey, no, I deserve that." He paused, then said, "I just wanted you to know I got in a program. I'm on Step Nine."

I rolled my eyes—hard. "Please stop talking."

"Wow, Riley, I expected better from you." His tone was derisive.

He wants to talk about expecting better from me? I looked at him, dumbfounded. "What?!"

"Be pissed off at me if you want," he said, the words rolling smoothly off his tongue. "But the Riley I know would at least let me tell her I'm sorry. Do you even know what Step Nine is?"

I stared at the set, looking away from Connor. "No."

"Step Nine means I have to atone, whenever possible, for the hurt I caused other people." He stepped in front of my line of sight, with a frown that made him look like a sad puppy. "Rye, I hurt you. I know I did."

I lowered my voice, hoping he'd do the same. "Connor, you don't have to do this."

I didn't care if he wanted to apologize. I didn't want to forgive him. I still shook every time I thought about how our relationship had ended.

On the set, the director was shouting to the bandmates: "Okay, now burst through the doors!" All at once, the cells sprang open, and each band member came out, carrying an instrument and leaving their straitjackets behind. The zombies started giving chase right away. I watched pointedly, looking anywhere but toward Connor.

"Riley, seriously, listen to me," he said, "I'm trying to tell you I'm sorry. I lied to you. I cheated. I did terrible things in pursuit of my addiction, and I regret every moment of pain my affliction caused you."

My nose wrinkled in disgust. Even his apology was evasive, trying desperately to avoid responsibility. I wanted to tell him that it wasn't his affliction that had caused me pain—it was his actions. But more than that, I just wanted him to go away.

"Apology accepted," I said flatly. "Don't you have work to do?"

"Hear me out," he said, reaching out to my shoulder. "Just last week, I was thinking about you, wishing I had your number so I could atone. And just like that, here you are. It's like fate or something."

The director's loud Boston accent ripped through our conversation. "Hey, Jax, get your head in the damn game," he said. "The redhead will be there when you get done."

I felt suddenly embarrassed. Jax seemed to be looking at the stage, now, but had he been watching me? What did he think—and did he see Connor trying to touch my shoulder and get close?

I brushed his hand away, bristling. "It's not fate, Connor. It's bad luck. And you're too late anyway—I've moved on."

His nose wrinkled, and he lifted an eyebrow. "Oh, really? Who is he?"

Shit. I'd said too much, and I didn't really want to blab to Connor that I was sleeping with America's next top rock god. I pressed my lips together. "That's none of your business."

"I bet he can't give you what I can. Remember how you always wanted to go to Ibiza?"

Don't, Connor. Just don't. "Yeah," I said, my eyes starting to well up with tears. "I was all ready to go that Christmas when you broke up with me. Thanks for the memory."

"Well, don't get so sad, because we can still go," he said, his chest puffing out with ego. "My work is sending me out there to hammer out a contract with an A-list director—but I can't tell you who. Never know who might be listening."

I gave him my best I-don't-give-a-fuck smile. "I don't care. Those dreams are done, Connor." Turning my heel, I started walking toward the soundstage exit.

"Riley, don't walk away from me," he pleaded. "I still have it. Remember the day you gave this to me?"

He held up a silver keychain with the Eiffel Tower on it—total tourist kitsch, but I'd bought it for him, right before everything fell apart. I stopped in my tracks and looked down, overcome by the memories.

"Remember what I gave you?" He moved closer to me, bringing his face close to mine. "We could still make it work."

I felt a wave of panic and reached into my pocket for my lifesavers, only to realize they were still on the bus. *Just my luck—especially when Connor's the reason I have them in the first place.*

I whirled back toward him, enraged. "Let me make this clear to you," I said, feeling my hands start to shake. "Get out of my life, Connor. I don't care where you go, I don't care what you do. Just stay the hell away from me."

His mouth twisted into a crooked, angry smile. "God, you've changed a lot, but you're just as crazy as I remember."

I pushed back a wave of nausea. "And you're just as big a narcissist."

"Nice. Real nice, Riley," he said, his voice rising with resentment and rage. "I apologize and you start your paranoid psychobabble. You always were a grade-A cun—"

BAM!! A punch landed on the side of Connor's skull, sending him reeling to the floor. "What the fuck?" he screamed, holding his head in his hands.

The tattooed, sun-kissed arm that took him out could only belong to one man. "Jax!" I said, startled. He'd approached before I'd even noticed—which meant, I realized with embarrassment, that Connor and I had been making a bigger scene than I'd realized.

Jax's dark eyes searched me. "Are you okay?"

I was shaking and on the verge of a panic attack, but I didn't want Jax to know that someone like Connor could affect me that way. "I'm—I'm fine."

"Good," he said, then turned and called to the security guards on the fringes of the lot. "Get this joker off my set. He's trespassing and he's harassing our tour accountant."

On the floor, Connor moaned in pain as security rushed in and lifted him by the arms, starting to drag him out. He shook his head as if clearing his vision and yelled at Jax, "What the fuck was that about? I was just having a friendly conversation with an old friend. Do you know who I am?"

Jax held up his hand, and the security guards stopped dragging Connor away for a moment. Jax glared at Connor with a dangerous glint in his eyes that I'd never seen before. "I don't give a shit who you are and I don't give a fuck what you *thought* you were doing. You made Riley upset. That's all I need to know." He waved the guards away, "Get this asshole out of here. For his own sake."

Connor continued to rant, "Well, I see she's got her claws into you too. Man to man, don't say I didn't warn you. She's fucking crazy!"

Even after all these years, his words could still hurt me.

Jax tensed but I put my hand on his arm, my eyes starting to sting. "No, Jax. Please. Just make him leave. I'm—I'm really sorry I ruined your shoot."

Even though Jax was still tense, he didn't make another step towards Connor. He watched until security dragged Connor out of sight and then turned back to me.

"Don't worry about it," he said, his eyes kind and gentle, but filled with concern. "We'll talk later."

As he walked back to the stage, where the rest of the band was waiting, I found a seat and collapsed into it. Jax said not to worry, but that was impossible—after what had happened today, he'd want to know about my history with Connor. But if he found out the truth, what would he think of me? Jax didn't need more drama in his life. Besides, what would the rest of the band think of this? When Jax convinced me to sleep in his bed, he told me the band would be cool with it, but that was before what happened in Vegas and before their music video shoot had to be interrupted because of me.

I'd gone from looking forward to the evening to dreading it—and all because of Connor.

I took a deep breath, then another, but it didn't help. Fighting back my tears, I curled up into my chair and waited for the shoot to end. No matter what tonight brought, I knew one thing:

I needed my lifesavers.

Chapter Twenty

SEEING THINGS

That evening, I walked up the stairs to Jax's room, while the band milled around chatting after they had wrapped up their shoot. I'd been thinking of the Fortress of Solitude all afternoon and evening, telling myself that I'd feel better as soon as I got a chance to lay down and collect my thoughts.

I pulled back the covers and huddled in against a pillow, and almost immediately collapsed, crying. I couldn't shake the memory of Connor. Not just how he'd treated me, but how he'd made me treat myself. I'd spent so long trying to forget him, to make myself someone better than the person I used to be.

A soft knock rapped against the door.

"Hello?" I said, trying not to sniffle.

"It's me," I heard Jax's voice respond, quietly. I curled up in a corner of the mattress, facing the wall. I couldn't look at him right now—I didn't want him to see me as a fucked-up, crying heap.

"Don't come in here."

I heard the door open and quickly tried to wipe my eyes and get my hair out of my face.

Jax climbed into the bed and crawled to my corner, then put an arm around me tenderly.

I shook my head, burying myself deeper into the covers. "I don't want to talk. I want to be alone."

"We don't have to talk," he said, his voice was soothing and soft, "but you shouldn't be alone. Not when you feel like this."

I couldn't say anything—I was too overwhelmed. Instead, I let him hold me as my body shook and the tears flowed down my face. The tears gave way to howling, uncontrollable sobs and he held on tighter.

"Next time something like that happens," he said. "I'm going to follow the badass Riley playbook and get out the pepper spray."

I smiled and tried to laugh, but my voice came out ragged and hoarse.

Maybe Jax thought that I was a badass, but he had never seen me like this, barely able to hold myself together. When he first met me, I'd picked a lock to get backstage and then left him with blue balls. He had met badass Riley.

But that wasn't me.

Badass Riley was just who I wished I could be. Today was proof of that. I'd pepper sprayed a thug, played cowbell on stage in front of thousands, and rode a motorcycle without a helmet, but still—I couldn't stand up to Connor. I could pretend to be brave all I wanted, but underneath it all I couldn't get over the pathetic person I was in the past. What would Jax think once he learned about the real me?

I let out a long sigh. "I—I guess I owe you an explanation, huh?"

"You don't have to tell me anything," Jax said, combing his fingers through my hair slowly. "When I saw you so upset because of that piece of shit, I didn't ask what he had done to you because I didn't need to. If anyone ever makes you feel that way, they have to go. If you want to tell me about it, I'm here to listen. If you don't want to tell me, that's fine too."

I looked up at him, searching his eyes for any hint that he was lying to me.

Jax looked right back at me, his gaze open and sincere. He brushed a strand of hair out of my face. "Whatever you choose, I'm never going to let anyone make you that upset ever again. I promise."

Even though Jax and I hadn't known each other that long, but there was something happening between us. We both sensed that. He had proven he was committed to me beyond the silly games we played, but I was still hiding who I really was from him.

Jax might not think of me the same way after he found out but I still had to tell him. It wasn't fair for me to lead him on, to let him think that I was someone that I wasn't.

I took a deep breath.

"We dated for over two years," I said quietly. "It was a long time ago."

Jax's strong hand slid over mine and squeezed. I turned toward him, and quickly tilted my head down so he wouldn't see my face red from crying.

"The first six months were incredible," I said, a half-smile breaking through my tears with the memory. "I'd just started college, he was a junior. He introduced me to all the right friends, got me into the right parties. We had a blast, but then we had a fight."

I felt Jax's body tense up, and he held me closer protectively.

"It wasn't—it wasn't like you might be thinking. He didn't hit me, or anything," I said, the recollection still too fresh in my mind. "He just stormed out when I got mad at him. And he didn't come back. I found out the next day that he'd gone out and slept with another girl."

He grimaced, and nodded for me to continue.

"I was furious. But he—he was totally calm, and he said I was being irrational. He started twisting around everything I said." My voice was flat, and I tried to keep myself as calm as I could. *Deep breaths*. "He said he thought we were broken up, said it was my fault he cheated. He said I'd broken up with him when I yelled at him. Somehow, he convinced *me* to beg for *him* to come back."

"He sounds like an asshole." Jax's teeth were gritted, but he held me tighter in his arms.

"I know that, now," I said, drying my tears with the back of my hand. "I just didn't when I was nineteen."

Jax shook his head.

My eyes brimmed over with tears again. "So I got back together with him," I choked out. "I know, pathetic right? But at the time, I was just so happy that he took me back. It was only a couple months later when I started noticing little things. He was spending all his time on his phone, and he put a password on his laptop."

"Did you ask him why?"

"Yeah. He said he had a project for work, and that the laptop password was in case his computer got stolen. It was all just plausible enough to be true."

"But you stayed suspicious. You're not stupid."

"Yeah. At least, I thought I wasn't stupid," I said, my voice bitter at the memory. "Connor changed all that."

"Why?" Jax growled, the anger palpable in his voice.

I squeezed the pillow in front of me. It was hard to talk about, and my words were slow to come out. "He denied everything. Worse than denied. He told me I was being crazy. Being controlling, paranoid, you name it. He told me I was sick in the head, that I needed to see a psychiatrist. A—And I believed him, Jax."

He started to say something, but I cut him off. "I mean, he was right wasn't he? I was the one who got back with him even after what he did, right? I—it's so stupid," I said feeling my eyes sting. "I was so stupid."

"You're not crazy or stupid," Jax said, his jaw muscles working. "He was gaslighting you, messing with your head, making you doubt yourself."

I felt my body tense with anxiety. "That's exactly what it was like," I said, my hands balling into fists. "It got to the point where it was hard to sort out what was real and what wasn't. I was gullible. I was stupid."

Jax suddenly looked stricken and shook his head, letting out a long exhale. "Fuck. I didn't realize."

"Didn't realize what?"

"How bad it was for you when I pulled that stunt with the groupies," he said, cringing at the memory. "I had no idea it would actually hurt you. It was just supposed to be a joke."

Embarrassment flooded through me. "I shouldn't have taken it the way I did," I said, my cheeks getting hot. "I just thought I wasn't good enough. Connor wrecked my confidence. 'No one wants a crazy girl,' he'd tell me. He used to say he was just in it for the crazy girl sex."

Jax reached out and wiped away my tears. "So why'd you finally ditch him?"

A shiver ran through me, and I was silent for a long moment.

"I—I didn't," I said at last. "He ditched me."

"What?"

"And when he did, I didn't even know what was real any more. He'd lied to me for so long that I thought I deserved it."

Jax's eyes got sad, and he ran his fingers through my hair, waiting for me to continue.

I closed my eyes. "I was on a class trip to France. We barely talked the whole time. Fought a bunch before I went, but he told me to bring back the kitschiest tourist souvenir I could."

"What'd you get him?"

"Eiffel tower keychain, tacky fake silver. Five euros."

"Good choice."

"Yeah. I gave it to him and he said he had a gift for me—" my voice broke, but I cleared my throat. I didn't want Jax to know this part still bothered me. "It was this ring, a ruby with diamonds around it. He said it wasn't an engagement ring, but close."

"So this was pretty serious."

"I thought so. Until my best friend told me a week later that they'd slept together while I was away."

He cringed. "Fuck."

"I was so angry." I still remembered the night in vivid detail—the yellow dress I'd been wearing, the way my right heel blistered as I walked through the night on my new shoes. "I went to his house to scream at him and when I did, he laughed in my face."

He looked surprised. "Wait, what?"

"He told me that my best friend was obsessed with him. That they hadn't done anything, but that she had tried to come onto him when I was gone." The tears were falling onto the pillow, now, and I couldn't stop them. "When I finally got him to admit what he'd done, he told me that it was because I hadn't paid enough attention to him. And that I wasn't doing enough to look good. He twisted everything back to being my fault and I actually tried to apologize."

"Tried to?"

"Yeah. He took the ring back, kicked me out without even letting me get my shoes. I had to walk two miles with bare feet just to get back home."

"What a piece of shit."

"I should have gotten angry at him, I know that now," I said, my voice stronger. "Hell, I bet the ring was fake."

"I'm surprised you didn't get revenge," Jax said, his scarred eyebrow lifting.

"Maybe I would have if he'd done it today," I said. "But I was so messed up back then."

Jax closed his eyes and sighed, then brought me close and kissed the top of my head.

"And then I—I went crazy." I said, cringing at the memory.

"You weren't crazy, Riley. That's just what Connor wanted you to think."

"No, Jax.," I said. "You don't understand, I mean, *crazy.* I barely ate, barely slept. My grades fell off a cliff and I worried everyone who cared about me . . ."

His eyes, now, were focused far off in the distance. "When people like Connor change who you are, there's only one thing you can do."

"What?"

"You cut them out of your life," he said. "Then you don't talk to them again, you don't think about them again. Look, you spent two years with him, right?"

"Yeah."

"And in that time, you were doing other things, too. You had classes. You had parents. You had hobbies."

I nodded. Where was he going with this? "Sure, I—"

"So those things all happened. But *he didn't.*" Jax's gaze was intense. "Understand? Any time you remember those years, you remember the parts without him. Like cutting someone out from a photo."

I was quiet for a minute. "I guess I just don't think of those years at all."

We sat in silence for a while, Jax gently stroking my hair. Since he got me talking about it, I might as well tell him the whole story. I cleared my throat and started again, "After a semester of grades that almost kept me from getting a job after graduation, I finally saw a psychiatrist. He gave me my lifesavers, and that—that helped a lot."

"Lifesavers?" Jax squinted quizzically at me.

I took the orange bottle out of my pocket. "Yeah," I said, giving the pills a shake. "The first time I took a Xanax, I could finally breathe again, you know? So since then, I think they might have actually saved my life."

Jax looked at the pill bottle. "I . . ." he started to say, then seemed to tense. "Never mind. Go on."

"I got my act together, after that," I explained. "I got straight A's. I buckled down. Everyone thinks I'm this put-together person and it's like I'm the only one who knows that I'm still this pathetic girl some asshole could break, just because he wanted to."

Jax shook his head angrily. "Don't say that Riley. You weren't anything like that when I first met you."

"Yeah well, Connor was such a button up, clean cut guy . . . I thought he was different, but he taught me that guys were really all the same. So after that, well . . . I switched to bad boys. They don't pretend to be romantic or lie about how committed they are to you or about sharing your dreams when all they're doing is screwing you behind your back. With a bad boy, what you see is what you get, and I guess it helped me get a lot of my confidence back. At least, I thought it had. Until today."

"Look at me, Riley," Jax said, his voice low.

I turned my face away from him harder. "I've been ugly crying." I felt my eyes, dry and hot, and knew they must be red. "You don't want to see this."

He lifted my chin until we were at eye level, but I kept my eyes squeezed shut. "Riley, look at me. Now."

His voice was so soothing that I couldn't help opening my eyes and seeing his black, gentle ones staring back at me. "I'm glad you told me about Connor," he said. "And I know you wish it hadn't happened. But you don't need to feel ashamed. Not around me."

I looked down. "I acted like an idiot. I should have dumped him a year and a half before I did."

"That doesn't make his lies your fault."

"When he came to the set today, I just . . . I hated it," I said, ripples of anger flooding into my body. "I thought I'd put it all behind me, but when I saw him today, it was like I would never get over this part of myself. What if I'm just that weak, pathetic person deep down?"

Jax shook his head. "No, that's not you."

"I walked home barefoot after my scumbag ex kicked me out. How is that not pathetic?"

"Riley, you're the most badass woman I've ever met," he said, his eyes wide and intense. "You're strong, you're brave, and you don't take shit from anybody. The fact that some asshole lied to you a long time ago and made you feel weak is on him, not you."

Jax pulled me to him, pressing his lips hard against my forehead and hugging me so tight that I could barely breathe.

I squeezed him right back wishing that we would never have to let go of each other. "Thanks, Jax," I whispered into this chest.

He loosened his embrace and a fragment of a laugh escaped his mouth. "You know, when I came up here, I was worried you were about to break things off with me."

My eyes opened wider. "What? Why?"

He ran a hand through his hair, "I was afraid I might have overreacted when I threw that punch."

"You didn't."

"Yeah, but now I have a big regret." His eyes were shining, now. I felt like I'd never seen him looking quite so gorgeous.

"Oh? What's that?"

"That I didn't throw a harder one," he growled, his hand making a fist. "I wish I'd broken his fucking face after what he put you through."

I took his fist in both my hands and brought it close to my mouth, then kissed it softly. He turned his head to look at me, surprised.

"You did just right," I said softly, remembering how Connor had looked when he was laying on the floor. "I don't think he'll be bothering me again—not for a long time, anyway."

The Xanax bottle rested near my hand, and I realized I still hadn't taken one today. I twisted the bottle between my fingers, thinking about the pills inside and set it down again.

Chapter Twenty-One

WET 'N' WILD

I woke up, startled by a strange sound. Sunlight beamed through the window, and I saw that I was in Jax's room. The strange sound came again, except louder. This time, I could tell it was a moan. Seeking out the comfort of Jax's arms, I rolled over and realized that it was him moaning, deeply and painfully, his face strained. His eyes were squeezed shut and his head was flopping back and forth over a damp halo of sweat on his pillow.

"Jax," I said softly to him, unsure what what to do. "Jax, it's okay, everything's okay."

I gently rubbed my hand on his tense arm, hoping I could calm him down.

He went silent. I brushed aside his damp hair and faintly kissed his temple. I whispered into his ear and continued rubbing his arm gently until his body relaxed down into the bed and his breathing returned to normal. If this is what happened when he slept, I could see why he didn't get much of it.

I studied Jax's face. He seemed peaceful now, as if whatever nightmare he'd experienced never happened. I flopped onto my pillow, relieved.

Judging from the light streaming through the window, I could tell that it had to have been close to noon. It was unusual for me to sleep in so late but yesterday's incident had been exhausting, both mentally and emotionally. I looked at Jax snoring quietly, and then slipped out of bed to wash up.

The bus was parked, and I couldn't hear any of the constant music, video games, laughing, or partying that I was growing accustomed to while on tour. The band appeared to be out, and even Bernie was gone too.

I peeked out the blinds and discovered that we were in a vast parking lot. Past rows of cars and behind a tall privacy fence, bursts of water shot up twenty feet into the air and I could make out the tops of what looked to be waterslides and lifeguard towers. I realized that we were stopped at a water park, which was probably where the rest of the band was having fun.

It was a gorgeous day out, and I was eager to join them, but I still wasn't sure what they thought of what happened yesterday at the music video shoot. Jax told me after our talk that the band didn't think much of it. He had said that when he went back to the soundstage he just told the band that some random creep was bothering me so he got rid of the guy. Even though Jax was convinced that they bought the story, I was still worried about what the band might think if they realized that Jax and I were becoming more than just friends. The last thing I wanted right now was to create drama or make things awkward on the bus.

Still, I couldn't avoid them forever, and I knew I'd be kicking myself for weeks if I missed out on all the fun in the sun. So I exhaled deeply and made my decision.

I went into the bathroom and slipped into my bathing suit. I found myself grinning from ear to ear remembering how this bikini top initiated my post-concert kissing ritual with Jax. I left the bathroom and checked to see if Jax wanted to go, but he was still sleeping peacefully. I was tempted to wake him but felt he deserved a good rest after clocking out my ex and then listening to me unload my baggage all night. *Poor guy.*

After giving him one last peck on the cheek, I left the bus and headed for the park. At the gate I discovered that it was a pirate-themed water park named Blackbeard's Lagoon, and I was pleasantly surprised to learn that the band had already paid for my admission. That was thoughtful of them. I figured they'd probably expensed it to the band's account, but these tickets were a far cry from thousand-dollar flutes of champagne, so I was more than okay with their decision, even if it did make some extra work for me.

Inside, as I strolled the place seeking out the band, I noticed fountains sculpted like pirates standing on open treasure chests everywhere. Most of the staff sported eyepatches and bandanas. People were laughing and screaming as they slid down twisty slides and walked plank-like diving boards into a huge pool with plastic vines and foliage designed to resemble a lagoon. Next to the pool, rowdy teenagers manned controllable water cannons from inside a pirate ship and they fired attacks at unsuspecting parkgoers. After passing the same peglegged pirate fountain for the third time, I still saw no sign of the band.

I considered stopping under a lone palm tree for a break, when I heard "Riley! Over here!"

Turning sharply, I saw Kev waving me over to the rest of the band sitting around a wooden picnic table partially hidden by a big umbrella.

"Found you guys!" I said, approaching them and trying to act like nothing was on my mind. "Thanks for buying my ticket."

Sky, dressed in a polka-dot string bikini, shot me a bright smile. "No problem. We saw this place and just had to treat ourselves after our long day of filming. I figured you'd be down once you woke up and left the Fortress of Solitude."

Chewie jumped off the table. "Riley, awesome, now we can do it."

"Do what? Don't tell me you need me to make more buttons."

Chewie laughed and pointed a futuristic raygun at me. He made machine gun noises with his mouth, pretending to shoot me. "Fuck buttons, we've got more urgent needs, like a water gun fight! And now that you're here, we've got even teams."

I brightened. It was exactly the type of fun I needed to take my mind off of yesterday. "Sounds like a blast, and a good way to cool off today, count me in."

"Excellent!" Chewie squirted his raygun at the concrete right in front of my feet, trying to intimidate me.

"Watch it, Chewie," I said, smiling devilishly. "I grew up playing Duck Hunt, so I'm an excellent shot."

"Well, go grab a gun and let's put those skills to the test." Chewie cocked his raygun. "They rent the guns out right over there. We'll be waiting here, locked and loaded."

"Alright, I'll be back," I said, doing my best Terminator impression, and then I headed over to the water gun stand to wait in line. It occurred to me that this was the first time I was really hanging out with the rest of the band. Most of the tour I'd been either working by myself or hanging out with Jax.

A firm hand gripped my elbow. Surprised, I yanked my arm away and spun around. "What th—"

"Riley, there you are," Jax said, with concern etched into his face. "I've been looking everywhere for you."

I brought my hand to my pounding chest and exhaled in relief. "I'm right here." I was glad to see him out of bed and enjoying the park. But he was still wearing the shorts and shirt he'd slept in. Looking into his dark eyes, I sought out any sign of his earlier nightmare. "Are you okay?"

"I'm fine, I was worried when you weren't there when I woke up."

Jax was so sweet; he must've thought I was still feeling bad about Connor. "Aw, sorry, I didn't know when you'd wake up so I came to check this place out. Isn't it wild? I'm loving this whole pirate theme. Arrr!"

He looked around, as if suddenly noticing we were in a water park and then returned his sight to me. "Good. If you like it, I'm all for it."

Even though his face had softened, I could sense an uncertainty in his voice. "Is there anything you want to talk about?"

"No . . . I just wanted to make sure you're safe."

"How can I not be safe when I've got *you* as my personal bodyguard?" I asked with a big smile, swooning over Jax's concern for my safety. "The rest of the band and I are having a water gun fight. Care to join us?"

Crossing his arms, he squinted in the sunlight. "Now that I know you're fine, I think I'm just gonna go back to the bus and write."

My turn in line came up. I was impressed with their selection, and I ended up outfitting myself with two high-powered pistols that came with extra clips that I tucked into my bikini bottoms. "Oh, quit being such a party pooper. It'll be fun."

He shook his head slightly. "I'm not really in the mood."

I could tell he needed to have some fun too. "Guess I'll just have to get you in the mood." Inspired by our Wild West horseback riding trip, I brought up my pistols in a quickdraw motion and squirted Jax in the chest.

He casually looked down at the big wet spot on his chest then lifted his eyes back to me, a grin slowly spreading over his lips. "You're asking for trouble."

Seeing his expression lighten, I closed one eye, took careful aim, and fired a round at his stone abs. "Bullseye," I said with satisfaction as the contours of his six pack appeared through the wet cotton.

He pulled the shirt over his head and tossed it aside, baring the ink on his chiseled torso. With a twinkle in his dark eyes, he said, "Okay, now I can't be held responsible for my actions."

"Should I be worried about that?" I asked playfully. But with his shirt off, I didn't know if *I* could be held responsible for my actions either.

"Depends. But first I'd better arm myself." He turned to the water gun vendor and picked out two double barrel water guns. He bent his arms and held up the guns, framing his face with them. "Gotta make sure I've got enough firepower."

"Looks like you've got more than enough firepower right there," I said, pointing to his biceps. I was tempted to give them a firm squeeze, but I restrained myself, wary that the band might see me feeling him up.

We moved away from the stand and headed back toward the band as Jax said, "You know that was a risky move soaking me back there."

"Oh yeah?" My brow lifted. "Does that mean you're going to punish with me a spanking now?"

"It's a very real possibility," he said, low and guttural, making me bite my lip at the sound of his voice.

"Well, I don't think I did anything wrong." I flipped my hair behind my ear. "You can't come into a water park and not expect to get wet."

"I don't see that as one the water park rules," he said, pointing with his gun at one of the many signs posted throughout the park.

"It's an unwritten rule." I playfully shoved his arm. "Besides I could tell you needed someone to cheer you up. And I figured I owed you since you were sweet enough to cheer me up yesterday."

He stopped me and his penetrating gaze sought out my eyes, sending a flutter through my stomach. "Guess that means I owe you one now too." He lowered his face and brought his lips to mine. The slightest brush of his lips sent a tingle sizzling straight down to my curled toes and I had an overwhelming urge to reach out and wrap my arms around him. But instead I pulled away.

I looked at him with wide eyes. "What are you doing, Jax?"

"I'm kissing you, what does it look like I'm doing?" he asked with a confused look on his face.

"Just . . . can we keep the PDA under wraps until we get a better sense of the band's feelings on this? Can you do this for me?"

His lips curved downward and he furrowed his brow pensively. But then his face relaxed and gave a mischievous smile. "Whatever you say, Pepper, but you know that's going to be hard, since I want you constantly."

I could see he didn't like it, but I was happy that he listened and was willing to do something he didn't want to do. I smiled. "Save it for later, Stud. And thanks for understanding."

As we resumed walking back to the band, I couldn't help but notice women turning their heads to stare at us. Or more specifically, turning to stare at Jax's taut, ripped body. They lowered their shades, licked their lips, peeked out from behind magazines, and fanned themselves with those magazines. A sudden self-consciousness arose in me over how I stacked up in Jax's mind next to these women openly flirting and flaunting their fit, tanned bodies.

From out of nowhere, a tanned and pretty brunette in a designer bikini stepped in front of Jax. "Oh my god, it is you! You're Jax Trenton! I'm your biggest fan! Would you take a selfie with me? Pretty please?"

I could sense Jax's lack of enthusiasm at the proposal, but he nodded and posed with the lady as she snapped a selfie with him before she bounced away, obviously ecstatic. As I kept walking side-by-side with Jax, I realized that these women openly ogling his glistening body wanted *my* man. And Jax didn't want any of them—he wanted *me*. I threw back my shoulders and stuck out my chin proudly. Keep dreaming ladies.

The band came into sight, and I tried to bury the thought that them seeing Jax and me together would raise some questions in their minds. When we came up to them, I forced a smile and said, "Look who found me . . . "

Chewie groaned. "Oh great."

"What's wrong?" I asked.

"Now the teams are gonna be all lopsided," Chewie said, his mouth wrinkled.

"Well," Kev said with his hand on his chin. "Me and Chewie are like sharpshooters, Sky not so much. I haven't seen Jax play, but he's good at everything so I'm sure he's skilled. And Riley, you claim to be this Duck Hunt-trained master shot—"

"Damn straight," I chimed in.

"So how about us three," Kev pointed to himself, Chewie, and Sky, "versus you two."

"We've got more guns though," I said, noting how Jax and I were each dual-wielding. "We've got the advantage."

"Yeah, but we've got a secret weapon that you guys don't."

"And what's that? A hidden stash of water balloons?" I asked, spinning the water pistols on my fingers.

"It's a little thing called 'chemistry'," Kev said, blowing on his knuckles. "We work together like lions in a pride. You and Jax are lone wolves."

Jax waved away Kev's comment. "If that's what you think, prepare to get schooled. We've got more chemistry than a keg of gunpowder."

I looked at Jax warily. I was a little worried that he was giving away too much about us to the band, but I was also eager to prove that we could work well together.

We agreed on teams and terms, did some trash-talking, and then the two teams separated, with each one heading to opposite sides of the park.

Once we were in position, Jax and I started our hunt, seeking out each band member like an elite SWAT team. I quickly discovered and shot a surprised Sky trying to blend in with a bunch of kids by an octopus shooting water from its tentacles. Then Jax pointed out Chewie standing guard by the pirate ship. I nodded and snuck across the ship, hoping to get the jump on him. Instead I emerged to him gunning straight for me.

I held up my guns, ready for a duel, when suddenly Jax came swinging by on one of the lagoon's plastic vines like Tarzan, shooting Chewie's sunglasses off his face. Chewie slumped away defeated.

I spotted Kev across the pool by a row of lounge chairs. Jax went into commando mode, using finger gestures to indicate we should split up. He pointed back and forth between me and his eyes, signaling he was watching me. I snickered at how seriously he was taking this.

We split up and maneuvered around the pool. Kev spotted us and took off running. After a brief chase, we managed to trap him between a water-logged jungle gym and the lockers. He spun around and held out his waterblaster, alternating his aim between the two of us. Jax and I squared our guns on Kev and slowly circled him in a Mexican standoff.

Kev suddenly let out a battle cry and jumped to the side as he squirted me in the stomach. But Jax was on him in an instant, nailing him with both guns.

I was upset that Kev managed to shoot me, but in the end I was glad our team won. Jax and I celebrated with a high-five followed by a butt bump and a chest bump.

"Wow, I stand corrected. You guys do have chemistry," Kev said panting to catch his breath from running around. "You guys know each other's movements so well. It's almost like you're an old married couple."

"Oh, we're just friends," I said quickly, and then laughed uncomfortably. "And barely ones at that."

Great, that was just perfect. Not suspicious at all.

Kev raised a skeptical eyebrow that I pretended not to see. I hurried to think of a distraction to change the topic.

Inspiration struck and I casually walked over to Jax. With a big grin I said, "I'm sorry, but I'm afraid this is totally necessary."

He cocked his head. "What's totally necessary?"

I grabbed his arm with both hands. "I've got him, hurry up! Blast him!"

"Hey!" Jax struggled against my grip, but I knew he wasn't using his full strength. "What are you doing? You're on my team, let go of me."

"Nope, you brought this on yourself for being so damn good." I laughed as Sky, Chewie, and Kev surrounded us and then unloaded their guns on Jax. I got hit too, but I didn't mind it; it was like dousing a winning coach with a cooler of Gatorade—sometimes you get some on yourself.

But their streams quickly petered out.

"Ahh I'm tapped," Chewie said disappointedly.

"Me too," Kev replied as he frowned and looked at Chewie.

Like mirror images, Kev and Chewie both looked at each other, smiled, and silently nodded. They each grabbed one of Jax's feet. I continued holding onto his arm as Sky picked up on the cue and latched onto his other arm. With great effort, we hoisted him into the air.

"What the hell are you guys doing?" Jax asked, sporting a big smile on his face.

They say muscle weighs more than fat, and Jax's body was a testament to that, since it seemed like he was made out of solid concrete. We struggled to carry him over to the pool a few feet away. At the edge, we swung his body back and forth, building some momentum.

"One, two, three!" I shouted and the four of us tossed Jax into the pool. He hit the water and sent a splash up higher than my head.

We waited for a few seconds before Jax's head popped out of the water. He ran his hands through wet hair, pulling it out of his face. He lifted himself out of the pool as water cascaded down the grooves of his pecs and abs. Soaking wet, he stood there and stared at us.

"Those teams were even more lopsided," he said before flashing us a big smile. "Still took all four of you to take me down."

"Yeah, but it got the job done," I said, smiling and wiping my hands.

"Way to go, Riles, bringing down the champ," Chewie said as he held up his hand. I high-fived him.

Laughing and catching our breaths, we headed back to our spot to dry off. As we walked, Sky placed her hand on my arm and stepped in close to me. "You know, normally, it'd just be the three of us out here playing around, since Jax never joins our little roadside excursions. But personally, I subscribe to 'the more the merrier' mantra, so I'm glad you're here and you're getting him out of his Fortress of Solitude."

Her kind words made me feel warm and fuzzy. "Aw, thanks."

Back at the lounge chairs, Chewie snapped a wet towel at Kev, who turned around and snapped Chewie back. Sky put on a pair of white sunglasses that covered half her face while she sprawled out on a lounge chair to soak up some rays.

I watched them with amusement as I started drying out my hair. "It's awesome that you guys can just stop the bus wherever and hit up a water park. More jobs need to offer water park trips during the workday." But then an unflattering image of Palmer in a speedo flashed across my mind and I shuddered.

"Although coming here with my boss would be pretty gross."

They all laughed. Kev started wiping sunscreen across his bare, muscular chest. "Yeah we're always down for some fun. And it helps that unlike most bands, we all get along pretty well. Usually." Kev rolled his eyes over at Jax who narrowed his, but then Kev smiled warmly at me. "You know, it almost feels like you're part of the band too, Riley."

I felt my face flush. Kev could be such a sweetheart.

"That's me, cowbellist extraordinaire." I pantomimed playing the cowbell in an exaggerated fashion for a few seconds. "But seriously, I'm glad you think I'm fitting in so well. You've all made me feel so welcome on the tour."

"Word," Chewie said, nodding and patting water off his pale arms with a towel. "Yeah, because otherwise, it'd probably be pretty awkward."

I looked at him, confused. "Otherwise what'd be awkward?"

"I mean it'd be awkward if we weren't so cool, considering what's going on with you and Jax."

I froze. "What do you mean?"

"You know," Chewie said.

My pulse raced. I blinked rapidly. "Oh you mean since we're becoming friends?"

Chewie stopped patting himself off and gave me a wry look. "No, I mean, considering that you two are a thing."

The towel I'd been using to dry my hair fell to the ground. An unwelcome weight pressed against my chest.

"I—I don't know what you're talking about," I said. My eyes darted around, avoiding anyone else's eye contact, and I spotted an ice cream stand. "Hey does anyone want any ice cream?"

"It's pretty obvious, Riley." Chewie smiled. "We've known about you two since Vegas. It's all good."

I glanced at Jax and he shrugged. Apparently he didn't know about it any more than I did.

"You all know?" I asked tentatively, and they all nodded, " . . . and you're all okay with it?" I twisted my fingers. "I don't want to cause any drama."

"So long as we keep rocking," Chewie said, "I'm down for whatever. You're a cool chick, Riley, and I think you'll be good for this big guy."

"Yeah, I think you two are cute together," Sky said, her brow arched high above her sunglasses. "You've got this whole Bonnie and Clyde vibe."

"I'm happy for you two." Kev added, his blue eyes sparkling in the sunlight. "Don't worry, we'll keep this just in the band. We know it might be weird with you being the tour accountant and all."

I exhaled deeply. I was relieved that the band was being so cool about it and I was happy that it was one less thing I had to worry about. This now meant that Jax and I didn't have to hide the fact that we were together. I looked at Jax and he wore a big, satisfied grin.

"Aw, thanks guys," I said. "That means a lot to me to hear you say that."

Jax smacked his hands together. "Cool, now that that's settled, let's get back to enjoying this water park."

Chapter Twenty-Two

ICE CREAM

I felt drained after all the running around from the water fight. Sky stayed sprawled on a lounge chair tanning herself while Kev and Chewie continued chasing and shooting each other with their water guns.

I started heading away from the pool area but Jax grabbed my arm and looked at me with a frown on his face. He grabbed Sky's bottle of suntan lotion from a lounge chair. "Wait, before we go, come here. Your skin needs sunscreen."

"I rarely get any color so I could always be working on my tan . . . but my skin is pretty sensitive, so thanks," I said. It was sweet that he was thinking of me. All the fun we'd been having must've distracted me from applying any.

Pulling my wet hair to the front of my neck, I turned around and felt Jax's presence up close behind me. I heard the lotion squirt. Even though I was expecting it, I was still shocked by the sudden coolness of the sunscreen he slathered onto my back. I started swaying along to the movement of his hands against my body. I wanted to feel them everywhere across my skin, all at once.

He reached around me and rubbed his hands across top of my chest, getting dangerously close to my bikini top. I felt his warm breath on the back of my neck as he said, "I like this bikini a lot more when I'm holding it in my hands."

His soft whispering into my ear made me melt into a puddle of desire. "Too bad we're not in the bus' hot tub."

"It's the perfect time to sneak away," he growled into my ear, his hands still kneading the lotion into my chest. "I need you now."

Quivering with arousal, I licked my lips at the primal urgency of his voice. But as badly as I was aching for him, I still wanted to stay in the park for now, since we were having so much fun. "The hot tub will be there waiting for us, let's just finish enjoying the waterpark." Pulling his arms to the side, I grabbed his hand and kissed the back of it then I turned around to face him.

Smiling slyly, he said, "You know better than to think that I'm that easily discouraged."

The fact that we were standing there having this discussion meant I was well acquainted with his perseverance, but he had to have been equally familiar with my stubbornness by now. "Later. I promise. Besides, just because the band is cool with us now doesn't mean we need to rub it in their face." Grinning, I slipped the suntan lotion bottle from his hand. "You want me to get you too?"

Jax shrugged. "My skin doesn't burn, but it's good to keep my tattoos from drying out."

I squirted the sunscreen into my hands and wiped the white lotion up and down both of his tatted arms. Dabbing out a bit more sunscreen, my hands swirled it over his naturally bronzed chest and I bit my lip as I fingered his nipple rings. My palms moved lower against his washboard abs and I traced the V-shaped groove of his pelvis muscle. His muscle lines hypnotized me and my hands almost continued going down his shorts before I shook my head and stopped myself at the last second.

When I finished, I looked up and saw that several women had been greedily watching my show, whispering to each other.

Jax turned to see where I was looking. He let out a low chuckle when he saw the women. "Don't worry about them. They're just jealous because you're a rock star's girlfriend."

Girlfriend? The word sent a jolt of excitement fluttering to my belly. Was that what he thought of me now? Even though it was intimidating that we had come so far, so fast, I could probably get used to the idea.

Jax grinned at me, giving me a quick wink.

I glanced over at the women staring at us again and felt a burst of pride, knowing that they all wanted to be in my position.

I sighed pleasantly. It seemed like everything was in its right place. Jax and I were going well, the band approved of our relationship, my employers still didn't know about us, and the budget was under control. And to top it off, I was a shoo-in for that bonus with a very real possibility for a promotion. It was as if nothing could go wrong.

The sunscreen's initial chill quickly faded, and with the sun beating down on us, I wanted something to cool me down. But it would've been silly to go jump in the water after applying all this sunscreen since it would just wash right off. Looking around, I spotted an ice cream stand across from the water slides. I'd suggested it earlier just to get the band off the scent of what was between Jax and me, but now it really did sound like a good idea. "Ooh I'd love some ice cream right now. Let's go get some."

Jax shook his head slightly. "How about some funnel cake instead?"

"No way, it's too hot for that. Come on, let's cool off with some ice cream."

He studied my face with discerning eyes and after a moment said, "Fine, let's go." He grabbed my hand and we headed over to the ice cream stand.

I leaned into Jax as we strolled past teenagers playing with water guns. "I'm so relieved we don't have to hide us being together anymore."

"Yeah, I'm relieved too," he said, his eyes darting around at the ice cream cones that people had in their hands.

I impatiently stepped to the back of the long line. People walked away from the counter with big swirled curlicues of vanilla and chocolate soft serve, making my mouth water more and more with each one I saw.

"I can't wait for mine—it's been ages since I've had some soft serve. I think I'm going to get the vanilla-chocolate swirl. How about you?"

"Vanilla," he answered immediately. "I want vanilla."

"That's surprising. I definitely would've pegged you for more a chocolate sort of guy."

He shifted on his feet and rubbed the back of his neck before stopping and flashing me a grin. "You should know by now that I'm full of surprises."

"It's true. And I like your surprises, they're sweet and thoughtful." I crossed my arms and stuck out my bottom lip. "It's stupid surprises like Connor yesterday that suck."

He brushed my damp hair behind my ear and looked me deeply in the eyes, comforting me with his warm gaze. "Forget about him, Riley. He's nothing. He's less than zero."

"I know, Jax. Thanks again." I stepped up on my tiptoes and gave him a quick peck on the lips. "For everything."

We finally got to the front of the line and I ordered my ice cream. Jax paused for a brief second and then ordered a vanilla cone. When the server handed us our twisting towers of ice cream, Jax's face lit up.

As soon as we started walking away, I immediately started licking at mine, savoring its coldness and enjoying its sweet flavor. I couldn't help but notice that Jax was holding his cone in front of him and watching it intently.

"If you don't eat it soon, it's going to melt all over your hand," I teased him.

"I'm appreciating it," he said still staring at it. "It's not everyday you get a chance to appreciate a perfectly shaped ice cream cone."

"Shouldn't you be appreciating it with your mouth instead of your eyes?"

He finally looked up and turned to me with soft eyes. "Ice cream's a lot like childhood. It goes by so fast that before you get a chance to appreciate it, it's gone forever. All that remains is dirty hands and fleeting memories of lost innocence."

I grinned, savoring the cold sweetness of the ice cream in my mouth. "I'm having a hard time imagining you as anything close to innocent."

"We were all kids once," Jax said quietly. He paused for a moment before he returned my smile with a little smirk and took a lick of his ice cream.

A cold trail of melted liquid crept down my hand, so I returned to enjoying my treat before it was all lost to a fleeting memory too.

We walked back to where the rest of the band was relaxing. Sky was still tanning on a lounge chair by the pool while Chewie and Kev ran around squirting each other with their water guns. I was amazed at how much energy Kev and Chewie still had to run around like little kids.

Chewie chased after Kev, who jumped over Sky reclining on a lounge chair. "What the hell?" Sky yelled. "Can't you two go play your games on the jungle-gym with the other kiddies?"

Kev stopped in front of Jax, and then Kev turned to face Sky. "Sorry, just trying to get away from the Abominable Chewman."

While Kev was standing there apologizing to Sky, Chewie took aim and fired away. Kev ducked. Chewie's watergun stream sailed over Kev's head and hit Jax's ice cream, knocking it off the cone and splattering it across his bare chest.

The look of childish innocence on Jax's face immediately vanished. His nostrils flared and his chest heaved as the melted ice cream dripped from his pecs to his abs.

Kev stood up, looked at the mess on Jax's chest, and his face scrunched up. "Whoa, Jax, sorry about that. Who would've thought Chewie's aim would be that good?"

"What the fuck, man?" Jax tossed the empty cone at Kev. "I just got that ice cream and you ruined it— you fucking ruined it."

"Jax!" I cried, but before I could stop him, he grunted and angrily shoved Kev.

Kev stumbled back a few steps. His arms came up to balance himself, but his foot hit the edge of the pool and he tumbled backwards into the water, sending up a splash in his wake.

My jaw dropped. Sky ripped off her sunglasses, and even Chewie looked shocked as they rushed over to help Kev. Sky shook her head and turned to Jax. "What's wrong with you? It's just some ice cream."

Kev pulled himself out of the pool, refusing anyone's help. "What a dickbag. Jeez."

Jax blinked his eyes repeatedly, as if awakening from a daze. "It's—fuck it, I need to get out of here." He turned and headed toward the exit, leaving me with my mouth hanging open in shock.

I felt compelled to apologize on behalf of Jax. "Sorry, Kev," I said, putting my hand on his wet shoulder and smiling apologetically. "Are you okay?"

"Thanks, I'm fine," he grunted, his pride still sore. As far as I could see, the only part of him that was hurt. "It's not your fault. I don't know what the hell got into that asshole."

"Has he ever done anything like this before?" I asked as Chewie handed Kev a towel.

Kev wrapped it around himself and Chewie shook his head. "No—I mean he's always been moody, but all of us got along pretty well."

Sky nodded in agreement. "This is the first time I've seen him this upset over something so stupid. I don't know what's gotten into him."

I sucked in a deep breath and pinched the bridge of my nose. I was deeply concerned about Jax and the way he acted. It just didn't make any sense that a guy like Jax would get so upset over something as trivial as spilled ice cream when we were having so much fun just a little while ago.

I decided to go after him. Whatever was on Jax's mind, maybe I could cheer him up, or at the very least, calm him down.

"You guys should enjoy the rest of the waterpark. I'll see if I can talk to Jax," I called over my shoulder as I headed out to look for Jax.

Chapter Twenty-Three

TALK

When I finally spotted him, he was walking fast through the parking lot, a couple hundred yards ahead of me. No matter how hard I picked up my pace, it seemed like he was always going faster. I saw him vanish into the bus when I was still only halfway through the huge lot.

When I finally got to the triple-decker at the far edge of the parking lot, I wasted no time in heading for the stairs.

I tiptoed up to Jax's room, then stood near the door, trying to figure out what was going on inside.

Silence greeted me.

I wondered if he was napping—or fuming. I took a deep breath. *Here goes nothing*, I thought as my hand lifted to knock.

Just as my knuckles were about to rap against the door, it opened, and Jax emerged. Still dressed in his waterpark clothes, he had a shirt and pants draped over one arm and a towel over the other.

"Jax—" I started.

"Not right now," he said, his voice gruff. "I need a shower."

I sniffed at the air and realized we both still smelled like chlorine. Before I could even answer him, he had already turned away and was walking down the stairs.

My brows furrowed. *Well, that wasn't great*. With a sigh, I opened the door to Jax's room and then gasped at what I saw inside. Torn sheets of paper lay all over the bed, and everything on his shelf had been knocked down onto the floor.

Whatever was wrong with Jax, I knew I couldn't leave the room the way it was. I started picking up the pieces of paper and setting them in a box on the shelf. I grabbed his guitar, put it back where it belonged, and smoothed the sheets across the bed.

I sat on his bed, waiting for him to finish his shower and come back, hoping a little cool-down time was all he needed to be himself again. When the handle twisted and he pushed the door open, I looked up to see Jax step into the room. He was wearing a fresh set of jeans and a t-shirt. One of his eyes twitched as he saw that the room had been cleaned up.

I wanted to talk but I had no idea what to say. "Did you have a good shower?" I heard the words coming from my mouth, but I felt like I was far away.

"Yeah," Jax said, his face barely moving. "Not enough hot water. But close enough."

We sat in silence, each of us looking at the wall.

Outside the bus, faint cheery music from the water park played. My hands fidgeted on my knees. Jax stared toward the door, looking like he wished he could leave.

"So how are you feel—" I started.

Jax's voice broke in. "Do you want to watch a movie?"

I turned my head toward him curiously. *A movie?* "I . . . sure. What movie?"

His hand had moved to a binder full of Blu-Rays before I'd even finished talking. He thumbed through the discs, then pulled one out. I leaned to see if I could read any text on its surface, but he popped it into the player before I could make anything out.

Without a word, he crawled into the bed and sat beside me. The disc played, and a logo appeared, followed by a flurry of black bird wings. Text popped onto the screen:

The Birds

Another Hitchcock movie? It seemed like Jax watched them a lot, maybe he saw them as the film equivalent of comfort food. I felt suddenly hopeful. If Jax wanted to watch something comforting, maybe he'd be willing to talk afterward.

After a few minutes, I had snuggled in against Jax. A woman in the movie was riding on a boat toward a harbor, when out of nowhere, a seagull swooped down and attacked her, making her head bleed. I winced at the gull's bite—not just because it looked painful, but because the aggression coming out of nowhere reminded me of Jax shoving Kev into the water.

I looked at Jax who was staring at the screen, but his stony face gave away nothing. What was going on in his head? I couldn't figure it out, and it was driving me a little crazy. Nothing had happened that was out of the ordinary, but he'd snapped at Kev as if Kev had actually meant to knock over his ice cream and then blew it way out of proportion.

My eyes flitted back to the screen nervously. My general feeling of anxiety intensified with every sharp swell of music and every seemingly ordinary dialogue line. Even a scene with a children's birthday party seemed ominous—and then it happened. Like a flash, a flock of seagulls descended on the children, and the party guests all ran screaming into the house.

I jumped at the sudden attack and quickly felt embarrassed. If this was how I was feeling as the movie started, how was I going to sit through the whole thing?

"Hey, Jax?" I said quietly.

"What?" He sounded annoyed.

"Can we stop the movie for a minute?"

Without a word, he flicked a button on the remote control. Two actresses were suddenly paused on screen, gazing into the sky apprehensively. Jax kept looking straight ahead at the still frame.

I hesitated. He was clearly still in a bad mood, but I didn't know how to stop it without finding out what was wrong.

"What happened out there?" I asked, trying to stay as neutral as possible.

A smile slid across his face, charming, wide and completely fake. "So I overreacted," he said, his voice a breezy brush-off. "He'll do something to get me back later. Don't worry about it."

He reached toward the remote again.

"When I was a kid," I said, fast enough to stop him from pressing the button, "My family had this cat, Gonzo."

He looked at me, puzzled.

"He was my best friend when I was little." I closed my eyes, remembering. "He'd sleep on my bed every day. But then, one day, I laid down in my bed and he bit me. Hard."

Jax tilted his head. "I don't understand . . ."

"Gonzo kept doing it, more and more. My parents were furious. They yelled at him, tried shutting him away when he bit. Nothing worked. So they decided to put him to sleep."

"Oh." He averted his eyes and his mouth turned down. "I'm sorry."

"When we went to the vet, I was sobbing," I continued. "But the vet said Gonzo wasn't biting because he'd turned mean. He had an infection, and we were hurting him whenever we tried to pet him."

Jax looked back to the movie screen and his glance fell to the remote. "Okay. So what happened?"

"We gave him some antibiotics, and he was as good as new."

He squinted at me and picked the remote back up. "I'm . . . glad the story had a happy ending?" he offered.

"I'm glad, too," I said, my voice stronger now. "When Gonzo bit me, we shouldn't have asked why he was being mean. We should have asked what was wrong. It would have saved us all a lot of pain."

Jax stiffened, and his head turned toward me slowly. Looking straight into my eyes, he asked, "Why are you telling me this?"

I met his gaze. He'd helped me talk about Connor—now it was my turn to help Jax. "Because you weren't acting like yourself earlier. And because I don't want to wait for it to boil over again for us to talk about it."

"Don't worry about it," he said. "It's just something I need to deal with."

"What is?"

"It's . . . not about the band, and it's not about you."

"Then what *is* it about?"

His glance went back to his hands, which were fidgeting in his lap. I'd never seen him looking so nervous. "I've never talked to anyone about it," he said. "And I'm not starting today."

I couldn't take that as an answer—if I pretended to let it go, I knew it would just gnaw at me the way Connor's secrets had. "Jax, if we're going to be together, I can't deal with you hiding your feelings any time the going gets tough," I said, keeping my voice as gentle as I could. "I—I told you about Connor. I told you what that relationship did to me."

His body tensed. "And you think I'm just like him."

"No, I know you're not," I said softly, reaching out a reassuring hand. "But you're keeping secrets from me, and that hurts. Maybe if I'd never met Connor, it wouldn't hurt so much. But I can't help how I feel now."

"And I can't help being the person I am," he said, folding his arms across his chest.

My vision blurred with tears, but I didn't let them spill over. "Please, Jax?" I asked. "I just . . . I don't want to have to go back to therapy. I don't want my life to be all about secrets and lies."

"I'm not keeping secrets," he said brusquely. "I just don't tell my whole life story to people I've only just met."

I recoiled, and felt one of the tears I'd been trying to hold back roll down my face. "Fine," I said, trying to keep the hurt out of my voice. "I guess that's how it is."

"Shit," he said, looking suddenly ashamed. "I'm sorry. I shouldn't have said that."

"You're right. You shouldn't have." I wiped the tear away with my sleeve.

"I just—I never do this kind of thing."

"What?"

He sighed and shrugged, shaking his head. "Talk about myself."

I clasped my hand around his and looked into his dark eyes. "Jax, tell me straight up. Do I mean anything to you? Or am I just a novel alternative to your regularly scheduled groupie programming?"

He closed his eyes. "You shouldn't have to ask that. You mean a lot to me, Riley. More than you know."

Frustrated and confused, I blurted, "Then why can't you talk about it? Don't you trust me?"

"I trust you more than," he paused, then squeezed my hand, "more than anyone. And more than I should. It's not that."

I felt myself crumpling inward. "What *changed* between us, Jax? I feel like you were open with me before and now you're not."

His voice rose aggressively. "It's got nothing to do with you! Why don't you get that?"

"Then what's it all about?" I asked, practically pleading. "Help me understand."

A tortured half-smile twisted his mouth. "Help you *understand*?" he asked, his words punctuated by a sad, staccato laugh. "Riley, you're never going to be able to understand."

His condescending tone made my cheeks hot with anger. "Stop talking to me like I'm a child," I said sharply. "Dammit, Jax, stop pushing me away!"

His scarred eyebrow raised almost imperceptibly, and he took a deep breath. "Riley, what did you do for your fourteenth birthday?"

I tried to remember. Was this Jax's way of giving me a story back in exchange for the one I'd told about Gonzo? "We went to Applebees," I said, then corrected myself. "No, wait. That was the year of the disastrous sleepover. Mina gave Chloe a haircut so bad she actually cried."

His eyes closed softly and he nodded. "For my fourteenth birthday I . . . woke up on a park bench," he said. "I'd been saving cans for days, hoping to have enough to get twenty, thirty, maybe even forty bucks from the recycling center. I wanted a real meal, at a real restaurant."

My eyes were wide, but I couldn't say anything. Jax had been homeless at fourteen?

"When I woke up, I found out someone had stolen the whole bag I'd saved," he said, his body starting to rock back and forth gently. "The sky was grey. My stomach was growling. And all I could do was . . . scream."

I realized the tears had started falling down my cheeks again. Jax opened his eyes back up and looked at me. "I know you want to understand what I've been through," he said, reaching up a hand to dry the tears. "But our pasts are different worlds. Some things . . . you can't understand. And you don't want to. You're lucky."

He was right. There was no way I could understand how he'd grown up. I'd never been out on the streets before. I'd never even been close. "I'm really sorry, Jax," I said. "I didn't know."

"Well, now you do."

I looked uncomfortably at my lap as a full minute passed by quietly. "I . . . one thing I don't get," I said, breaking the silence. "What did your fourteenth birthday have to do with Kev and ice cream?"

His expression darkened. "Riley, didn't I tell you not to ask about it?"

"Yes, but—"

"Good."

"Look, Jax, we have different pasts, but that doesn't mean we can't talk now. I'm right here."

"You don't get to win this one, Riley. Drop it." His expression was flat, unreadable, and he turned away.

Frustrated, I rolled over in the bed. I wanted to be a good girlfriend—I wanted to help Jax get past his fears instead of hiding from them. But no matter how hard I tried, he wouldn't budge.

I couldn't help hot tears from rolling down my cheeks. I wiped them from my face in a hurry, embarrassed that I was crying over something like this, but as I did, more came rolling down. Why was I getting so upset over this? I never would've imagined

Jax shutting me out would hurt as much as it did. But the more I thought about it, the more I realized just how far I'd fallen for him.

Jax had been right when he said that we hadn't known each other for that long, but it felt like so much longer. My fear all this time had been what would happen if I gave in to him, but now for the first time, I began to fear what would happen if I lost him.

I curled into myself. It was like the pillow wall had been put back up and Jax, laying beside me, was a million miles away. With the pain in my chest eating away at me, I began to worry that I was getting myself in too deep. The more time I spent with Jax, and the closer we became, the more he'd be able to hurt me.

Chapter Twenty-Four

ALONE

I tossed and turned most of the night in Jax's bed as he slept soundly next to me.

Thankfully, I must've dozed off sometime in the middle of the night since the next time I opened my eyes, sunlight streamed through the windows. Frustrated from my fitful night's sleep, I rolled over and realized I was the only one in bed.

"Jax?" Still woozy, I rubbed my eyes and scanned the room. There was no sign of him.

We still hadn't spoken since our troublesome talk yesterday and both of us went to sleep angry at each other, all of which made his absence worrisome. The last time I woke up and he wasn't around, he'd been planning our hotel getaway at the Palms. And while he could've been out making similar arrangements to make up for being so walled-off yesterday, I couldn't shake the feeling that because of how we left things, this time it was different.

I wanted to know where Jax was, so I got up to look around the bus. Something was off though. There were no other footsteps, or music blaring, or any sounds of any sort.

After not finding anyone on the first and second floor, I went up to the sundeck and saw that we were parked amidst a grove of trees nestled in between rocky hills. In between the trees, I could see white stone columns and rows of red seats built into the hillside. It was The Roman, tonight's historic outdoor venue. It was one of the hottest places to hold a concert in Los Angeles. And tonight's show was special because it was going to be recorded for a live concert DVD.

I figured the band must've gone inside the venue to practice early and Jax was with them. Still though, it would've been thoughtful if he would've at least left me a note or something.

Even though Jax and I had issues we needed to work out, he'd made it clear that he didn't want me to push him to talk, so I figured I'd wait until he decided to broach the subject.

Because of all the headaches and hanging out during the past few days, I had a lot of catching up to do before tonight's show so I went through my morning routine and then shifted myself into work mode. I spent the whole day on the bus' first floor couch, tossing around my laptop, hastily shuffling through papers, and shooting off brusque emails to my co-workers.

Later that afternoon, as I stretched out my stiff back, my phone started ringing. I eagerly grabbed it, hoping it was Jax calling to apologize.

But it was only Jen. Even though I'd gotten my hopes up for Jax, I was still happy to see her name show up. I answered and we chit-chatted for a bit. It was great to catch up with her and hear all the latest gossip about Hans Peterson. The whole time, though, she wouldn't stop pestering me about Jax. Reluctantly, I gave her a few juicy snippets. But once I let a little slip out, I couldn't stop, and I spilled everything that'd been going on. After I finished bringing her up to speed, including telling her how I woke up alone this morning and haven't heard from Jax all day, there was a silence on the other end.

Jen cleared her throat. "I'm not trying to make any waves here, Rye, but as one of your very good friends, I feel like I should say something. Now, I know you're the expert on bad boys, but I just watched this documentary on TV about them. This is how it always starts. First they wall themselves off, then they cut themselves loose. And usually with no explanations or anything."

"Oh stop, you're over-exaggerating," I said, letting her words fly out the other ear. I knew she meant well, but I also knew that Jax and I had something special. "Trust me, Jax might be a bad boy, but he's . . . different."

"If you say so, but if things go south, don't say I didn't warn you."

After we said our goodbyes and hung up, Jen's words haunted me. *First they wall themselves off, then they cut themselves loose*. But I knew Jax wouldn't do that to me. I thumbed around on the phone's screen, ambivalent over whether I should text Jax. I wanted to see how he was feeling, but I was resolved to let him make the next move. I tossed the phone down and went back to work.

I worked for a little while longer when muffled laughs and footsteps trickled up from the door. I held my breath, anxiously waiting to see if Jax was coming up the stairs. Chewie, Sky, and then Kev burst in from the stairwell. Kev looked a little irritated. I was guessing that Jax still hadn't made up with Kev because I knew he hadn't apologized yesterday. I wanted to ask about it, but I also didn't want to open up any closed up wounds.

"Hey guys, ready for the show?" I asked, keeping my eye on the door. When Jax didn't appear behind them, I realized that he must've stayed behind in the venue, maybe to keep practicing.

Chewie smiled. "Wait 'til you see how hard we're gonna rock The Roman." He started headbanging for a second, and then stopped and said, "Man, I'm probably gonna win an Oscar once they release the DVD."

I couldn't help but smile at Chewie's exuberance. "Can't wait to take it all in from the sidelines. So what have you guys been up to all day? Practicing for tonight?"

"Nah, this entire tour's been one long practice sesh," Chewie replied with a blasé wave. "They've got this badass arcade in there and I've been wasting these two in videogames all day."

Kev rolled his eyes. "You won one game, Chew. One."

"Yeah, the final winner-takes-all game," Chewie said, confidently crossing his arms.

Sky shook her head at the two of them. "How's your day going, Riley? Thought you'd be off spending it with Jax before the show."

The sound of his name made me sigh. I wished things were good enough between us to be on a date right now, I'd much rather be laughing and drinking with Jax than working and lamenting here on the bus by myself. "Nope. I've been working all day keeping your wallets stuffed." I paused. "Actually, I thought Jax was with you guys . . ."

Sky's usual perky smile withered away and she furrowed her brow. "He's not here? That's odd. He wasn't answering his texts so we came back, hoping to find him here."

Jax isn't with the band? Was he avoiding me? Was he avoiding everyone? I suddenly worried that yesterday's conversation had upset him so much that he went out to brood with his phone turned off. My stomach began to twist.

"Um, yeah," I said, "he's not here. I haven't seen him all day, and I haven't talked to him since last night."

"Yeah," Kev said, crossing his arms. "I haven't heard from him after pushed me into the pool either."

"Well he did tell me he overreacted about that," I said. "And I'm sure he'll make it up to you next time you see him."

"We'll see," Kev said, with a hint of disbelief.

I felt a little embarrassed admitting that I didn't know where my boyfriend had been all day long. *What kind of girlfriend goes an entire day without knowing her boyfriend's whereabouts?* I didn't like being so out of the loop. I couldn't help feeling like this had shades of Connor written all over it—me sitting around twiddling my thumbs waiting until he decides I'm worth his time. I could feel myself getting flustered, and I realized I needed to clear my head.

Sky glanced at her watch and then scrunched up her face. "Fuck. We need to do a soundcheck, and we need to do it like right now."

"Yeah, this is a huge show tonight." Kev raked his fingers through his blonde hair. "Our set has to be pitch perfect."

I'd told myself I was intent on letting Jax contact me first, but since he hadn't been with the band and he hadn't called me all day, I decided that it'd be a good idea to check in with him. "I'll call him and see if he answers for me." I pulled out my phone and dialed his number. My nose wrinkled when it went straight to voicemail. "Hey Jax, just here with the band. You're needed for soundcheck. Either give me a call or I guess you can just meet up with them inside. Okay. Bye."

I hung up, dismayed by how weird my voice sounded in my ears. I tried being as nonchalant as possible, but I couldn't help sounding a little rattled.

Sky tilted her head quizzically. "That's not good. This is our first outdoor gig of the tour, so he knows we need him for a soundcheck."

"I have faith he'll turn up," I said, unsure of the words as they left my mouth.

"Let's hope so," Sky said with a calmness in her voice that belied her visible irritation. "Well, Jax or no Jax, we need to do a soundcheck now. It'd be nice if he graced us with his presence." She paused. "Riley, would you have time to search The Roman to see if he's off hiding anywhere?"

"Will do."

"Thanks!" Sky said as they hopped off the bus, all of them mumbling concerns about Jax's whereabouts.

Slightly troubled, I packed up my work and left the bus shortly after them to seek out Jax. I had no luck asking the roadies, and a hopeful search of the venue turned up squat. It was getting close to showtime, so I had no choice but to reluctantly inform the band of the bad news.

I clenched up my fists and headed toward the stage, rueing this feeling of failure. Jax's disappearing act upset me, and this prolonged silence was starting to cut into me deeply. How would we ever be able to resolve our issues together if his immediate reaction was to run away? If this was how he dealt with all of his problems, I didn't know how long I could endure it.

As I grudgingly approached the stage, I heard the disjointed music from the soundcheck along with the band's grumblings into the mics as they voiced their frustrations about Jax not being around to offer up his input and expertise. A roadie sang and played guitar in Jax's stead, but he was woefully underwhelming in every aspect. At the same time, the film crew prepped their cameras and lighting equipment to record the concert video and the director cursed up a storm about having to guess the camera angle positioning for Jax's towering physique.

I grimaced listening to the band struggle, but the first opportunity I had, I waved to get their attention. They all stopped playing and looked at me with high expectations written all over their faces.

"Any luck?" Sky asked into the mic, her brow raised optimistically.

I wrung my fingers and shook my head slightly. "Sorry, I couldn't find him anywhere. He just vanished."

Glowering, Kev tossed his guitar down and stormed off the stage.

"Thanks anyway, Riley," Sky said, as she and Chewie called it quits a bit more gracefully and disappeared backstage.

I gnashed my teeth together. Jax's absence was getting even more disturbing. Him not being here for soundcheck was already interfering with tonight's performance, and it wasn't like him to put the band on the backburner.

The second they left the stage, the audience started piling in and I decided to follow the band backstage to sweat it out with them.

I flashed my VIP badge at the security guard and headed past the darkened wings of the sidestage. At the green room door, I knocked on it and then peeked my head through. The band was all moping around on black leather couches.

I felt like apologizing to them for Jax's disappearance since I had made him more upset when I tried talking to him. Still, I wasn't ready to share the intimate details of our relationship with the band.

"Anybody get a call from him?" I asked.

"Nope," Kev said, idly strumming an acoustic guitar.

I bit my lip. "He knows how important this show is, right?"

"He better goddamn know." Kev plucked harshly on the strings. "This live concert DVD was *his* genius idea."

Sky checked her watch. "I hope he shows up soon. That film crew was really vocal about wanting to start on time."

"How much time do you have left?" I asked.

"The show's supposed to start any minute now," Sky said, her words dripping with disappointment. "But we can push it back half an hour or so. After that the film crew gets a pay bump."

"Fuck." I leaned against the doorjamb and slightly banged my head against it. It was one thing for bands to start their shows late—hell, it seemed like it was standard operating procedure for the music industry—but I had a feeling this film crew didn't tolerate lateness. "And if he doesn't show?"

"We'll have to cancel the concert," Kev said soberly.

It felt like the floor dropped out on me. If they cancelled the show, it'd mean we'd have to send out refunds to all the ticket holders and it'd utterly wreck the band's budget moving forward. Plus we'd have to eat the cost of the film crew and negate any potential income from future sales of the DVD. Cancelling the show was not an option.

"There's still plenty of time left," I offered. "I'm sure Jax will come walking in any second now . . . " Laughing nervously, I pointed to the doorway, naively hoping he'd magically walk through.

Tapping my foot, too much on edge to stay still, I started pacing back and forth in the green room, anxiously checking my cellphone every minute. A queasy feeling emerged in the pit of my stomach, and every minute that brought us closer to cancellation made the queasiness grow stronger. *How could Jax do this on such an important day?*

A terrible thought snuck into my mind. What if Jax was doing this to hurt me? Was he trying to prove that he was still a loner who wouldn't be tied down by our relationship? I shook my head. Given how much Jax seemed to care about me, the idea seemed too far-fetched.

I watched as Kev strummed his guitar so roughly that I thought he was going to snap the strings. Sky stared ahead frowning as she ran through chords on an acoustic bass while Chewie puffed on a joint, filling up the room with a cloud of smoke.

Half an hour passed and the pay bump for the film crew went into effect. It was going to be a hassle making room for that in the budget. And that hassle would become the headache from hell if they canceled this show.

A knock on the door startled us. We all exchanged expectant glances and I headed to open the door. I didn't think Jax would bother knocking, but there was always a chance . . .

I opened the door to a middle-aged woman standing there with red wavy curls tangled in a headset microphone. "Last call for showtime."

It was the concert producer, Ms. Deetz. I recognized her nasally voice from having a pleasant phone conversation with her regarding the show's ticket pricing.

"Since we're an outdoor venue," she continued, "we have a city-mandated Midnight Power Down Policy, which is stipulated in the contract. Once the clock strikes twelve, it's lights out. So it's now or never folks. What's it gonna be?"

Unsure how to respond to her, I spun around and saw the band huddled together in the center of the room. Their disillusioned faces spoke volumes.

Kev threw his hands in the air. "Fuck it. Let's do it without him. I'll sing the songs."

Sky crossed her arms and gave Kev an unimpressed look. "You know that's impossible."

"She's right," Chewie said, scratching the back of his neck. "You rock, Kev, but fuck, we need Jax here."

"Fuck this noise." Kev kicked the couch. "I can't believe we have to do this."

Sky exhaled loudly. "Looks like we're going to have to cancel. I'll give the bad news to the fans. Hope I don't start a riot."

She trudged out of the green room and we all followed. It was one thing to cancel a show in Anytown, USA—but canceling one in L.A. would be a disaster. Every trendsetting gossip blog, radio show, and podcast in the city would blast the band back into obscurity. It seemed like in one fell swoop, Jax's absence was going to destroy all the Hitchcocks' hard-earned hype.

As we dragged our feet to the stage, the crowd's chants and cheers echoed through the darkened wings of the sidestage. No one said a word and I felt absolutely terrible about everything.

A shadow shifted from a recess and for a split second, I thought I saw a ghost. I looked again but didn't see anything.

But then, from the dark corner, a voice growled, "Everybody ready to rock The Roman?"

Jax suddenly stepped into the light and I breathed a heavy sigh of relief at the sight of him. Dressed in leather pants and a tight black t-shirt with his dark eyes glittering in the backstage lighting, he looked ready to jump on stage.

"Jax!" I cried.

He acknowledged me with a brief smile. I wanted to smile back, but his sudden calm and collected appearance, combined with his day-long lack of communication and last minute arrival, left me too pissed off to manage a smile.

"There you are!" Sky shouted, with her hand over her heart. The relief on her face quickly faded into anger and she punched Jax in the shoulder. "You pompous asshole. I was just about to cancel the show!"

"Dude, finally," Chewie said, slapping Jax's back. "Thought I'd have to be a one-man band up there tonight."

"Now I'd pay to see that," Jax said. Turning to Kev, he held out a small package wrapped in brown paper. "Hey, Kev, I just wanted to apologize for yesterday. There was . . . there was a problem, but it's gone now. I cleared my head and it's over. We cool?"

Kev eyed the package skeptically. "There was an even bigger problem today."

"I'm here now and everything's good to go," Jax said, shaking the package for Kev.

A smirk crossed Kev's lip and he accepted the package. As he slowly unwrapped it, he revealed some sort of electronic device. I had no idea what it was, but Kev's face lit up. "Holy shit, an original Craftmaster Treble Booster? It's impossible to get one of these nowadays. My guitar's gonna sound so sweet now. Thanks, man."

"It was no problem," Jax replied, shrugging it off.

Kev stuck out his hand and said, "Okay, now we're cool."

Both smiling, the two of them shook hands.

The band started heading toward the stage and despite my relief that Jax was back and had made up with Kev, I couldn't help but stew in anger. His disappearance was the sort of untrustworthiness I came to expect from guys like Connor. I'd thought Jax was above and beyond that sort of behavior, but I guess I was wrong. And if running away and not discussing our problems was the only way Jax knew how to deal with things, I didn't know how long we'd be able to keep this up. I needed to talk to him before the show.

I grabbed his arm and held him back. "Jax, where've you been?"

He ran his fingers through his black hair and shrugged. "I had to make amends with Kev."

I waited for him to say more, but when he didn't, all my pent up frustration came bursting out. "I know sometimes you need your space but why didn't you call or text me? I've been worried about you all day. You could've at least let me know where you were."

Jax grabbed my shoulders and kissed me on the forehead like nothing was wrong. "I'm here now, aren't I?"

"That's not the point! We need to talk about this, maybe not right at this moment, but you can't just pretend like nothing is wrong when you disappear for an entire day and almost blow off your own concert."

"Don't worry about it, Pepper," he said, giving me a small smile and a wink. Then he turned and strutted out onto stage as the crowd erupted into cheers, leaving me standing there by myself.

I stood there in disbelief trying to process what just happened. I couldn't believe he had the balls to disappear all day, leave me worried sick, almost screw up the show for *his* band, and then act as if it was no big deal. Confused and hurt, I wrapped my arms around myself, wondering where things were headed with us.

On stage, the band exploded into the first song. It was even more energetic, bombastic, and sexual than usual. Within the first few minutes, a woman rushed out on stage. A security guard quickly caught her before she was able to reach Jax, who continued singing and playing without missing a beat. I could tell it was going to make for a great DVD.

I wanted to enjoy the show, but Jax hurt me. I felt like he tossed me to the side like a dirty tissue while he swaggered around on stage, being his typical seductive rock star self, as if nothing had happened.

I promised myself to have a serious talk with him after this show, even if it meant risking everything we've built together thus far. The status quo was simply not going to work, and I was far too stubborn to drop it. But the thought left me deeply distressed, since if we were unable to talk about our problems, I couldn't picture a scenario where we'd be able to work as a couple. But I clung to the hope that Jax cared for me enough that he'd be willing to talk to me, to open up to me, and let me into his world.

I paced nervously backstage during the show, barely hearing the music above the buzzing in my ears. Whatever was going on with Jax, it was clearly not just going away on its own. As the band took their post-encore bows, I waited for my chance.

Jax, guitar over his shoulder, walked offstage to his dressing room. I took a deep breath, steeling myself for this conversation. Even though I knew it wouldn't be easy, I didn't think I could take another day like this.

I didn't want to give Jax another chance to blow me off until later. I burst through the dressing room door without knocking. His back was turned to me, his ass looking unbelievably taut in the leather pants from the second act.

When the door clicked shut behind me, he whirled around, wearing a grin, until he saw me waiting there, scowling. With a casual raise of his eyebrow, he took off the leather pants and slid on a pair of distressed dark-wash jeans. He was completely, maddeningly silent.

I tapped my foot anxiously while he put his street clothes back on, but he made no sign of being willing to talk to me—or even acknowledge that I was in the room.

"Do you just want to pretend like none of that ever happened?" I finally asked, exasperated.

Still looking away from me as he ran a comb through his hair, Jax said, "None of what?"

I felt my eyelid twitch. "Do you have *any idea* how freaked out the band was?" I asked as my voice rose. "They were less than a minute from calling off the whole show."

"That's on them," he said with a shrug, not meeting my eyes. "If they can't trust me by now, that's their problem. I was here on time for curtain, ready to go."

I shook my head in disbelief. "What's gotten into you? Your band needed you. Where did you go?"

He gritted his teeth, and I saw sweat beading above his brow. "I just needed to be alone, Riley," he growled. "Can't you understand? Alone? The bus is small enough as it is, and I'm sharing my space. I needed to clear my head."

What was that supposed to mean? Was he trying to blame his disappearance on our sleeping arrangements?

"It's not good enough, Jax," I said, trying to keep the hurt out of my voice. "You didn't see how worried everyone was. Do you know what all those ticket refunds would do to your profits, not to mention your publicity? The venue would have been furious. The label would have been furious."

His eyes closed. "Stop it. I don't want to hear about this."

"Then start telling me what's going on! Where were you? Why did you disappear today?"

He wouldn't open his eyes. He wouldn't say a word. He just sat there, still as a stone. I wanted to cry.

"Is this—is this about us?"

"What?"

"I figured it was coming," I said, feeling the words tumbling out of me as the tears flowed. "The tour leg will be over soon, and then I'm going back to New York, and you'll want to break things off before then."

He walked toward me and put his hands on my shoulders. "I don't know what we'll do when the tour stops." I felt my stomach sink. "But I don't want to break up. I promise, everything between us is fine."

"It is *not* fine," I said sharply, then sighed. "I—I know you don't think I can handle whatever's going on, but you're wrong."

He looked away, a thousand-yard stare that made my heart hurt. *What did this to you, Jax?*

"Is it drugs? We can get you into treatment. We can do whatever you need to do. Whatever it is, let's face it together."

His face contorted into a sad smile. "You're too good to me," he said softly. "But I promise you. The only drugs I've done on this tour, you've seen me do."

I didn't understand. Why all the secrecy? Why had he changed so much in a few days? "I can't *help* you, Jax," I said as a heaving sob escaped my chest. "I can't help if I don't know what's going on."

He stepped back, and when he looked at me again his eyes were cold. "You're blowing this way out of proportion. So I've been in a bad mood for a couple of days. Why does that mean you have to fix me all of a sudden?"

I swallowed, willing myself to stop crying so I could talk. "I know what a bad mood looks like. This is something else. I know it is."

Anger glinted in his eyes. He started to say something, then stopped. I saw his hands curl into tight fists as his eyes closed and his breath became slow and steady. When his eyes opened again, they were different, somehow—softer, back to the Jax I'd fallen for.

"I'm sorry," he said, looking ashamed. "I'm not going to tell you that you're seeing things. You deserve better than that, after what that asshole did to you."

I reached out to his shoulder, my heart beating fast.

He took a slow, deep breath, then another. I leaned against his chest. *Jax, please, if you were ever going to be open with me . . .*

His breathing was almost meditative. It took everything I had not to ask more, not to push—I knew by now that if Jax was about to tell me, the worst thing I could do would be to push more.

Just as the silence was becoming unbearable, he spoke quietly. "Okay. I think I can handle it now. I've got it under control."

I felt almost shaky with relief. He was finally going to tell me about his demons. I squeezed his hand. Whatever he said, I was going to be ready.

"Let's go back to the bus," he said, his tone louder and less intimate, as if we were in public. I was suddenly confused. Had someone come in? But as I looked around, it was just the two of us.

Then again, Jax knew better than most that dressing room privacy could be interrupted at any time. "You're right. This is a bad place to talk about personal stuff."

He looked taken aback, and his brow arched skeptically. "Talk? I thought we were done talking about it," he scoffed. "I told you, I've got myself under control. I'm not going to blow up again. You can take my word for it."

"What?" I asked, feeling like I'd just gotten whiplash. "Jax, I thought you meant you could handle talking to me about what happened."

His body tensed, veins popping from his taut muscles. "No. And that's not going to happen. Let's just go back, Riley."

I stood my ground. "I'm not going back until you promise me we can talk about this. I don't know if we can be together if you refuse to even talk when you're so clearly upset!"

He looked into my eyes. "Then I guess the bus leaves without you. Listen, Riley." He reached toward my face, tender even as his words pricked my heart like needles. "I don't do threats, and I don't do ultimatums. You've got a spot waiting for you on the bus whenever you want it. But you don't get to tell me what I have to talk about."

I felt trapped—not wanting to push too far, but unwilling to let his secrets stay between us. Wasn't there a compromise? Wasn't there a way we could both get what we wanted? "I—you're right, Jax," I said as he laced up his boots. "I'm sorry I tried to push you. I don't need you to open up at once, but for god's sake, I need *something* . . ."

His dark eyes pierced through my soul as he stood there, looking at me. For a moment, a strange expression flickered over his face. *Maybe I got through to him after all*. Then, before I knew it, the strange look went away.

When he spoke again, his voice was hoarse. "I'm sorry I couldn't give you what you needed, Riley." Slinging his guitar strap over his shoulder, he left the dressing room.

I thought my heart would break into a thousand pieces.

Chapter Twenty-Five

OVER

Breathe. Riley, just breathe.

I walked toward the bus, determined. My eyes were still dry and red from crying, but I'd cleaned myself up as much as I could in the dressing room mirror.

Jax didn't want to open up, no matter what. But the more I thought about it, the more I realized that for me, losing him was not an option. I wasn't about to give up the best thing that had ever happened to me because of a few bad mood swings.

That meant I'd have to tell him I was sorry for pushing too far. The words of the apology turned over in my head, forming as the bus door opened.

I set my purse down as soon as I got inside and walked toward the bathroom for one last red-eye check. As I opened the bathroom door, I heard footsteps coming down the stairs. My stomach churned with anxiety as I saw Jax's boots at the top of the stairs. *Shit.* I wanted to talk to him alone, not out in the public areas of the bus.

"Oh," I said, trying to keep my cool as he stepped onto the first floor. "I was just coming up to—"

With a shake of his head, Jax let out a sad sigh. His eyes were stormy, unreadable, but he extended a hand toward mine. "Riley, we . . . we need to talk. Take a ride with me."

My fingers turned to ice as his clasped around them. I didn't know what he wanted, but I knew *we need to talk* never meant anything good. "Okay," I breathed, trying to keep myself from shaking. Had I pushed him over the edge? Was it already too late for us?

Wordlessly, Jax led me off the bus and got his motorcycle off the trailer. I followed behind him, in agony.

"I'm really sorry," I said as I watched him untie the bike. "I didn't mean what I said before—what I said about not being able to be with you."

His eyes scanned over the bike once before he threw his leg over the seat. "I know." His voice was quiet, and he wouldn't meet my eyes.

I got on the bike behind him, feeling almost limp, exhausted. Jax tried to start the engine but it sputtered, stalling. After he gave it another kick it roared to life and we started on our way.

By the time we'd ridden a few miles in the warm summer air, I was clinging tight, hoping to remember every detail of the ride. *This could be the last time.* The shopping centers and bright lights of the city were flying by us, and I held onto Jax tighter as we wove through luxury cars—a Ferrari, a Lambo, two identical Bugattis driving side by side.

The warmth of his body in my arms felt bittersweet. In a lot of ways, I'd never fit with someone the way I fit with Jax. I'd certainly never fallen for someone so fast. But it looked more and more like this clear southern California night was the night it would all fall apart.

I knew I should try to hold on to the moment. But all I could do was think about when it would end.

As I watched the landscape around us for a clue as to where we were headed, I saw the expensive, designer brands give way to middle-class neighborhoods and malls. Then, after a few miles on the freeway, my hair whipping in the wind, we got off at an exit that looked nothing like the places we'd come from.

Broken beer bottles littered the off-ramp, and as we came to a stop, I noticed that the stop sign was riddled with bullet holes. My heart skipped a beat as I looked around, but I didn't see anyone—no cars, no pedestrians, not even a stray cat or dog.

This neighborhood looked nothing like the places we'd been to during the tour so far. Ramshackle trailers and tiny, run-down single-story houses crowded against one another. In the distance, dogs barked, and the grass grew long and unkempt in yards where concrete blocks held up the rusting remains of old trucks.

Jax rounded a corner and narrowly avoided a burned-out wreck of a car. It didn't look like it had burned recently. Why had no one cleaned it up or removed it?

Why was he taking me somewhere so desolate? We were totally alone, and no one knew where we were going. My pulse pounded in my ears as he slowed the bike down.

"What the hell?" I said, feeling the panic start to rise at the back of my throat. "Jax, does anyone even live around here?"

"People live here. It's just too dangerous to go out on the street unless you have business to do." He kept his eyes on the road, never looking back toward me.

My mouth was dry. "Wait, you know this place? Where are we going?"

As if to answer my question, he slowed the bike to a crawl, then stopped. He slid off the bike without saying a word, and I looked around, confused.

"Jax, what are you doing? Why are we stopping here?"

The bike's headlamp illuminated one of the strangest and ugliest houses I had ever seen. It looked like a collection of trailers from different eras—at least half a dozen in total—but instead of sitting next to one another, they had been connected together in a lurching, zig-zagging pattern.

"Get off the bike, Riley. I need to show you something." He walked onto the mostly dirt lawn, away from the road.

Something about the house seemed wrong. It wasn't just the shoddy construction or the way the trailers clashed. My instinctual alarms were going off: Desolate area. Bullet-ridden signs. Nobody knew where we were. I'd hurriedly left without my purse and cell phone. It was all adding up to a terrible, Hitchcockian vision in my head. I wanted to scream. I wanted to run away. I wanted to do anything but get off the bike and walk around with Jax.

Jax extended his hand for me to get off the motorcycle, but I just looked at him with wide, terrified eyes.

I saw a sad smile come to his face. "Don't be scared," he said, his voice gentler than I expected. "This is where I grew up."

I gasped. Was he joking? "Really?"

"Yeah."

The look of shame on Jax's face made me feel guilty that I'd ever doubted him. I got off the bike and tried to act normal as I walked across the lawn. "It looks, um . . . cozy."

He raised an eyebrow. "You don't have to sugarcoat it," he said. "It looks like a pile of fucking trash. And it always has."

There was nothing I could say to that. I studied his face, waiting for him to say more. I watched as his face shifted, almost imperceptibly, and realized that he'd started to shake. Fury, pain, grief, shame—I didn't know which one he was feeling, or if all of them had mixed together, but he was quaking with it, his breaths hard and steady.

"I don't know who lives here now, but my dad used to live here—before he went to prison. He was always into something or other," he said, each word halting. "He lived here with me and he never . . . ever . . . let me forget how angry he was at me."

I approached closer. We were in the place Jax had run away from, the place where his nightmares had started. But what had happened in those walls?

"Why was he so angry at you?" I asked.

"It started when . . ." he trailed off. Suddenly, his face became a mask with a thousand-yard stare. "Look, I thought I knew, once. But after a while, I stopped asking. He didn't have to have a reason. I think he was just . . . like that."

"God, Jax," I said, my voice dropping to a whisper. "I'm so sorry. I'm sorry I pushed you."

"You didn't know. You were trying to do the right thing. I'm just too fucked up to talk about it. That's what this house did to me, Riley."

I shuddered. My parents had always been there for me, helping me when my life became chaotic, supporting me when I went to therapy to get over Connor. I couldn't imagine what it'd be like to have grown up in a house like Jax's.

"So you just stayed here until you could run away."

"Yeah," he said, his eyes haunted as they roamed over the connected trailers. "It was my own personal hell."

"And I forced you back here," I said, wincing with a sudden rush of shame as I said the words. I'd thought Jax's problems were on the same level as mine—a bad ex, or a stupid mistake when he was young.

He turned around, looking at the neighborhood. "I never wanted to come here again," he said, his voice threatening to crack. "All I ever wanted to do was forget. Start over, you know? But the closer we got to Los Angeles, the harder it was. Every venue, every mile driven, it all brought us closer to right here. To where it all started."

I stayed silent, waiting for him to finish. His piercing eyes studied the mishmash of trailers intensely.

"This morning," he said, his jaw working, "I couldn't sleep. Every time I closed my eyes I saw—I saw his face and I—I had to go for a ride, clear my mind. I knew I could have told you or maybe Sky or Chewie but I just—I couldn't"

I put a hand on his back. Even through his clothing, I could tell that his muscles were tense.

"And that thing yesterday with Kev was," he started, but then took a deep breath and shook his head, "it was stupid. Just stupid bullshit. It had nothing to do with him."

I nodded softly. I couldn't believe how stupid I'd been, or how pushy I must have seemed to Jax. "I should have listened to you more. I'm sorry."

He turned back to me and stepped close, until we were almost toe to toe. Looking into my eyes, he said, "I know you wanted to help. You thought you could help me move on if I faced the past. You thought you could help me make sense of it." He wrapped me in his arms, and I buried my face in his chest. "And I know you meant well, but . . . I don't *want* that. What happened to me didn't make sense, and it never will. I buried my past because I wanted it to stay dead."

His words tore at my heart. I stepped back to look at him. "Do you just want to bury it forever?"

Jax looked away. "I knew it would happen. As soon as I told you, it'd be alive again. All of it, my whole past—"

"No!" I said vehemently. "I won't bring it up. I won't even mention it, not ever, not if you don't want me to. I promise."

He touched my cheek and his face was so sad that it made me feel like crumpling to the street. "It doesn't make any difference," he said, his voice gentler than I'd ever heard it. "Even if you never talked to me about it, I'd see it in your eyes. In the way you look at me."

The words hurt, but his face made it clear that he truly believed it wouldn't be the same after this. I wasn't sure if he was wrong.

"Jax, I—"

He lifted my chin until our eyes were inches apart. "So I couldn't—I couldn't tell you before and still look in your eyes. But I had to make a choice. It was either my past or you. And I chose you."

My eyes filled with tears. "That means a lot. It means everything."

His dark features hardened. "If you'd asked me before the tour started whether I could look someone in the face who knew where I came from, who I was before . . . I'd have said no. But that was then."

I realized that I was holding my breath in.

"Now . . ." He pondered for a moment. "Now I couldn't stand to lose you."

The humid night air felt still and quiet around us. Only reedy cricket chirps and distant motorcycle engine rumblings disturbed the silence as we looked into each other's eyes.

"I won't keep asking about the past anymore," I said. "I promise."

A half-smile moved across his face. "You can ask whatever you need to. You just need to understand if I don't always want to answer."

I looked up and moved my lips closer to his, hearing the distant rumbling of motorcycle engines. "It's a deal."

His mouth felt like being reborn. Jax's lips were urgent, eager, fierce—I wanted his kiss desperately, but it was clear he *needed* mine. We lost ourselves in each other, right there on the lawn in front of Jax's old house, ignoring the revving engines and the insect buzz.

He wrapped me in his arms, kissing me with the intensity and joy I'd been missing for days. There were no more secrets between us, no more lies, and as his lips searched my mouth, I moaned with lust and relief.

When our lips finally broke apart, I looked up at him almost shyly. For once, he had an almost boyish grin on his face, innocent and playful.

We were going to be alright.

The distant motorcycle engine noise suddenly got louder and headlamps illuminated us as a group of bikers turned down the street. Both of us turned to look at them, but as soon as I did, I was nearly blinded by the bright lights.

Jax's face tightened, and he moved between me and the bikes. One of the bikers, a guy with a red bandana and missing teeth, rubbed at his scraggly beard in a way that made me shudder with disgust.

"Can we go back to the bus Jax? I don't feel safe here," I said.

He looked slowly from them to me, and then back to them. "You're right," he said at last, casting a sidelong glance at his bike, easily twenty yards away. "Come on. We're getting the hell out of here."

Chapter Twenty-Six

THE REAPERS

Jax grabbed my hand and we hurried across the dirt yard, heading toward the curb where he'd parked his bike by the sole streetlamp that was lit on the block.

"Hey, ain't no need to go nowhere, honey," the biker with the red bandana shouted over the roar of their six idling motorcycles in the middle of the street. "We're just 'bout to get the party started."

I shivered in revulsion at Bandana's drunken drawl and picked up my pace as I sidestepped empty beer cans.

Jax must've seen the worry on my face because he said, "They're probably local drug dealers. This neighborhood was overgrown with them when I was a kid. It's why most people stay inside." He squeezed my hand gently. "They're just trying to mess with us. Ignore them."

Everything about Jax's childhood filled me with more and more grief. But his calmness kept me steady, even if an inkling of apprehension bubbled just under my skin. I tried to make the best out of the situation. "Well at least they can't rob me since I left my purse on the bus. But let's just get out of here."

We finally reached his motorcycle and hopped onto the cushioned seat. Safely on his bike, I rested my head on his back and took one last look at the jerry-rigged trailers that served as his childhood home.

I was grateful that Jax brought me here and opened up to me, even though the story about his dad left me completely heartbroken. But that was the past, and we still had our entire future ahead of us.

A sudden silence filled the air as the bikers all turned off their bikes and left them parked in the middle of the street. The way they aligned their bikes looked like it was going to be tricky for Jax to weave his bike through. I was about to tell him that backing up might be a good option instead, but a quick glance behind me revealed some deep potholes in the street.

The sound of shattering glass echoed through the neighborhood. One of them must've thrown a bottle.

Twitching with an urgent desire to flee, I wrapped my arms around Jax's waist. "I'm ready whenever you are."

He jammed the key into the ignition and kicked down on the bike's starter.

The engine revved for a second but quickly sputtered out. The failing motor sounded like a dying animal and I desperately hoped it was just a one-time glitch.

"Uh . . . Jax . . . ?" I asked, trying to mask my concern.

"It can be a little tricky sometimes," he said coolly. "No biggie."

All six bikers simultaneously slithered off their bikes and started strolling towards us. One had a long, braided goatee, another was bald with a drooping mustache that covered his mouth. Another had a face completely covered in tattoos. One wore a sleeveless leather vest covered in patches, while one wore a spiked helmet. And then there was Bandana, who seemed to be the gang's mouthpiece. Wearing faded leather and ripped denim adorned with chains and spikes, they seemed more dangerous than any other bikers I'd seen before. And every step across the potholed asphalt they took made my heart pound harder and faster.

I gripped onto Jax even more tightly and he kicked down on the bike's starter again.

This time there was only a soft click, and it sounded as if something important was broken. I gulped.

"Boss didn't say he was inviting over any fine-ass foxes tonight," Bandana said as he rubbed his chubby belly. "But I can't say I don't like it."

My skin crawled at his skeeviness. *Why the hell are these guys bothering us?* We weren't there to bother any of them. Jax was right, maybe if we just ignored them, they'd leave us alone.

"Everything okay, Jax?" I asked softly, trying to ignore the approaching thugs, but the quiver in my voice betrayed my nervousness.

"Everything's fine." His voice was sharp and low, but he thankfully didn't sound discouraged.

"Everything sure don't sound fine," Bandana said as he led the gang towards Jax's stalled bike. "Tell you guys what. We'll entertain the fine lady while you go take a walk. Maybe you'll luck out and find a mechanic to fix up your Big Wheel."

I felt Jax's body flex up at the guy's words. "My bike's fine," Jax said back to him. "We'll be out of here in a second."

The bikers let out spine-chilling laughs as they stopped in the street and formed a semicircle around the bike. Up close under the streetlamp, they seemed even more intimidating. They all had faces made for mugshots, with wild eyes that seemed to act like radars for mindless violence. I could make out a big patch they all wore on their chest of a skeleton in a purple hooded robe clutching a sickle with one bony hand and a naked lady with the other. It had the words *The Reapers* written beneath it.

My stomach twisted. We needed to get out of here now.

"Hurry, Jax," I cried, patting his arm.

"I'm trying," Jax replied. He was beginning to sound frustrated. Once again, he turned the key and kicked the lever, but the bike failed to start.

"See kid, the thing is," said Bandana, "the cops don't come around here, so we gotta solve our own problems. And when little shits like you start snooping around, that means we got ourselves a problem on our hands. So, first things first, we're gonna hold you two under a citizen's arrest and give this little tart here a thorough strip-search."

"Back off," Jax barked.

Bandana took a mean swig on a bottle of booze, but kept his beady black eyes trained on Jax. He pulled away the bottle, wiped off his scruff, and said, "What the fuck you say to me? Who the hell you think are, trying to boss me around? We just told you that we're in charge around here. Looks like we're gonna have to teach you how to respect the local authority."

His threat sounded real, and I feared if Jax didn't get the bike started a fight was going to break out.

The thugs started tightening the semicircle around us. The thug wearing the spiked helmet whipped something out of his pocket and started flailing it around, making metallic clinking sounds with it. His hand stopped moving and a piece of metal protruded from his fist. I gasped when realized it was a butterfly knife.

Jax suddenly leapt off the motorcycle and grabbed my arm, pulling me off with him. My heart felt like it was pounding in my throat. I held onto Jax as we stepped away backwards, not wanting to take our eyes off the thugs. They blocked off the street and sidewalk, and the only direction available to us was back toward the trailer homes of Jax's youth.

Jax shielded me with his arm as we backed up. "Stay close, Riley."

"Look, we don't want any problems," Jax said, "but if you think you're going to start something, we're sure as hell going to finish it."

I pulled on his arm and whispered, "I think we can make a dash for it if we head to the left."

His dark eyes darted to the side and he nodded slightly.

He nudged me, and we turned and hurried past the left edge of the thugs' semicircle, as I snugly held onto Jax's strong arm. I held my breath, hopeful we'd make it past these thugs and their bullshit.

I suddenly felt a hand wrap around my arm, yanking me back.

"Leave me the fuck alone!" I shouted as I spun around and tried twisting my arm free from the biker with the gross face tattoos. I lashed out like a caged animal and tried kicking him in the balls, but he dodged my foot.

Like a flash of lightning, Jax's arm shot out and clocked the guy, sending him staggering back. I tried to stop myself from trembling in fright, but I knew these guys were going to be seriously pissed.

"Stay there, Riley," Jax said, stepping forward and forming a human barrier between the bikers and me.

"Looks like we gotta teach you some manners now," Face Tattoos said. He cracked his knuckles and spit blood. "We're gonna fucking break you in half now. And if you're lucky, we'll even let you watch what we do to her."

They all swarmed closer in on us as an anxious shaking rippled through my body. Jax reached beyond me and held out his hand. He turned his head back quickly and whispered, "Keep trying to start the bike, I'll draw them away."

I reached in his hand and found the motorcycle keys.

Spiky Helmet swirled around his butterfly knife. Jax got into a fighting stance and drew them out further into front yard, away from the street and the bike. The glint of the streetlight reflected off the blade's sharp edges and a panicked breath caught in my throat.

Holding up the knife, Spiky Helmet charged at him. Jax stood tall until the last possible second before sidestepping the charging biker. But he left his foot out and tripped the thug. It sent the biker's helmet flying off as he fell forward. His chin smacked off the sidewalk and scraped against the concrete, leaving behind a trail of blood.

I yelped at the cracking sound of jaw hitting concrete. No. I had to keep cool and get this bike started so we could get out of here. I slammed the keys into the ignition and gave the throttle and gave the pedal a vicious kick. A weak sputtering sound came from the engine, even worse than before.

Shit!

Turning towards the fight, I saw Jax leap forward and tackle one of the bikers. He held down the thug with one hand and pummeled his face as the other bikers rushed towards him.

Even though I knew I had to keep trying with the bike, I wasn't going to let Jax take on the thugs alone. Looking around for something I could use to my advantage, I noticed that next to the street was a gravel driveway filled with sharp heavy rocks. I hustled over, squatted down, and held up the bottom of my blouse, filling it with as many rocks as I could fit into it and then quickly ran back to the bike and tried the starter pedal again. This time, the engine rumbled more loudly, but still didn't start

Over on the front yard, the burly bald biker ripped Jax off his buddy, and him and Jax wrestled around in the dirt of the front yard as the other bikers kicked them.

I picked out a jagged rock from my blouse, took aim at the bikers, and launched it. *Miss.* I did it again. *Miss.* Everyone was moving around so fast that it made it difficult to hit them.

I whipped another rock and finally managed to hit the guy with the long braided goatee in the eye. He clutched his face as blood splurted out.

I stepped closer and hurled a handful of rocks at the bikers. They rained down like meteors, nailing a few guys in the head.

Bandana turned and saw me. "Now *you* think you're tough shit?" He threw his bottle of booze at me.

I ducked and the rocks fell out of my blouse as the incoming bottle went twirling over my head, landing in the front yard a few feet away.

Howling and grunting, Jax went absolutely apeshit on Bandana. Thankfully he was beating them so badly, they all forgot about me.

Frantic, I tried the bike again, panic rising in my chest. Nothing. Dammit! When were we going to catch a break?

Jax was still holding his own against the bikers, but they just kept getting right back up and going at him. They must've been so drugged up that they weren't feeling any of the pain Jax was dishing out.

I knew Jax was a fighter, but I didn't know how much longer he could keep fending them off. He wasn't superhuman. Yet there he was, with blood splattered all over his white tank top like a butcher after a hard day's work.

The bike didn't seem like it wanted to cooperate and I didn't know if Jax could hold out forever. Even though I didn't have my purse or pepper spray with me, I wasn't going to sit on the sidelines and watch these animals beat the man I loved to death.

I distantly registered the word *love* in my mind before adrenaline surged into me as I rushed towards the bikers.

A loud rumbling sound suddenly filled the humid air and I stopped in my tracks. I turned and saw an old beat-up Cadillac with a fucked up muffler spewing smoke out the back. It stopped in the street by the row of bikes with its headlights illuminating the fight.

A man stepped out of the car and whistled so sharply I thought it'd burst my eardrums.

The bikers all suddenly stopped and dropped their fighting stances. Even Jax froze, still gripping onto one of the bikers' jacket.

Jax's fiery eyes went wide as the color drained from his face.

It looked like he was staring at a ghost.

Chapter Twenty-Seven
ONE SMALL LIE

Jax

Twenty-two years ago.

Jax's breaths were coming fast. His skin was too hot. He was running with all his might, desperately hoping he wouldn't get caught. But he was getting tired and his legs were beginning to feel a tingliness and burning in them. His chest felt sharp and achey. And worse of all, he knew the person chasing him was faster.

He looked to his left and saw a wall of gray not far off; he looked to his right and saw the same. He had nowhere to go except forward, but forward was full of big colors he couldn't run through. He had to make a difficult choice: climb the big colors or try to run around them.

It would slow him down if he climbed, but Jax was good at climbing. He'd climbed up the huge tree in his backyard many times whenever he was scared because it was safe up there. There were a lot of leaves he could hide behind, and it was high enough that nobody could reach him.

If he continued running, he knew it would eventually be over for him.

I can't get caught. I can't let him catch me.

He dashed up the brown steps and lost one of his shoes. The sticky straps on both of them had broken off long ago. He felt lucky that his shoes had stayed on his feet for this long because they usually fell off quickly whenever he ran.

He didn't look back or try to get it. He had to keep moving. He climbed another set of steps and raced toward the yellow and orange striped entrance he'd been looking for.

When he got there, he sank down to his butt, his nerves on fire. The noise in his ears sounded like roaring. His eyes widened as he looked down.

This is it. I'm going to make it. I'm going to get away. If I just push myself forward . . .

He pushed himself forward, but a strong grip on his shoulders stopped him.

"GOTCHA!"

Jax turned his head to look behind him and saw green eyes and a giant grin. He recognized the tiny spots across the boy's nose and cheeks.

"Nooo!" Jax screamed, kicking his legs and flapping his hands in disappointment that his friend, Michael tagged him.

Michael laughed. "Gotcha. Cops win!" Two fingers pressed against the back of Jax's head. "You're under arrest!" he heard Michael cry followed by a spitty explosion sound as the two fingers fired.

Jax laughed and slid down the bright red to the bottom, all the while patting his mouth with his hand as he tried making the sound that Indians make.

Michael followed him with his hands raised in the air in victory and crying, "YIPPEEEE!"

Jax turned to Michael. "Okay, you got me, Michael. My turn now?"

Michael looked down at Jax's feet and pointed to his sock with a hole in the front, large enough for the big toe to poke through. "Haha! Jax, you lost your shoe again!" Michael slapped his own knee and bent over, continuing to laugh.

Jax looked at Michael's shoes. They looked clean, and they looked so cool because they had

Transformers on them. Jax wished he could have shoes like those. Moments later, he went to get the shoe he had lost and came back to Michael.

Before they could start another game, there was a loud, screeching sound. Jax saw Mrs. Appleton blowing the whistle around her neck. "Okay children! Recess is over. Your mommies and daddies are here to pick you up!"

Michael cheered and ran to the entrance where his mom was standing. She had yellow hair and a big smile on her face. She hugged him when he got over to her. Then she gave him a cone with white swirly ice cream on top.

Jax saw his dad's black car sitting on the other side of the street. He couldn't see his dad inside because the windows were dark, but he was pretty sure Daddy was inside. He could tell it was Daddy's car because Daddy's car was always the one with the fins on the back so it looked like a shark.

As Jax was leaving the playground, he heard his name being called.

"Hey Jax!" Michael's mom said. "We have an extra one. Do you want it?"

Jax's eyes lit up. He nodded eagerly and rushed over. "Thanks!" he said as he took the ice cream.

After Jax and Michael said their goodbyes, Jax took a few licks. It tasted so good, he couldn't imagine anything tasting better. He couldn't remember the last time he'd had ice cream.

Jax carried his treat as he walked across the street to Daddy's car, careful to watch out for other cars driving by. He walked around to the other side and opened the door carefully.

He stood on the curb, staring at Daddy in the driver seat, unsure if he should get inside. Sometimes Daddy got mad when he got inside without asking first. But then sometimes Daddy also got mad if he didn't get inside quick enough.

"Hi Daddy," Jax said, as a sort of question.

"Get inside," Daddy said.

Jax released his breath and hopped inside. It seemed like Daddy wasn't in a bad mood right now, which made him happy.

"So, how was school?" Daddy asked.

"Awesome!" Jax cheered. "We made pictures. And we made them with wet, icky stuff that had a lot of colors. Mrs. Appleton said we have to let them dry, so I can't show you today. But tomorrow I can show you."

Daddy chewed something in his mouth for a moment. "You play with that other boy?"

Jax put his finger to his mouth as he thought about his day and who he played with. "Um, who?"

"You know, the one with the mom over there," Daddy said pointing out the window. "That hot lady with the nice butt."

"Oh! That's Michael's mom! She gave me this!" Jax held up his ice cream.

Daddy kept his gaze out the window. "Yep, that's the one." Daddy rolled down the window a little bit and spit brown stuff from his mouth.

"Yeah, I played with Michael. We played cops and Indians!"

"Who won this time?"

Jax hesitated. He'd had so much fun playing with Michael that he'd forgotten that he should've taken it more seriously. He thought about telling the truth, but was afraid of how Daddy might respond if he told Daddy that he lost. "I won, Daddy."

Daddy was quiet for a moment. "Are you telling the truth, Jax?"

Jax suddenly felt like ants were crawling all around in his stomach, eating at the few bites of ice cream that were there. He looked away. "I—I don't know."

"Don't lie to me, boy," Daddy said with a scary voice.

"I—I almost won."

"So you lost?"

"Yeah, but—"

Jax's head smashed into the side window with a crunching sound. He cried out in pain as the world flashed bluish-green.

"I told you not to lie to me, boy. Why don't you ever listen?"

Jax's head pounded. It hurt so bad that he wanted to scream, but he bit his lip to avoid crying. Daddy didn't like crying. All he wanted was to make Daddy happy, but he would always mess up and Daddy would get angry at him and have to punish him for being bad.

"Sorry Daddy," Jax mumbled, fighting back the tears in his eyes. He was so disappointed in himself. He deserved it. "I'll try harder next time."

Daddy took a deep breath.

Just as Jax thought Daddy was going to calm down, Daddy's arm shot out. Jax's head slammed into the window again. And again. And again. And again . . . He didn't know how many times he heard the crunching sound because after a while everything went from bluish-green to black.

When he opened his eyes again, he figured he had fallen asleep and just woken up. His head throbbed and ached all over. It felt like a T-Rex had played jump rope on his head while he was sleeping and now an Indian was banging on it like a drum. The ants from his belly were now crawling all over his eyes, making it hard to see.

He slowly turned to look at Daddy in the driver seat and saw that Daddy's face was no longer red and scrunched up. Daddy didn't look angry anymore.

"Put on your seatbelt, Jax," Daddy said. "I don't want you to get hurt."

The world was still fuzzy and spinning, and Jax wasn't quite sure he understood the words that Daddy had said even though he knew he had heard them.

Belt. Seat. See what bells? . . . There are bells ringing in my head but I can't see them . . .

After a few seconds, Jax somehow managed to do as he was told.

He looked down at his shirt and saw the ice cream had spilled all over it.

As Daddy started driving, Jax tried scooping the white ice cream mixed with red drops on his shirt into his mouth. He thought that if he ate enough, the ants would crawl out of his eyes and go back to his stomach, and then he would be able to see better. But after a few gulps, he realized he couldn't eat anymore. The ice cream tasted like metal.

It made him want to cry even more. He bit his lip harder and balled his fists into his shorts. His eyes felt stingy and wet, but he wouldn't let the tears come down. He wasn't going to blink. He wasn't going to disappoint Daddy and make him angry again.

Crying would just make it worse.

Chapter Twenty-Eight

BURN

Riley

The bikers had stopped fighting and turned their attention toward the source of the whistling—the man who had gotten out of the black Cadillac.

The man had wild shoulder-length hair, grayed with streaks of white. The maroon shirt he wore was unbuttoned, and beneath it was a stained beater that protruded a bit over his belt. His jeans looked worn. His face had bags and deep lines; he looked like he was past his forties, but despite his age, there was something about him that was striking. I couldn't put my finger on it.

The man began walking over. "What's going on here?" he asked in a deep voice. His words lacked any trace of uncertainty, his question more like a command than an answer.

I looked at Jax. His brows were knitted together tightly, his eyes were wide, and his mouth was a thin line. He looked shocked, anguished even, as if he recognized the man coming toward us, and that the man was a ghost. A sudden dread coiled in my stomach.

The streetlamp began to flicker, casting menacing shadows along the empty street. With each step closer the man took toward us, it felt like the night air was getting thicker.

The group of drunk, half-beaten bikers backed away from Jax, each stepping to one of two sides, parting almost in reverence to make a path for the man. I hurried over to Jax to be by his side.

As the man approached us, his shadow eclipsed both me and Jax. I could see now that he was as tall as Jax, and his shoulders were just as broad, if not broader.

He came to a stop a few feet in front of us. "Huh?" he grunted, his dark eyes boring into each of us in turn. "Who the hell are you guys?"

"Darrel," Bandana said as he settled by the man's side, "this asshole's trying to look tough in front of his girl."

I moved closer to Jax, afraid something bad might happen. Although we'd been outnumbered before, Jax had been able to handle all of them by himself. But now, it seemed like their boss was here. Darrel sent off real bad vibes. I didn't know whether it was in that look in his eyes that seemed like he was assessing you, identifying your weaknesses, picking apart your flaws, or in the confident way he walked, like a man who possessed no fear. Whatever it was, I could sense that he was a man capable of being extremely dangerous.

I touched Jax's arm for security, but he didn't so much as turn his head to acknowledge me; he just kept staring forward with blazing intensity, at Darrel, as if he sensed the same danger as I did.

"Oh?" Darrel stepped forward, narrowing his thick, gray eyebrows as he studied us. "What are you guys doing here?"

I looked to Jax for a response, but his jaw was clamped tight. He seemed to be trying as hard as he could to restrain himself from speaking. His mind must've still been on the fight.

"We were trying to leave," I said, in an attempt to defuse the situation.

One of Darrel's brows raised. "Were you now?" He casually looked at the other bikers who were holding injured limbs and tending to open wounds. "Seems unlikely. In fact, it looks like you were trying to cause trouble in my neighborhood."

The hairs on the back of my neck raised at his accusation. And that he referred to this area as *his* neighborhood disturbed me. A part of me had hoped that the appearance of this man would stop the fighting for good, but I started to get the sense that his arrival had just made the situation worse. Much worse. I had to choose my words carefully.

"We didn't mean to," I offered. "We were just acting in defense. We're sorry."

"Don't apologize," Jax growled, surprising me. His clenched teeth were bared, and his eyes were fixed on Darrel like a hawk. "We did nothing wrong."

Darrel didn't look the least bit intimidated by Jax. He took an easy step forward, violating Jax's personal space. My body tensed. Darrel studied Jax's angry face for a moment. Then surprise gripped his expression. "That scar on your eyebrow . . . how'd you get it?"

Jax's teeth ground audibly. His hands tightened into balls by his side. A spike of fear rippled through me from the thought that he was preparing to throw a punch. I grasped his arm, silently urging him not to. If there was a chance we could get out of here without having to fight again, we had to take it. I didn't want any more violence. I didn't want Jax to get hurt.

"It's you, ain't it?" Darrel asked, his sunken eyes now wide.

Jax's fists were coiled so hard they were shaking. But then I felt his leg tapping against mine and realized that his legs were shaking as well. I felt terrified and confused. I couldn't tell whether Jax wanted to bash Darrel's face into a bloody pulp or run far, far away from him.

Darrel smiled, the deep lines around his eyes and mouth twisting sinisterly. "After all these years, my good-for-nothing son that ran away from home has now come back. I'd been thinking that you would've been dead by now. Didn't figure you'd last out there."

Son. The word Darrel used sliced into my brain. *Oh god, Darrel is Jax's dad.*

The resemblance finally hit me. The two men were almost eerily similar. I could see it in their builds, in their facial structure, in the deepness of their voices, and most of all in the intensity of their dark eyes. Looking at Darrel was like looking at a future version of Jax, but a drug-worn, menacing version.

How long had it been since Jax last saw this man? Wasn't he supposed to be in prison? If Jax had already run away from home by the time he was fourteen, it must've been at least ten years ago. My chest constricted as the weight of this unplanned reunion sunk in.

"I'm glad I could disappoint you," Jax snarled.

Darrel moved to within a foot in front of Jax, showing no fear of being hit by his son. "You've come to get back at me huh?"

I studied Jax's reaction. I could see it in the tortured look on his face. He wanted to say no. He wanted to deny coming back here for revenge, to deny coming back to revisit the demons from his past. But the sight of his dad in front of him now, the man who'd tormented him as a child . . . a part of him did want to take revenge now. A part of him wanted to inflict all the things that were done to him back on to the man who did them.

"Look at you now," Darrel growled as he eyed his son from head to toe. "You're a disgrace—a goddamn embarrassment. You make me sick, wearing those tight leather pants like some sort of faggot."

"Screw you," Jax roared. "You don't know shit about me!"

"I know you're weak," Darrel replied, staring Jax down. "Always were. Always will be."

"I'm not afraid of you anymore," Jax bit out, a swell of emotions billowing beneath the surface. "You can't scare me like you used to."

Darrel's eyes widened and his lips curved into a grin. "Oh, look at this. Seems like little Jacky boy has grown some balls on him now." Laughing in a way that sent shivers down my spine, he turned his head to look at the other guys. "The boy's all grown up."

All the bikers laughed.

When Darrel turned back to face Jax, his arm came in a wide hook, bashing Jax across the face.

Jax, taken by surprise received the full force of the hit. He grunted in pain, inadvertently pushing me away as he staggered on his feet.

"Don't you ever talk to me like that!" Darrel shouted, his eyes red with fury. "You hear me?! Didn't you learn anything I taught you, boy? Respect your elders."

While Jax was bent-over, recovering, Darrel hopped a step raising his boot backward and kicked Jax in the gut. A gust of wind escaped Jax's chest, and he collapsed to the ground, clutching at his stomach.

"Stop!" I cried, running to tackle Darrel before he had a chance to kick Jax again.

Just as I was about to tackle him, my head twisted violently.

SMACK!

For a brief moment, there had been enormous pressure on the side of my face, pushing my eye toward my nose until it felt like my eyeball was going to pop out of its socket. I faintly registered my feet lifting off the pavement and my body crashing to the ground like a rag doll. My cheek suddenly burned like a clothes iron had been pressed against it. Dazed, I faintly recalled the image of the back of Darrel's hand coming out of nowhere and smashing into my cheek.

"Riley!"

I recognized the roar of Jax's voice above the ringing in my ears. Through blurry vision I watched Jax stagger toward me, spitting blood from his mouth.

Two other bikers immediately pounced on him. They began punching and kicking Jax on the ground.

"Teach him a lesson, guys," Darrel hollered.

Suddenly the two men attacking Jax went flying backward, and I saw Jax rising to his feet, crying out in rage. The other four men ran toward Jax with their fists raised. Jax knocked them back one by one, but taking a few hits himself in the process.

When Jax turned his attention to Darrel, Darrel reached behind his back and pulled out a gun. "I wouldn't do that if I were you."

Jax froze when he noticed the gun pointing at him. Immediately, someone tackled him to the ground and started beating him. The other guys joined in. Jax tried to fight back, but he was being overpowered. He curled into a ball, desperately trying to protect his head with his hands as the bikers kicked him with their heavy boots.

Darrel walked over to Jax and pointed the gun down at him. There was an audible click as Darrel cocked the gun.

"No!" I screamed.

As Jax struggled to get to his feet, Darrel swung the butt of the pistol across the back of Jax's head, knocking him facedown to the pavement. His body became still.

When I saw Jax wasn't moving, I screamed.

Darrel spit on Jax. "You're a pathetic excuse for a son," he said. "Makes me sick just looking at you again."

Fire boiled in my veins. I was going to kill him. I was going to kill Darrel.

Before I could scramble to my feet, hands grabbed each of my arms and another one yanked my head up by my hair. The bikers cackled like hyenas. "Let's have some fun with her now," one of them said.

Darrel came over, knelt to eye-level, and squeezed my cheeks between his fingers, turning my face from side to side as he assessed me. I struggled with all the energy I had, thrashing my arms and legs to escape, but the bikers' strong hands restrained my movements.

I spit in Darrel's face and stared daggers at him. I wanted to punch him in the face. I wanted to claw his fucking eyes out.

He casually wiped his face clean with his thumb then inhaled through his nose and spat back onto my forehead, making me scream.

"This bitch is feisty," he said coolly to the guys restraining me. "She'll bite your dick off if you try to have fun with her. Better to let her go." He smiled at me right before his fist slammed into the side of my face.

I collided with the pavement, my ears ringing, and my jaw radiating pain.

"Let 'em be," Darrel said to the bikers. "She can go with him. He likes to run like a coward, so I say let him do it."

The bikers murmured their agreement, then each took turns spitting on Jax's motionless body sprawled across the pavement.

"C'mon," I heard Darrel shout. "Let's go inside. I've had enough looking at these two."

The thugs obediently followed Darrel toward the house, their footsteps growing fainter.

When I could no longer hear them, I struggled to my hands and knees, desperate to get to Jax. My head felt swollen and dizzy. I tried to get to my feet, but suddenly the world began to turn sideways. I cried out as I crashed back to the ground, landing on my elbow. Fighting to keep myself steady, I gave up on standing and crawled over to Jax.

I touched his face. "Wake up Jax," I cried desperately.

"Riley . . . ?" he mumbled, a trail of crimson staining the side of his mouth.

"It's me," I said, as tears rolled down my cheek. I was so relieved to hear his voice. I didn't know what I'd do if he hadn't responded. "It's me, baby. It's me."

"Are you okay?" he said slowly, his eyes half-open.

I carefully brushed his hair out of his face, trying my hardest not to break down. He was in much worse condition than I was. I needed to be strong for him. "I'm fine, Jax, they're gone now. Let's get you out of here okay? Can you stand?"

"I might need some help," he muttered before spitting some blood out of his mouth.

Draping his arm over my shoulder, I helped him to his feet, the both of us wobbling for a moment before we steadied ourselves. We limped over to Jax's motorcycle. When it failed to start again, I shrieked and kicked it angrily half a dozen times until it finally revved to life. I cursed myself, wishing that I had done that sooner.

Jax wasn't in any condition to drive, so I helped him onto the backseat while I climbed on as the driver. I'd never driven a motorcycle before, but I was confident that I could do it after having ridden with Jax.

I took a deep breath, feeling my sides ache as I did so. We were going to get back to the bus. We were going to leave this place—this horrible place where Jax's demons lived.

It was all quiet on the streets once again. The gnarled shadows from the flickering streetlamp still looked menacing as they lapped at fresh blood stains on the ground.

My eyes stung. This had been my fault. If I hadn't pushed him, he would've never come back here, and all of this would've never happened. Jax would've never been hurt. I couldn't help a horrible feeling of guilt from knotting in my stomach. Jax had helped me beat my demons, and all I did was push him into getting beaten by his own.

I didn't fully understand it before, but now I knew why Jax wanted to keep his past buried. Why he never wanted to face it or make sense of it. You bury your demons to starve them, to weaken them because they're too strong to face directly. After a while, you get stronger and the demons get weaker. When the demons are on the verge of death but refuse to die, you dig them up and strike the final blow then give them a proper burial. For most people this works. But the thing is, some demons never weaken when you bury them. Sometimes, they get stronger.

Jax could never face his demons and win. At least not alone, he couldn't.

As Jax leaned against me on the rumbling bike, his soft, irregular breaths blowing against my ear, I knew nothing would ever be the same between us after tonight. If only we could rewind everything, to go back to that beautiful night in Las Vegas when it seemed like nothing could get between us.

Then I remembered how the bikers spit on Jax while he laid on the ground, broken and bloodied, and uncontrollable fury rushed through my veins. My hand tightened around the throttle as I struggled to contain the storm of emotions building inside my chest. No one was going to hurt the man that I loved and get away with it.

No, this wasn't fucking over yet.

"Jax, wait here. This will just take a second," I said as I stopped the bike.

"Riley . . . no . . . don't get hurt."

Even as injured as he was, Jax was more concerned about my well-being than his own.

"I won't," I said quietly, trembling with sorrow and rage.

After I eased him down on the bike, I walked over to the bottle of whiskey one of the bikers had thrown at me earlier. I picked it up and brought it back to the bike. I tore the hanging bit of fabric from my blouse sleeve and stuffed it into the opening of the bottle. I took Jax's lighter from his pocket and lit the end of the sleeve hanging out of the top.

On the bike, ready to go, I secured Jax's arms around me and raised the flaming bottle above my head.

"What are you doing?" Jax managed.

I lifted his bruised hand to my mouth and kissed it tenderly. "Burning away the past."

Then I threw the flaming bottle toward the house.

Thank you for reading!

If you could spare a moment to leave a review it would be much appreciated.

Reviews help new readers find my books and decide if it's right for them. It also provides valuable feedback for my writing!

Sign up for my mailing list to get discounts, exclusive teasers, and to find out when my next book is released!

http://eepurl.com/sH7wn

Other books by Priscilla West

Forbidden Surrender
Secret Surrender
Beautiful Surrender

Wrecked
Rescued (Wrecked Book Two)

36146528R00196

Made in the USA
Lexington, KY
08 October 2014